The Day After Never

Covenant

Russell Blake

Books@RussellBlake.com

ISBN: 978-1535207096

Published by

Reprobatio Limited

Author's Note

The Day After Never originally started out as a trilogy. I had a story that could be told in three episodes, each roughly 75K words, and my plan was to tie up all loose ends by the end of the final book.

Unfortunately, that's not how things turned out.

As I wrote the third installment, an idea began to percolate, and by the end of this volume it was clear to me that I'd have to either write a fourth book, or this one would need to be double the word count, making it almost *War and Peace* length. That didn't seem viable, so I decided to make the trilogy a four-part series, where I deal with the additional plot items that arose during Covenant's creation in the final book.

Chapter 1

Duke lay on his stomach near a tiny stream, crossbow in hand and night vision goggles in place. The black nylon straps of the harness enveloped his head like a medieval torture device. Flashes of lightning crackled on the northern horizon, pulsing on the periphery of the night sky like artillery in a distant battle, though the storm was too far off to hear any accompanying thunder.

He'd been in position for a good half hour, waiting patiently for dinner to show itself, secure in the knowledge that it was a matter of time before some unwary animal came in search of water and ended its stay on the planet. He had gotten into the nocturnal hunting routine quickly once he and Aaron had reached his hidey hole in the foothills, and they'd dined on rabbit and venison since they'd arrived.

Duke had abandoned the trading post, hauling everything he could fit on an overloaded cart. He'd rigged several solar panels at his simple two-room cinder-block bunker, which provided sufficient power during the day to recharge the scope and operate the radio as well as a small refrigerator that barely kept their food below room temperature. He missed the conveniences in his old home but realized he'd made the right choice; the danger from the Locos had become too substantial to ignore. There was no question in Duke's mind that the trading post had already been looted, but he felt nothing when he thought about it – the place had served its purpose, and he could open another one elsewhere once any heat had died down.

He'd put out a warning call on the radio the morning he'd left, on the off chance that the kook in Artesia might be monitoring the airwaves, but when he'd gotten no acknowledgement, he had ridden into the wilds without looking back, Aaron by his side. In the end, the buildings where he'd eked out his existence for the last five years were just some walls and a roof on a godless stretch of nothing, and he held no regrets at leaving it behind. That was how life went in the post-collapse world, and he was grateful for every day that he awoke drawing breath – there were far too many who didn't each morning.

The hideaway, a former power line maintenance bunker that had long since ceased to matter, was tucked into the remote reaches of the foothills at the end of a dirt track that had washed away over the years and been reclaimed by weeds and prickly pear. But it had water from the stream, was on defendable high ground, and most importantly, was well away from the highway, and so relatively safe from the miscreants who used that strip of asphalt to visit terror on the unsuspecting.

A slight motion in the eerie neon green of his goggles drew Duke's attention to a clump of brush to his left. A gentle breeze from the north wrinkled the surface of the water, thankfully carrying his scent downriver, away from where he'd detected movement. He inclined his head slightly, careful not to move any more than necessary, and scanned the foliage.

A furry form eased into view, its leporine nose twitching and long ears cocked slightly back as it surveyed the surroundings, some primitive part of its brain warning it of a danger its eyes couldn't detect. Eventually thirst got the better of it, and Duke inched the crossbow forward – a relatively easy shot at fifteen yards, but not a given. He held his breath as the animal crept in fits and starts toward the water's edge, and he peered down the iron sights. His finger began gently squeezing the trigger, and then the hare was gone in a blur, startled by an explosion of gunfire from up the slope.

Duke rolled and forced himself to his feet in one seamless maneuver, his heart thudding in his chest as shots shattered the night. The higher pitched rattle of Aaron's AR-15 was answered by the deeper chatter of AK-47s – at least three or four, Duke guessed.

"Damn," he muttered as he retraced his steps toward the bunker, crossbow in hand, the landscape glowing neon green in the scope. In the days at the hideaway they'd had no trouble and seen nobody, but they hadn't relaxed their guard, sticking to shifts and keeping a watch for any sign of encroachment.

Based on the pitched gun battle taking place less than a quarter mile away, that lull in their misfortunes was over.

Duke stuck to a game trail and did his best to move silently along the dirt. The gunfire increased in volume as he neared the shoot-out. At the edge of the clearing beneath the building, he could make out muzzle flashes and counted four gunmen blasting away at Aaron's position.

He estimated the distance to the closest shooter and frowned – he would have to skirt the brush line to get close enough to be deadly with his Sig Sauer 9mm pistol. The Barnett Ghost 360 crossbow was astoundingly accurate when used with the carbon hunting bolts he favored, but he wasn't confident it would put a man down with a single bolt, whereas the pistol could place four rounds in an area the size of a soda can at fifty yards on a bad day. He pulled back into the thicket and moved north to where he'd seen the gunmen, and re-emerged almost directly behind the men.

Duke waited to confirm there were only four, and when he was certain of the count, slid the pistol from its holster and drew a bead on the nearest man, now no more than twenty-five yards away. He centered the sights on the man's back and squeezed the trigger. The pistol bucked three times in quick succession, its deadly bark blending with the nonstop firing from the attacker's AK. The crouching man fell forward, dropping his weapon, and Duke nodded to himself – one down.

The other three shooters hadn't noticed their associate's demise and were still firing away at the bunker with undiminished fury. Duke sidled to his right and aimed at the next attacker, who was lying on his stomach to shoot at Aaron. Duke adjusted the pistol slightly to compensate for the greater distance and put his second group of three shots between the man's shoulder blades. Two of the rounds shredded through his upper spine at an angle, exiting from the base of the front of his neck before being stopped by the hard dirt beneath him. The gunman flailed like a beached fish and then fell still.

At the bunker, Aaron must have noted the halving of the incoming fire because his AR-15 rattled at the two remaining shooters, the 5.56mm rounds slicing through the grass around them. One of the pair cried out as a well-placed shot took the top of his head off. One gunman remained. Duke held his fire – the angle was less than optimal for a kill shot. The shooter and Aaron exchanged a few volleys, and then, realizing he was the sole member of his group left alive, the attacker rolled onto his side and pushed himself to his feet.

Duke waited until the man was close and emptied the Sig Sauer magazine at him. The 9mm rounds punched into the gunman's chest but were stopped by the ceramic plate of his flak jacket, momentarily stunning him. He froze, and then a burst of automatic fire from the bunker cut him down from behind. Duke watched as the man's mouth formed an O and he pitched forward, his AK-47 sailing from his hands as though pulled by an invisible cord.

Silence settled over the clearing, and Duke called out to Aaron, "We got them all. You okay?"

A few seconds later Aaron's voice answered, "Yeah. You sure that's everyone?"

"I'll be there in a second. Don't shoot."

Duke made his way toward the bunker, pausing at each of the fallen attackers to toe their weapons well away. When he reached the building, he took in the bullet-pocked mortar around the door and windows and grunted. A grim-faced Aaron stood in the doorway, still holding his rifle.

"What happened?" Duke asked.

"They tripped one of the wires. Came up fast."

"Any idea who they were?"

"Negative."

Duke stepped into the room, ejected his spent magazine and slapped a new one in place, and went for his rifle, setting the crossbow by the door. "This is bad news."

"Gunfire will attract some attention," Aaron agreed.

"Let's check on the animals."

Aaron followed the trader to the area where the horses were corralled further up the hill and was relieved to find them unharmed. On the way back to the bunker, Duke's mind was processing furiously, his mouth a thin line, his eyes slits beneath a frowning brow.

At the killing field they quickly gathered the men's weapons. Their hair was long and unkempt, and all were Caucasian, with no facial tattoos or other identifying marks. Three had their eyes frozen open, their limbs already stiffening in death, and Duke's nose wrinkled at the stench rising from them – a combination of death, dried sweat, and lack of basic hygiene wafting from their tattered clothing.

"They aren't Locos or Raiders," Aaron observed.

"Yeah. Probably scavengers. Problem is there may be more of 'em."

"Could be."

"Which means it isn't safe here anymore." Duke's frown deepened. "Hate to ride at night, but I don't see much alternative, do you?"

"We can stay put and load for bear."

"If there's twenty of 'em, that's not such a good idea. Besides, as you said, the shots will draw every Raider and lowlife for miles around." Duke shook his head. "No, we got to pack up and git. Let's do it."

"Where we headed?"

"We'll camp north of here. There are some decent spots near the river. We'll figure out what to do next come tomorrow."

Aaron nodded. "Damn shame. I was just getting used to this toilet."

Duke threw a final glance at the dead men and then fixed Aaron with a worried stare. "I want to be gone in ten minutes. Pack everything we can carry. Leave the rest. The cart would slow us down too much and make us targets."

"Gonna miss the power," Aaron said, looking up at the solar panels arranged on the roof of the building.

"We can add it to our regret list. Now hurry up – time's a-wasting."

They made short work of hauling their possessions to the horses. After packing the saddlebags of all four animals, they mounted up, Duke with his night vision goggles in place to guide the way, and set off in the darkness, guns held at the ready.

They rode for three hours and set up their camp on the bank of the Black River near a spit of sand just above a rapid, the water rushing in the narrows before burbling over a scattering of boulders. Once their tents were pitched, Duke tossed Aaron some dried jerky, and they chewed wordlessly. When they'd swallowed their meager supper and washed it down with river water, Duke sat cross-legged in the moonlight, his AR-15 by his side.

"Least it isn't raining," he said, studying the horizon where the distant storm was playing itself out.

"So where do we go next?" Aaron asked.

"Beats me. But we can't go south, and there isn't much west. That leaves north."

"Loving's gone."

"Yeah, but there's more than Loving in that direction. We'll find somewhere we can put down roots and start a new business. Just got to be the right place."

Duke had a considerable store of gold, ammo, and weapons with which to start a new trading post, so he wasn't worried about adapting. His profession, like prostitution, was one of the oldest and always in demand. They would move carefully during the day and see what the future held. Maybe they'd find something up by Carlsbad, maybe further north.

"You want to take first watch?" Duke asked, his tone making it obvious that it wasn't a request.

Aaron nodded. "Four and four?"

"Same as ever." Duke handed Aaron the goggles and then unrolled his sleeping bag. The ground was hard, but no worse than the concrete floor of the bunker. "Wake me if you hear anything."

"Sure thing, boss." Aaron sat with his back against a tree and adjusted the goggles before scanning the surroundings.

Duke yawned again and, with his assault rifle by his side like a lover, closed his eyes and was asleep within thirty seconds, his soft snores rumbling in his chest as Aaron cocked his head to better hear over the river, the goggles lending him the appearance of an extraterrestrial.

"Hell of a way to end the run," he whispered to himself, and shifted into a less comfortable position so he wouldn't nod off.

Chapter 2

Lucas's side burned from the wound he'd acquired at the lake, but he ignored the pain as Tango followed Colt's horse through the darkness. They'd crossed the freeway intersection forty minutes earlier, and Colt had signaled for them to remain quiet until he gave the word that it was safe to talk. Once out of town, the landscape had transitioned from the blackened husks of warehouses and wrecking yards into a flat desert dotted with sparse groves of trees. The rain abated to a light drizzle, the trees of lightning that had illuminated the terrain blown east as the storm worked its way toward the great plains.

Colt held up a hand, barely visible in the gloom, and Lucas coaxed Tango abreast.

"We'll stop here for the night," Colt said. "Maybe get a few hours of sleep. Tomorrow's going to be a hard slog, so you'll need every bit of rest you can snatch."

"Think we're far enough from Roswell?" Lucas asked as Sierra, Ruby, and Eve materialized out of the rain.

"About four miles. That should do the trick. The locals avoid this area. Apache country starts at the five-mile point, but nobody wants to misjudge and stumble into their territory."

"Then it's safe?" Ruby asked.

Colt shrugged. "Safe as anywhere."

Lucas swung down from the saddle. "Come on. I'll help you with your tents."

Sierra nodded, helped Eve down, and lowered herself from Nugget. "This just keeps getting better, doesn't it?"

Lucas managed a tight smile. "We're alive. Everything else is gravy."

"Do you think they'll be able to follow us?"

Lucas wiped the water from his face. "They'll damn sure try. But they're going to have their work cut out for them. Rain's washed away our tracks."

Once the camp was made, they gathered under the trees and ate their rations. Ruby finished first and turned to Colt.

"So what can you tell us about Shangri-La? You've been there, right?"

Colt nodded slowly. "Yes. Not a lot to tell. It's a naturally protected enclave with power and water. The people are God-fearing and decent."

"Who started it?"

"The doctor who's working on the cure, a physician named Barnes, Elliot Barnes. Everyone calls him the Doc."

"He runs things?" Lucas asked.

"More or less. Everyone defers to him. Although there's always some disagreement on how to best accomplish things – that's true anytime you have a good number of people."

"How many?" Sierra asked.

"Probably pushing three hundred."

Lucas's eyebrows rose. "That many?"

"Yeah. We aren't recruiting. It's sustainable at that size. Bunch more and we'd run into resource problems."

"You trade with outsiders?"

"They have a confederate they work through in one of the nearby towns, but nobody knows that he's trading on behalf of Shangri-La."

"You say it's naturally protected. How's it set for weapons?" Lucas pressed.

"They have everything they need." Colt's tone wasn't inviting more questions.

"Are you one of the original members?" Sierra asked.

"That's right. I consider myself lucky."

"But you were living in Roswell," Ruby observed.

"I was sent there to wait for Eve. I infiltrated the town six months before we broke her out, and built the bar as a cover." He hesitated. "We have others outside of Shangri-La who gather info for us and keep us abreast of any news. But none of them know where it's located – they're all free agents."

"Just you," Lucas stated flatly.

Colt nodded. "That's right. Security. You can't tell anyone what you don't know."

"Makes sense," Lucas agreed.

"How far are we from it?" Sierra asked.

Colt smiled. "A ways."

Lucas grunted. "You mentioned Apache country. How are we supposed to cross it without a guide? You know the way?"

"Sort of. I managed it once. We'll be fine."

"Even without…Frank?" Ruby asked.

"That could get sticky, but we can level with the tribe if they stop us. They may not. It's a big area, and it's not like they have unlimited manpower."

"You don't sound confident," Lucas fired back.

"I'm not, but we'll play it by ear. They've been paid already, so we should be fine. It's not our fault if their man couldn't make it."

"Well, it sort of is, since it was one of our gang that gunned him down," Ruby said.

"We'll leave that part of the story out." Colt finished the last bites of his meal and rose. "If necessary, let me do the talking. Now get some rest. We'll leave at first light."

Lucas nodded and joined him at the horses. "You figure two days to cross their territory?"

"Maybe three. Not a lot of water for long stretches. No point in wearing out our rides for nothing."

"Makes sense. Anything else we need to know?"

"Next stop's Albuquerque. It's kind of the Wild West there, but we'll need to resupply and get the week's password."

"Password?"

"Guards will shoot on sight if you don't know it. They change it every week."

"How does whoever you're going to meet get it?"

"Radio. Got a guy in town whose job is nothing but keeping us posted on significant developments in the outside world. Albuquerque's a major trading hub, so he hears a lot of scuttlebutt."

"Who controls the town?"

"The local militia. Couple of criminal gangs tried to take it over, but they got overthrown by the survivors – pretty mean bunch, apparently, although I've never had any problems with 'em. Town's open to anyone that wants to trade, and the local posse keeps a tight rein on things. There are bars, whorehouses, the works, but they come down on you like a ton of bricks if you start trouble."

"Regular Tombstone, huh?"

"No new ideas."

Colt retired to his tent and Lucas rejoined the women, who were finishing up. Eve scooted over to him and looked up in the darkness. "Aunt Sierra and I want to say thank you for everything."

"No need, Eve. But I appreciate the sentiment."

Eve's eyes moved to his boots, and she shifted from foot to foot. "She likes you."

Lucas's stomach tightened and he glanced at Sierra, who was talking in hushed tones with Ruby.

"I like her too. And I like you. Now get ready to sleep. It'll be daybreak before you know it."

"My butt hurts."

"Everyone's does. You get used to it. Imagine how the horses feel."

Her eyes narrowed. "Why do their butts hurt?"

Lucas's mouth twitched. "I meant they're probably pretty tired. Now go to sleep, Eve. Sweet dreams."

He watched as the little girl tromped back to where the women were sitting. Sierra stood and took Eve's hand. Even in the gloom, the smile she threw to Lucas was unmistakable, and he nodded to her before moving to his own tent, upon which the patter of rain beat a steady tattoo.

Lucas slid into the three-man tent and zipped the entry flap closed, his mind on the young woman only a few yards away. His body signaled his interest with a stirring he hadn't felt for years.

"Eyes on the prize," Lucas whispered, pushing thoughts of Sierra out of his mind before they kept him awake the rest of the night. He would need to deal with the situation at some point, but this wasn't the time or place, and he closed his eyes and resolved to save the drama for another day.

Chapter 3

The lights of Houston's Crew-occupied downtown illuminated the night horizon. Huge refinery tanks behind a chain-link fence topped with coils of gleaming razor wire towered like monoliths against the backlit metro area. Once an oil traffic hub, the area was now all but abandoned, with only a few guards manning the outpost that protected the last of the viable diesel fuel in the Crew's possession.

The stainless steel of a single ten-thousand-gallon tanker truck gleamed beside one of the storage containers, dwarfed by the four-story tank. Around it a hodgepodge of empty crates and fifty-gallon drums littered the parking lot where they'd been emptied long ago during the looting that accompanied the collapse. Much of the chaos had been desperation, the wanton and haphazard destruction of a population as it starved and died. Between disease and pervasive violence, over ninety-five percent of the metropolis had perished before Magnus and the Crew had established order – of a kind.

Roving gangs of armed thugs had been assimilated into the Crew or executed without mercy. Some tried to escape conscription into the gang, but were hunted down; Magnus was savvy enough to be wary of their reappearance at a later date. His message had been clear and unequivocal – his was now the only law of the land, and you played by his rules...or died.

The surviving residents had been given the option of paying for protection or leaving to never return. Most stayed, there being no place better to go; the stories of the outlying areas were as grim as the piles of the dead that clogged the streets.

It was in this vision of hell that Magnus had set up court, doling out favors to his inner circle and arbitrarily punishing transgressions in mass executions that had taken on a grim pageantry, attended by the masses with the enthusiasm of gladiator matches in ancient Rome, ultimately cheered as the bloodthirsty spectacles became routine entertainment.

But as Magnus's grip on the territory tightened, resistance had organized. Determined men and women saw his reign as that of the anti-Christ – not much of a leap, as every form of atrocity, degradation, and perversion was pursued by the former inmates who'd been handpicked to be his lieutenants. Pedophilia, bestiality, slavery, torture, dark rituals with Satanic overtones and occult symbolism – nothing was off-limits in Magnus's vision of a brave new world, and the population lived in constant terror of their doors being kicked down and their sons and daughters dragged screaming into the streets, never to be seen again.

The resistance had grown organically, in cells with no connection to each other except through anonymous cutouts, but even with the secrecy many had perished when discovered. But that hadn't deterred the committed, and tonight, one of the oldest cells was planning a sabotage mission that had been developed over months of clandestine surveillance.

The fuel truck was Magnus's treasure – the last of the usable diesel in his possession. His technical staff had been working to bring a refinery back on line but so far had failed, with both the parts required to maintain the equipment and the technical know-how lacking. Fuel was his Achilles' heel, and if the cell could destroy it, the blow to the Crew could be severe enough to cause it to fragment as its members realized they weren't impervious to harm. Regardless, the Crew would lose its most precious commodity, which would hamper its dominance. It was widely known that Magnus had a substantial cache of fuel in reserve in case of an uprising and could transport hundreds of men to the farthest corners of his territory in a matter of days. That served as an effective deterrent, but if word spread that he was out of gas…resistance in other areas might be emboldened.

Five black-clad figures ran toward the fence, one with bolt cutters clutched to his chest. The moonless night had been chosen by their leader from an almanac, and they were practically invisible in the darkness. When they reached the barrier, they spread out, weapons raised, while the cutter went to work. Three minutes later, a gap large enough to slip through opened, and they eased through.

Once inside the refinery yard, they jogged toward the truck, using the discarded barrels and crates for cover. The guard post was distant enough that they wouldn't be seen, but they were taking no chances. They moved in fits and starts, pausing at strategic spots as they crossed the open asphalt.

They had nearly reached the truck when spotlights mounted to the roof of a darkened vehicle blinked to life, blinding them in the glare. A voice called out over a megaphone, "Freeze or we'll gun you down. No second warning. Drop your weapons, or you're history."

The team leader made a hand signal and threw himself to the side, trying to reach one of the crates for cover. A heavy machine gun opened up from the vehicle, peppering the pavement around the assault force. The cell gunmen fired in return using their assault rifles, but it was no contest, and the big .50-caliber machine gun shredded through their cover like tissue.

Thirty seconds later, all lay dead or wounded, their plate carriers having proved useless against the large-caliber rounds. The machine gun fell silent, and a tall, gaunt man stepped from the vehicle. Gothic script tattooed on his shaved head proclaimed his moniker to be "Snake." Below the name was the eye of Providence tattoo that paid homage to Magnus's fascination with the Illuminati, along with a pentagram. Six Crew fighters followed him from the big truck to the bodies.

Snake paused at the first corpse and kicked the man's chest with a steel-toed boot. The gunman beside him chuckled.

"Deader than my ex on Saturday night," Snake said with a grin.

Snake was one of Magnus's top men, in charge of security for the greater Houston area and one of his anointed successors in the event of his death. Snake took his job as seriously as though he were already running the Crew and took a personal interest in the attack on the fuel depot he'd gotten wind of from an informant.

One of the injured cell gunmen groaned, and Snake pointed his Desert Eagle at him and snapped an order to his group. "If he's not fatally wounded, patch him up so I can interrogate him. Same for the others."

In the end, three of the attackers had been killed and two wounded, both seriously, but not so badly they would die within the hour. It didn't matter to Snake – he only needed them breathing long enough to confirm what he knew about the cell so he could follow the chain of command to the person directing the attacks. He suspected an insider – someone within Magnus's organization with privileged knowledge – but he hadn't made his suspicions known yet, wanting to gather more information before he said anything.

But the attack on the truck had been too close for comfort. Its whereabouts were closely guarded, and this was its fourth home in five years. Nobody was allowed within a mile of the site, and it was shielded from view from the city.

Magnus had a leak. Of that Snake was certain.

And perhaps tonight he would learn something to point him in the direction of the traitor.

Chapter 4

Cano stared at the bloated corpses on the truck stop floor in stony silence. He moved to the front door and looked outside, where the outlines of Roswell's buildings glowed in the near distance as the sun's first rays reflected off their glass.

Luis approached, his boots crunching on the debris underfoot, and joined the Crew boss at the doorway. Pools of water from the rain that had only stopped an hour earlier quivered in the light breeze, and the air smelled heavy and damp.

"What's the plan?" Luis asked, his voice low.

Cano turned his head slightly. "We see if we can find someone who can identify these two. And we locate a radio and call for reinforcements."

"From where?"

"Pecos, obviously."

Luis's expression hardened. "We have barely enough men to secure the town."

"That's not my problem. I don't care whether the natives get restless in our absence or not. I'll deal with any insurrection when we return."

"What about Lubbock? Isn't it about the same distance from here?"

Cano stepped outside, ignoring Luis, who followed him out. The two remaining Crew gunmen carried their saddles from the depths of

17

the building. Luis rubbed his eyes with a tired hand and tried again. "How are we going to get the locals to cooperate?"

Cano scowled at him as though every question was annoying him further. "Let me worry about that."

"They have a reputation…"

Cano sneered, revealing several gold teeth. "So do I."

The men strapped their gear on their horses and set off toward town at a slow walk, the humidity stifling as dawn broke over the valley. Twenty minutes later, they arrived at a guard post manned by three civilians in camouflage fatigues and armed with AKs, the highway blocked by a cart loaded with bails of wet hay.

"That's far enough," one of the guards warned, weapon trained on Cano and his men.

"We're no threat. We need to do some bartering," Cano said.

"You don't look like traders," the lead guard said, his gun unwavering on the heavily muscled and tattooed Crew boss.

"Didn't say we were. Who runs this place? I want to talk to him."

"Who are you?" the guard demanded.

"My name's Cano. I represent the Crew."

The guard's face changed, and a tic twitched his left eye twice. Cano held his stare.

"What do you mean you represent the Crew?" another guard asked.

"It means you either take me to whoever runs this dump, or you'll wish you'd never been born."

A tense silence stretched between the two groups, and then Luis coaxed his horse forward a few steps. "Look. We need to find a radio, and we're looking for some help in identifying a couple of men who were killed out at the truck stop. We have no beef with you, and we don't want trouble. We'll pay for what we need and be on our way."

The guard studied Luis. "There's a trading post in town. Well marked. But you so much as look at your guns, you'll end the day in a box."

"Again, we're not here to cause any problems. Does the trading post have a radio?"

"No, but they can tell you who does." The man looked Cano up and down. "You have anything to do with the gunfight out at the lake? Early reports are saying there were a lot of guys that look like you."

"That's right," Luis answered before Cano could snap at the man. "We're after a group that stole Crew property."

"No trouble. Is that clear?" the lead gunman reiterated.

"Absolutely," Luis agreed. Cano remained silent.

The guard turned and gestured toward the town. "Head down the main street here. You'll find the trading post on the left about a half mile."

"Much obliged."

The guards moved the barrier out of the way, and Cano led his group through the gap. A few curious heads poked out from doors and windows as they made their way along the paved road, their horses' hooves echoing off the façades as they pushed deeper into Roswell. They passed the gutted remains of a fast-food restaurant that had been styled as a flying saucer, and Luis smiled slightly at the reminder of innocent times. Had it really been only five years since the world had collapsed? He felt decades older.

The approach to the trading post was lined with rusting vehicles, their tires flat and brittle from the sun, long since stripped of everything useful. The buildings were in decent shape compared to many cities, only a few with obvious scars from gun battles; most of the windows were boarded up or gaping like silent screams from a Munch painting. A pall of wood smoke from cooking fires hung over the street, and rivers of muddy water coursed down the gutters on both sides of the road. The bloated carcass of a mangy dog lay paws up in salute to the rising sun; a toddler sat nearby, poking it with a stick, laughing with another child at the unexpected entertainment.

When they reached the trading post, they dismounted and tied their horses to a lamppost that had been bent toward the ground at shoulder level. A painted sign for Tucker's Trading hung over one of the steel-barred windows, but the post was closed. Cano noted the heavy chain securing the entrance and sniffed the air, searching the street for the source of the smell.

"Eggs," he growled to Luis, who nodded.

"Yeah."

Cano walked to the end of the block, where several plastic tables had been set up on the crumbling sidewalk. A woman with skin the color of saddle leather nodded to them as they sat.

"That's the menu," she said, pointing at a blackboard leaning against the wall with a few items scrawled across it. "Prices negotiable, depending on what you got."

"Ammo," Cano said. "We want four of the biggest farmhand breakfasts you can manage."

She sized him up and named a price in ammunition.

Cano nodded and counted out the shells. "That do it?"

"Be back in a few with your food," she said, scooping the ammo into her apron and disappearing into the storefront.

Ten minutes later they were feasting on eggs swimming in grease, accompanied by a small mountain of fresh potatoes slathered with a pungent gravy. They ate like it was their last meal, cleaning their plates in no time. The woman returned to collect the empties and offered a grudging smile. "Anything else?"

"What time does the trading post open?"

"Oh, probably in about half an hour. Never know with Tucker."

"Can we get more water?"

"For another two rounds, you can drink as much as you like."

Twenty minutes later a short man with a small potbelly shuffled up to the trading post on foot, accompanied by three gunmen with the casual swagger of professional fighters. The man unlocked the chain, pushed the doors open, and disappeared inside.

Cano and Luis strode to the entrance while the two Crew thugs remained at the makeshift diner.

"You open?" Luis called into the dark space.

"Yeah. What you want?" a voice replied.

Cano stepped into the building, with Luis on his tail. The interior was bigger than it looked from the outside – a former auto parts store, based on the configuration. They approached a long counter and considered the steel racks of merchandise stretching into the gloom behind. The small man looked them over, a practiced half smile in place. "Help you with something?"

"We need supplies. Jerky, dry goods, water purification tablets. And information," Cano said.

"Got the first three," the man said. "Depends what you're after on the last bit."

"Couple of dead men north of here in a truck stop. I need to know who they are."

The little man shrugged. "First I heard of it."

"And we need a radio. Shortwave. Good antenna, not handheld."

"Don't have one. Sorry. How much jerky you want?"

"Enough for four men for...a week."

"Same with the rest?"

"That's right."

"Won't be cheap."

"Wasn't expecting a bargain." Cano paused. "What about the radio? Someone around here have one?"

"Over by city hall. Guy charges an arm and a leg, but it works. Look for the antenna. Can't miss it."

Several other men entered the trading post while one of Tucker's helpers was collecting the provisions, and Luis engaged with them, letting them know that they were looking for someone who could help identify the two dead men. The new arrivals seemed interested at the mention of pay, but balked when Luis told them where the bodies were – apparently nobody was willing to go north, outside the city limits, to check, no matter how attractive the offer.

Cano paid for the supplies with one of the AK-47s he'd retrieved from his fallen men, along with two STANAG magazines with sixty rounds in them – an exorbitant price, to be sure, but immaterial at the moment. He wanted the trader to know he meant business and wasn't playing cheap.

"You run into anyone who can help identify those two, I'd be grateful," Cano said.

"And how would that gratitude manifest itself?" the little man asked.

"Another AK, at least, for you. Same for whoever helps us."

The trader's eyes widened. "That's…grateful indeed."

"Spread the word. My men are at the corner breakfast place. Just have 'em ask for Cano, mention you sent them, and I'll take care of you."

The helper reappeared with his arm muscles bulging under the weight of the supplies. "Where you want it?" he asked.

"Horses are outside." Cano looked to the trader a final time. "Remember – money for nothing if you find someone to help me."

"Got it."

Luis and Cano led the helper to the horses. The young man set the bundles down and leaned into Cano. "I got a break for lunch. I ain't afraid to go look at no dead guys. You serious about the pay?"

Cano grinned. "Lightly used AK, all yours if you can identify them."

"If they were from around here, I can. I know everyone."

Luis sized up the man and estimated his age at somewhere around twenty. "We'll be over at the diner."

"I want two AKs. One for me…and the one you woulda given Tucker."

Cano and Luis exchanged a look, and the Crew boss nodded slowly. "That's reasonable. Same to me either way. You said you get off around noon? Can't slip away now?"

The man shook his head. "No way."

"All right. You know where to find us."

Luis and Cano watched as the young man headed back to the shop, and Cano began packing the goods into his saddlebags. "That's one problem solved."

"Assuming he knows 'em."

"Best lead we've got."

A tall man approached from across the street, hand on his sidearm – a Colt 1911 .45-caliber pistol in a worn holster that his expression said he knew how to use. He stopped in front of them and adjusted his ten-gallon Stetson.

"Howdy, boys. Heard you just arrived. Not going to be staying long, are you?"

Cano looked him up and down. "What's it to you?"

"I'm the sheriff. Don't want any trouble round here."

"We causing any?" Cano asked reasonably.

"Heard all about a gunfight out by the lake. Be best if you weren't here come sundown."

"Wasn't planning on staying."

The man nodded, his eyes hard. "Good."

They watched the sheriff amble into the trading post, and Cano turned to Luis. "Finish stowing this stuff. I'm going to find the radio."

"I wish you wouldn't pull any men from Pecos. We're thin on the ground there..."

Cano's voice was hard as iron. "Don't question me – you're here to do what I say, and that's all. Pack up and keep your mouth shut, understand?"

Luis choked back the fury that surged through him and dropped his head so Cano wouldn't see the murder in his eyes. He nodded once and moved away, fighting the urge to reach for his handgun and put a round through the man's skull. Luis reminded himself that even if he took Cano down, he'd have to face the pair of Crew gunmen, and the odds of prevailing against all three of them were slim.

Cano strode away, leaving Luis to stew at the insulting treatment, his back a further taunt and confirmation of Luis's subordination.

Luis counted slowly to ten, willing his heart rate back to normal, and began packing the goods. The long string of curses that ran through his head was as colorful as the flush that had suffused his face. Under normal circumstances, Luis would have already driven his knife into the Crew boss's heart, but now wasn't the time.

He would just keep his head down and wait.

Because eventually he'd have his chance, and then Cano would learn that he'd pushed the wrong man.

Chapter 5

Colt's horse swayed along in front of Lucas, its deliberate gait measured and even, the stride of an animal accustomed to covering long distances in a day with a minimum of undue exertion.

They had hit the trail at dawn, following the remnants of the storm as it moved northeast. The ground was still moist in patches, the earth unable to absorb any more, leaving the rest to the sun's rays. The heat had risen as the sky transitioned from salmon to purple to blue, and in some stretches they'd been surrounded by steam as the surface moisture evaporated – an eerie spectacle that added to the impression that they were closer to hell than to heaven.

They'd stopped periodically to rest and water the horses, allowing them to graze on what they could forage while Colt took bearings. He'd directed them toward the hills to the west, staying well off the cracked ebony ribbon of highway that stretched through the desert to the horizon. The going had gotten harder as they'd neared the hills, where the terrain grew more rugged and wild as the elevation increased, the route made doubly treacherous by the slick mud on the trail.

Capitan Mountain jutted into the sky to the west as the horses labored up the grade. The rest stops grew more frequent as it became obvious the animals were tiring as they ascended into thinner air. The white sand and occasional scrub gave way to patches of verdant growth, and then the landscape became an explosion of green fed by the storm, the plants thriving, if only for a few rare days.

24

Colt led them along a dirt road that was barely more than an indentation in the hills and then drew up short as they topped a rise and found themselves staring at a canyon filled with rushing water.

"Damn. No way across that," he said after a few minutes of staring at the wash. "It was dry when I was here before."

"Not anymore," Lucas observed. "Any bridges?"

Colt shook his head. "Just the main overpass at the highway."

"Then we either wait for the runoff to dry up, or backtrack and use the road."

Ruby cleared her throat. "We can't try to cross it? Find a shallow area?"

Colt shook his head. "Flash flooding like this is treacherous. Might just as soon lose you as make it." His face clouded. "We need to follow the canyon down to the highway and cross there."

Sierra frowned. "But you said the Apaches—"

"We have no choice. We're stopped dead until we make it across."

"He's right," Lucas said.

They wheeled their horses around and worked their way along the wash. An occasional hawk or buzzard overhead cast a fleeting shadow in the flattening landscape. An hour and a half later they arrived at the highway, where two overpasses crossed the canyon. They coaxed their horses across the broiling asphalt, weapons in hand, and exhaled a collective sigh of relief when they reached the far side.

Colt led them west again, his pace faster than before, as if trying to make up for the time lost retracing their steps. The dirt road they were following degraded to a trail that ran along the ravine before improving as it jagged north.

Ruby's horse screamed in alarm as its front legs slipped out from under it and the earth beneath fell away. She wrestled the reins as Sidney reared up on his hind legs, pulling back from the hole that had materialized without warning, her eyes panicked. Colt rode back to Ruby and froze when he saw the depression. He leapt from the saddle and helped Ruby get Sidney under control.

"What the hell was that?" she demanded as she dismounted,

panting hard from the sudden exertion.

Lucas dropped from the saddle and cautiously approached the hole. He knelt and used his Bowie knife to probe the edge of the dirt lip. When he looked up at Colt, his expression was dark.

"Trap. Woven reed mat supported from below with branches, over a pit. Can't tell how deep – there's a lot of water filling it."

Colt nodded. "And the way the mat's covered, you'd never see it. A neat trick – horse falls in, it stays in." Colt paused. "I've never seen one before. I had no idea they used them. I had a guide when I came south – he must have known where the traps were and kept us clear."

Lucas frowned. "We're too close to the road. They anticipated that anyone traveling without a guide would stay off the highway, and rigged the secondary routes." Lucas looked first to Ruby and then to Sidney. "You're lucky you were able to pull away in time. Although we need to check to see if his ankle's broken or just twisted."

Colt looked over the horse's front leg. "It's swelling, but not like a break."

"Walk him around some and see how he does."

Colt obliged, and within a few minutes it became obvious that Sidney could walk, but there was no way he would be able to support Ruby's weight.

"Poor Jax. Looks like he's going to have to do the heavy lifting again," she said. "We should transfer his cargo so it's only me."

They moved the saddlebags from the mule to Sidney, and after a reluctant start by Jax, the party continued toward the hills, the sun now well past the high point in the sky. Sidney limped noticeably as he followed in Jax's wake, but he soldiered on without complaint, sweat drying on his flanks.

Sierra called out to Lucas after a half hour, and he slowed for her to catch up.

"How much longer are we going to ride today?" she asked.

"Don't know. Probably until dark. Why?"

"Eve's tired, and so am I."

"You can doze in the saddle. But there's about twenty more miles we need to cover before we stop," Colt said from ahead.

"You have someplace in mind?" Lucas asked.

"That's right. There are some abandoned buildings off the highway. An old ranch. We camped there on my trip down."

"Twenty miles?" Sierra echoed.

"Afraid so. We need to clock fifty miles a day, and we've come no more than thirty."

"It seems like we've been riding forever," Ruby said.

"Get used to it. Three days of this before we hit Albuquerque, and a lot of it uphill, too."

Sierra groaned. "Why not cover it in four? What's the difference?"

"One more day for something bad to happen," Colt said. "And by the fourth day, we'll be out of water."

Lucas nodded. "We're wasting time we don't have. You want to doze, that's fine – I can take Eve for a while."

"No, I can manage. I...never mind."

Ruby adjusted her hat and gave the younger woman a sympathetic look. "Could be worse. At least you've got a horse. I'm stuck with Jax."

Jax turned his head slightly at his name.

Sierra had to laugh at the mule's beleaguered expression. "I think he's handsome."

"Well, he's getting the job done, and that's all that counts," Ruby agreed.

Colt cut off the banter. "Stay single file behind me, and if I stop, you do so as well. There may be some traps on the road, too, so I need to keep a sharp eye out."

"I can take point if you want," Lucas offered.

"No need. But I'll let you know if I get tired."

Lucas blotted his face with his bandana as Colt set off again. The rest of them followed in a ragged procession behind, Ruby and her gimp horse bringing up the rear. Lucas swept the horizon with his binoculars, but saw nothing but endless flatland to the east and craggy hills to the west. He probed the wound in his side with his fingers and was relieved that the bandage was dry, any blood clotted, his skin already beginning the healing process in spite of the demands of the ride.

Sierra pulled alongside him. "Does it hurt?"

He shook his head. "No. You did a good job." He glanced at Eve. "You holding up?"

The little girl nodded and gave him a tired smile, her face sunburned in spite of her oversized hat. He smiled back and turned his attention back to the trail, hoping that Colt's quiet perseverance meant he knew what he was doing. Lucas had calculated their rate of water consumption as well and had arrived at the same conclusion – barring a water source somewhere in the wilds, they would be out by the time they hit Albuquerque. And if they experienced any further delays, the experience would transition from difficult to deadly – he'd come across travelers who had died from dehydration only a few miles from water; distance in the desert was difficult to judge, even more so when one was desperately thirsty and in the end stages of life.

He kept his ruminations to himself, but made a note to talk to Colt in private to see if he had any plans he hadn't shared. If there was a river or a lake somewhere along their route, they'd be fine, but if he was serious about making Albuquerque before their water ran dry, they were risking everything on a plan where even the slightest delay or mistake could cost them their lives.

Chapter 6

Duke finished his breakfast and sat back against the tree that was providing welcome shade. He'd caught a plump bass that morning and cooked it over a low fire, and he and Aaron had eaten their fill, along with some rice boiled in brook water. Aaron burped from his position across from Duke, his AR-15 on his lap.

"That was great," Aaron said.

"Nothing like fresh fish," Duke agreed. "Nice enough day. Too bad we have to move. Body could get used to this for a while."

"I hear you." Aaron paused. "So when are we going to ride?"

Duke sighed. "I'm tempted to hang out another day, but that wouldn't be smart. Let's get a few miles under our belts and see what we find."

"Anything around here in particular?"

"Lucas's place is up by Loving. He said it got looted, but it may be okay to spend the night there. If it's still got a decent wall standing and good lines of sight, couldn't hurt."

"Won't the bad guys be looking for him?"

Duke shrugged. "Sure. But they've probably been over Loving and his ranch a dozen times by now. He's long gone, which even a bunch as dim as the Locos will figure out. Besides, it's a long way from Pecos. I don't see them parking a bunch of gunmen there on the off chance he shows up."

They mounted up and set their horses north, sticking to the ridgeline. From their vantage point they could see everything on the plains below them, and Duke spent much of the ride searching the horizon for threats.

They made better time than Duke had hoped, and it was late afternoon when they came across the remnants of Lucas's ranch. They rode through the entry, greeted by a dust devil twisting across the interior field that served as the courtyard.

Duke pointed at the iron gate. "Think we can wedge that into position for the night?"

Aaron regarded the metal slab, which had been knocked off its tracks. "Maybe. Might as well try."

They dismounted and put their backs into it, but couldn't budge the heavy barrier. Duke rigged up a rope to his horse, and Aaron did the same, and then together they were able to drag it upright and across the gap.

Duke inspected the result and nodded. "That should hold."

"Not if there's more than a couple of attackers."

"No reason for anyone to try. Look around – the place has been gutted. I'd bet word's spread among the scavengers there's nothing left."

"Hope you're right," Aaron said doubtfully.

"Me too."

The main ranch house had been ransacked, and not a stick of furniture remained unbroken or a window intact. Duke walked grimly through the house, leading with his rifle, and when he reached the master bedroom, stiffened at the doorway. Someone had defecated in the center of the mattress, and the room was thick with flies.

"Jesus God…" he exclaimed, and backed away.

Aaron glanced into the bedroom and shook his head. "Looks like the animals have been through this pretty good."

"Least the roof's in one piece."

"Think I'll take my chances in the barn."

"I'll be right behind you."

They were happy to find hay baled, dry but still edible. Duke unsaddled his horse and removed the saddlebags, and then did the same with his backup horse while Aaron followed suit.

Duke eyed the interior of the barn and hefted his gun. "I'll take first watch. Get some sleep. It'll be your turn before you know it."

"Shame he had to leave all this. You can see it must have been pretty nice before…before they got to it."

"Way the world works. No point in moaning over it; Lucas didn't." Duke paused. "He did what we're going to do: move on."

"That's probably healthiest. Nothing left now that the town's gone."

Duke shook his head. "Just some walls."

"We headed to Artesia tomorrow?"

"Might as well."

Duke made his way to the gate with his rifle and night vision monocle and set out three magazines by his side. He glanced at the time as twilight darkened the ranch and calculated five hours for his watch. That would put Aaron on deck at midnight, which was fine – five hours of sleep apiece would be adequate, if not ample.

Duke had survived on far less.

Motion caught his attention at the far side of the gate, and he raised the monocle. A big rabbit, skinny with youth, bounced into a nearby clump of bushes. Duke smiled to himself and shook his head at the tasty bounty only a few yards away – an easy shot if he'd had his crossbow, which he hadn't thought to bring. He picked up a rock and tossed it at the animal. "It's your lucky day, little guy. Enjoy it while it lasts," he whispered, feeling an odd sense of kinship with the rabbit, which was also doing its best to get by in a hostile world.

Chapter 7

Cano returned from using the radio and sat with Luis and the two Crew gunmen, who were visibly anxious as they waited for Tucker's man to show. It was nearly two when the gangly young man arrived in a rush, horse in tow.

"You got the guns?" he asked.

"Don't worry about that. We have them," Cano answered.

"Let's see 'em."

Cano rose and moved to his saddlebags. He withdrew two AKMs with folding stocks and held them out so the man could see them.

The young man nodded. "Name's Carlton."

"Let's ride. Wasted half the day in this dump," Cano said, swinging up into the saddle.

"Got to be back in an hour," Carlton said.

"You will be."

The group rode out of town and made for the truck stop, the sun blazing overhead through the muggy humidity. When they reached the parking lot, they dismounted, and Cano escorted Carlton into the interior, where the flies had multiplied a thousandfold in their absence, joined by rats and a plethora of insects in the consumption of the men's corpses.

Vermin scuttled away as they approached, and Carlton drew in a sharp breath at the overwhelming smell of putrefaction. The heat had done the bodies no favors, and the young man swallowed hard several times and barely made it three steps away before heaving up his breakfast.

Cano watched impassively as Carlton retched, and then moved to the corpses and leaned down to brush away a skin of maggots that had formed on their faces. He glanced up at the young man.

"You know them?" Cano growled.

Carlton peered at the corpses in the gloom and shook his head. "Never seen 'em before."

"You sure? Take a closer look."

Carlton wiped his mouth with the back of his arm. "That's okay."

"I wasn't asking."

Luis touched Carlton's arm and guided him nearer. "Breathe through your mouth," Luis advised, and Carlton nodded weakly.

Carlton regarded the first dead man for several beats and shook his head. "Nope." When he moved to the second, his eyes widened for a split second.

"What is it?" Cano demanded.

"I...I got to get outta here."

"Not before you tell me what I want to know."

"I'm gonna be sick."

"Then be sick," Cano said.

Carlton staggered away and bent over, supporting himself with hands on his knees as he dry heaved. The spell lasted fifteen seconds, and when he straightened, his tanned complexion was gray. "I recognize the second one."

"Who is he?"

"Seen him a couple times at the trading post. Apache. From up north."

"And?"

"They got a reservation or something up there. Own the whole territory. Bad news."

"Bad how?"

"You want to pass through, you got to pay a toll and use one of them. Frank — that's the guy there — was a guide. Used to bring ammo and weapons to swap at the trading post."

Cano digested the news. "How do you get in touch with them to arrange a guide?"

"They monitor the radio, I think. Never had to do it myself. Tucker may know."

Outside, the men gulped the warm air, but the stench of death lingered in their noses no matter how many breaths they took. Cano retrieved the AKMs and handed them to Carlton, who inspected them with practiced hands and nodded as he slid them into his saddlebags.

"Pleasure doing business with you," he said.

"You said maybe Tucker knew how to get in touch with the Apaches?"

"Yeah."

"How long you been working for him?" Cano asked.

"Three years, off and on."

"How much he pay you?"

Carlton looked away. "I get by. A slice of what we bring in."

"Big slice or little?" Cano pressed.

"I'm not rich or nuthin'."

"How'd you like to make some real money?"

"Doin' what?"

"Helping us."

Carlton held Cano's stare. "Helping? How?"

"You know these Apaches?"

Carlton shrugged. "Some of them, I guess."

"You ever been to Albuquerque?"

"Not since before…you know."

"We're headed that way. We're gonna need some solid hands."

"Already got a job."

"Not much of one, judging by your clothes and horse, kid." Cano mentioned a quantity of gold.

"You're bullshitting," Carlton blurted.

"Do I look like I'm joking?"

"You got it on you?"

"Got some. But I'm going to radio for more. I'm with the Crew. You know who we are?"

"I've heard of you."

"Then you know we have a lot of resources. I'm good for it."

"I...Tucker needs me."

"How long you have to work for him to see that kind of take? A year? Two? You can make that in a few weeks with us."

"I suppose I could tell him I gotta take a breather."

They mounted up and rode back into town. Cano and Luis accompanied Carlton into the trading post and waited until Tucker was finished with a customer to ask about communicating with the Apaches. When he was free, Luis took the lead, his bedside manner better than Cano's.

"Carlton was telling us that you may know how to contact the Apaches."

"You headed to Albuquerque?" Tucker asked.

"Looks that way."

"You have to put out a call on channel 19. They monitor it. But it ain't cheap."

"How much?"

"Depends on how many are going."

"Figure...five."

The trader named a figure in ammo. Luis frowned. "You serious?"

"They got a monopoly. Charge whatever they like."

Luis went back to Cano while Carlton had his talk with the boss. Luis told him what he'd learned, and Cano's scowl deepened.

"I've been thinking," Cano said. "It'll take four days, at least, for anyone to get here from Pecos. By then the trail will be cold."

"There is no trail. The rain."

Cano ignored him. "But we can assume they're headed north, based on the general direction they've been traveling. I'm willing to bet they're on their way to Albuquerque. If I'm right, I need to contact Magnus. He's got enough contacts to find someone there we can hook up with." Cano paused, thinking. "We'll need a few mercenaries. See who you can round up. Offer them the same pay as the kid. But get hard cases. I want killers, not a bunch of pussies, understand?"

"How will we pay them?"

"I've got enough gold to give them half now and half in Albuquerque. I'll let Magnus work out the rest."

Luis stepped out onto the sidewalk to wait for Carlton. The sheriff was speaking with the pair of Crew gunmen, whose expressions were unreadable. When the lawman saw Luis, he disengaged and wandered over.

"Thought I made it clear you boys should move along," he said.

"Yeah. We got that. You said by sunset, didn't you?"

"Not much time left."

"You see us after dark, then you maybe got a problem. Until then, chill. We're just hanging out."

The sheriff took a step toward Luis, hand on his gun. "Did you just tell me to 'chill'?"

"That's right. We aren't doing anything but waiting for our boss and trading with Tucker. There a law against that?"

The sheriff's eyes were slits. "I see you in the town limits one minute after dusk, you're going to be chilling in a ditch. Capiche, homeboy?"

Luis mad dogged the man, but the sheriff didn't flinch, his cobalt blue eyes hard as tungsten. Luis eventually looked away, reasoning that an escalation wasn't worth it. The sheriff must have sensed his near miss, because he walked away without comment, leaving the Loco on the sidewalk, waiting for Carlton.

The young man emerged a minute later. Luis stepped into the street. "Need to hire a couple more men. You know anybody?"

"Might. What do you want?"

"Hardest mofos you know. Stone killers. Good with a gun and a knife; seen combat."

"I know where to look."

"Yeah?"

"Bar near the town center. Rowdies is the name." Carlton nodded. "If anyone's interested, we'll find them there."

"Rowdies, huh?" Luis turned to the Crew gunmen. "Tell Cano I'll be back in a while. Let him know about the sheriff so we don't get caught in town."

Chapter 8

Lucas glanced up at the clouds overhead, a trailing remnant of the storm that had snuck up on them as they'd ridden east, and felt the first fine droplets of moisture land on his skin, the air charged with the electricity that presaged a cloudburst. The desert was still except for the hushed conversation of Ruby and Sierra. Colt was tending to the horses as Eve stood by. He wiped away the rain and stood.

"I'm going to look up ahead and see if there's any other trails we can take. This one's brutal," he said to Colt.

"Knock yourself out. You find something better, I'm fine with that as long as it leads northwest."

Lucas debated riding Tango but decided to let the stallion rest. He'd more than earned it, and Lucas could use the opportunity to stretch his legs. He shouldered his M4 sling and set off on a divergent path from the main trail, paying close attention to the terrain and any clues it could offer. After ten minutes of reconnaissance, he found a game trail that was every bit as bad as the one they were on, and was eyeing it skeptically when he heard a scream.

Colt.

Lucas broke into a run and sprinted back to the camp. Ruby was yelling instructions to Sierra, who was doing her best to calm Nugget. When Lucas arrived, Colt was lying on the ground in a ball, clutching his leg.

"What happened?" Lucas demanded.

"Rattler," Colt managed through clenched teeth. "Got me in the calf."

"What? How?"

"He was going to use the bathroom," Ruby said, pointing at a stand of bushes.

Lucas moved to Colt, pulling his belt free as he approached. He wrapped it around the bartender's knee and pulled it tight, and then handed Colt the end. "Keep pressure on that so the venom doesn't get a chance to circulate."

Sierra leaned into Lucas, her face white. "What are you going to do?"

"We don't have any antivenom. Let's get a peek at how bad it is."

Lucas unsheathed his Bowie knife and made short work of Colt's jean leg. He sliced up the seam to the knee with the razor-sharp blade and inspected the bite already discoloring around the two bright red punctures from the fangs.

"Looks like he got you pretty good. How big a snake?"

"Maybe three feet."

"That's a little bit of luck. It's the tiny ones that are the worst."

"Are you going to suck the venom out?" Ruby asked.

Lucas shook his head. "Nope. Doesn't do any good and increases the infection risk. Same with cutting the punctures."

"Then how do you treat it?"

"Afraid there isn't much we can do." He fingered the belt. "Even the tourniquet's a bad idea for more than a few minutes. Don't want you to lose the leg."

"So we just wait for me to die?" Colt asked.

"Most rattler bites aren't fatal," Lucas said.

"Most?" Colt looked down at the belt. "How about this tourniquet?"

"Probably best to loosen it up some."

"Then what's the point?"

"You can vary the pressure, slow the amount of venom that hits your bloodstream all at once." Lucas took another look at the bite. The discoloration was beginning to work its way up the veins toward

Colt's knee, and the area from his ankle up was almost twice the normal size. "It's swelling pretty good."

Colt grimaced and strained to see the wound. He regarded it without speaking for a moment and then nodded. "How long till I can ride?"

"Probably want to wait an hour or so, give your body a chance to process the venom."

Colt looked up at the sky. "We're losing the light."

"An hour won't kill us. We can ride harder later. Going to have to." Lucas paused. "Just relax. Keep your leg below your heart, and pulse the belt every five minutes or so."

Lucas stood and moved to Tango. Ruby followed him to the horse, glanced over at Colt, and then spoke softly to Lucas. "I don't mean to jinx this, but doesn't it seem like this trip is turning into a disaster?"

Lucas looked off at the endless desert. "Can't argue that one. But if it was easy, everyone would be doing it."

"I'm worried, Lucas."

He nodded. "Me too, Ruby, me too."

Chapter 9

A column of riders crested the rise. The men's faces were tanned the color of pecans beneath their cowboy hats, and rivulets of water from the tail end of the downpour streamed from the straw brims like tiny waterfalls. Eight in all, they toted assault rifles and wore flak jackets, their jeans faded from constant sun.

The Apache patrol worked its way west, one of many chartered with scouting the territory for interlopers trying to traverse the area without paying. The men were thin, with the rawboned look of men used to living hardscrabble off the land; the patrols operated in the field for weeks at a time before returning to the reservation headquarters for supplies and rest.

This patrol had been on the road for six days, entrusted with the southwestern boundary of the Indian nation. So far the trip had been uneventful, with no sign of life other than an occasional animal or bird of prey. The storm had made for unpleasant conditions, but the men rode without complaint, accustomed to anything nature could throw their way.

The lead rider slowed as he peered through the drizzle at a depression ahead in the wet sand. He raised a pair of ancient binoculars and scanned the area, and then stopped his horse and motioned to the rest of the party to do the same.

"One of the traps collapsed," he said, his voice low.

His second-in-command urged his horse forward until he was even with the lead rider. "Could be the storm."

The leader nodded. "Lot of water came down. Let's take a look."

The men rode to the trail and paused where the trap's corner hung in the pit below. Three of the men dismounted and made their way to the edge and stared into the hole. The leader pointed to the area near the opening.

"It wasn't the storm. You can see tracks – faint, but they're there. We're lucky they haven't washed away. This is recent. See?"

The second-in-command nodded. "Looks like at least five or six horses."

"But there's nothing in the trap," one of the men said.

"Could be it was a near miss."

The leader unslung his assault rifle and gestured at the tracks leading north. "They can't have gotten far. Mount up. We'll fix the trap later."

The men obeyed, and the patrol followed the hoofprints along the trail. The drizzle increased to a cloudburst and the tracks began to vanish as the rain scrubbed them clean. By the time the downpour lessoned to a mist again, the prints were gone.

The leader stopped again at a fork in the trail and scrutinized the ground. He signaled to one of his men to dismount and inspect the area up close. The man obliged and studied the trail, walking slowly for a dozen yards up each tributary before returning with a glum expression.

"Can't tell which they took."

The leader looked to his second-in-command with a resigned sigh. "Take half the men and follow the right fork. I'll take the left. Turn on your radio, but keep the volume down."

"I'll let you know if we find anything."

"Do that."

The tracker was swinging back into the saddle when the leader cocked his head, listening intently. He turned to his men.

"Did you hear that?"

The second-in-command shook his head. "No. What?"

The leader frowned. "A scream."

"Are you sure?"

"Yes."

"Which direction?"

"That way," he said, indicating the left fork. "Ed, follow us with the horses. If they're close by, we better do this on foot so they don't see us coming."

The leader lowered himself from the saddle and waited as his men followed suit. Thirty seconds later the leader began creeping along the trail, the men now in a single file procession behind him, guns in hand, faces drawn and earnest as the last of the storm blew past.

Chapter 10

Carlton seemed to know the men hanging around outside of Rowdies, who were smoking hand-rolled cigarettes that burned something other than tobacco. They looked Luis over, taking in his tattoos without comment. Carlton nodded to the nearest man.

"Busy today?"

The man shrugged. "Not much going on. Why?"

"Trading post's slower than molasses. Thought I'd show my friend here around."

"Friend, huh?" the man echoed, pointedly eyeing Luis. "You ain't from around here, are you?" he asked.

"That's right." Luis softened his tone. "What's that you're smoking?"

The man laughed. "Little of this, little of that. You know."

Luis smirked. "Yeah."

"You want any, you know who to ask."

"I'll remember that."

Carlton pushed through the swinging double doors and led Luis into a darkened room twice as deep as it was wide. A long wooden bar stretched along one side, and a collection of battered circular tables occupied the floor. The far wall boasted a dozen booths. Luis waited as his eyes adjusted to the gloom and followed Carlton to the bar.

A heavyset man with a leonine head of red hair regarded them from beneath bushy eyebrows.

"What can I get you fellers?" he asked, his voice a growl.

Carlton shrugged. "Whiskey."

Luis took in the bottles behind the man, lined up like soldiers for inspection. "You got any tequila?"

The man nodded almost imperceptibly. "Got no-name rotgut and some El Jimador, from Mexico."

"How much for the Jimador?"

The bartender named a figure in ammo. Luis nodded. "I'll take a shot."

The bartender took his time pouring the drinks into chipped glasses before setting them down in front of Luis, who slid several cartridges to him in trade. The bartender inspected the rounds and grunted affirmation, and Carlton and Luis raised their glasses.

"To the road!" Carlton said. Luis didn't respond, too busy surveying the men in the room, some at the bar behind the young man, others seated at the tables. Carlton took a pull on his drink and coughed. Luis downed half his tequila in a swallow and didn't blink, savoring the burn as the fiery liquid slid down his throat and warmed his stomach. He set down his glass and looked at Carlton.

"So what have we got here?"

Carlton twisted to appraise the patrons and nodded at a hulk of a man at one of the tables, his bulk barely fitting in his chair.

"That's Quincy. He might fit the bill. Meaner than a pit viper. But he likes to drink."

"That's okay. No booze on the trail. Desert makes an honest man out of everyone. Let's talk to him."

"Sure."

Carlton carried his drink over to the big man and pulled up a chair. Quincy peered at him with bearlike eyes, his untamed beard and scraggly long hair giving him the appearance of a vagrant, and nodded. "Carl." He shifted his attention to Luis, and his expression clearly conveyed he didn't like what he saw. "Who's this?"

"Name's Luis," Luis said. "I'm looking for a few good men."

Quincy's expression didn't change. "Don't swing that way."

45

Luis laughed and sat down across from the big man. "Didn't figure you did."

Carlton cut in. "He's looking for gunmen."

Quincy smiled, revealing rotting teeth. "That right? For what?"

"Heading north. Looking to put together some fighters."

"Who you planning to fight?"

"Whoever we have to. We're looking for some folks that stole some property from us."

"Who's us?"

Luis looked around to ensure nobody was eavesdropping. "You hear of the Crew?"

Quincy's eyes widened. "Course. You Crew?"

"That's right."

"Long ways from home, aren't you?"

"That's why we're hiring. We don't want to wait around for backup."

"How far you headed?"

"Far as necessary. You have any tracking experience?"

"Sure. You pick it up pretty quick out in the wild." The big man frowned. "What's the pay?"

Luis told him. Quincy drained his glass and burped before setting it down and leaning forward. "You're shitting me."

"No. I'm serious."

"Who do I have to kill?"

The corner of Luis's mouth twitched slightly. "Whoever we tell you to."

Quincy shrugged. "Works for me."

"I thought it might. Half in advance; half at the end of the job."

"Done. When do we ride?"

"Soon." Luis studied Quincy's face, which looked like he'd been beaten with a meat hammer. "You know anyone else might be interested in the deal?"

"That pair," Quincy said, indicating two men in the back of the bar at the last booth. "Rodriguez brothers. Got quite a rep. You heard of 'em?"

Luis shook his head. "No."

"I have," Carlton said. "Nothing good, either."

"They know their way around a gun, and they ain't shy," Quincy said. "Just got to keep an eye on 'em, is all." He coughed. "Spent some time in the joint. Murder's the rumor."

Luis nodded. "I'll be back in a few." Luis swiveled toward Carlton. "Stay here."

Luis approached the men, who watched him as he neared with the dead stare of the prison yard. Both were whippet thin, with wisps of black facial hair on their upper lips and chins. The taller of them sported tattooed teardrops beneath his left eye and barbwire inked around his neck. The other had a scar running down the side of his face from his ear to his nose, the one eye sagging slightly either from the injury or the stitching.

Luis inclined his head to the men. "Got a minute?"

"Depends," the older of the pair answered.

"Got a proposition."

"If it don't involve pay, good way to get yourself hurt."

"It does."

The older man gave him an oily smile. "Then have a seat."

Luis did and tossed back the rest of his tequila. "What are you drinking?"

"Whatever you're buying."

Luis waved for the bartender, pointed at his glass, and held up three fingers. The man nodded and went to work. Luis sat back in his chair and studied the two men. Both had junkie pallors, their faces pockmarked and cruel, and their eyes periodically darted around the room with animal cunning.

"You spend a long time inside?" Luis asked.

"Some," the one with the tattooed tears replied.

"Where?"

"PNM in Santa Fe. Four years."

"Level Five?"

The man shook his head. "Six."

"Brutal."

"It was okay."

The bartender arrived with the drinks and Luis counted out more ammo for him. When he was done, he raised his glass.

"I'm Len. That's Marco," the older one said.

They threw back the tequila. "Now that's what I'm talking about," Len said appreciatively.

"I have a job for two guys who don't mind a fight."

Len nodded. "I'm listening."

"I'm after some people who stole from my group. The Crew. I have to get them back. You don't steal from us."

Len nodded again. "Magnus's outfit. Houston, right?"

"Almost all of Texas now. Clear to Pecos."

"How much, and for how long?"

"Probably a week or so." He told them what Cano had offered. They exchanged a glance.

"That's for a week or two?" Len asked.

"It could get snotty."

"Hell, I'd walk through boiling lava for that. Where do we sign up?" Marco said.

"Guy running the show has to approve you. Name's Cano."

"Sounds good. When and where?"

"You got horses?"

"Of course."

"What kind of shape are they in?"

"Good enough."

"Any problem following orders? Cano doesn't put up with crap."

Marco shrugged. "He's the boss. We do what he says."

"And what I say."

"Right."

Luis stood. "You know the breakfast joint down by the trading post?"

"Sure."

"Meet me there in an hour."

Len threw a glance at Quincy. "You thinking of hiring him?"

"Already did. Why?"

"Dumb as a stump."

"Not asking him to think."

"It's your money."

"You have a problem working with him? Any bad blood between you?"

Len shook his head. "Nah. Just sizing up the competition, is all."

"We're going to be riding hard. No booze or dope."

"Fair enough. When do we get paid?"

Luis explained the deal to them and told the pair where they were headed.

Marco's eyes fixed on his. "You got a guide?"

"No."

"Bad idea."

"We're working on it. That a problem?"

Len tilted his glass to his mouth to get the last few drops and then tossed it on the table with a clatter. "If you say it ain't, then it ain't."

Luis allowed himself a small smile. "Right answer."

Carlton and Quincy looked at him quizzically when he returned to the table and sat down heavily.

"They're on board," Luis said, and checked the time. "Damn. Going to be dark in a couple hours. We need to get back." He told Quincy to meet them at the diner, and he rose. Carlton joined him, and they stepped out into the sunlight, blinking from the bright contrast to the dim bar interior.

The sheriff was standing across the street, now with two more men. He held out his index finger and pointed it at Luis, and then moved his thumb down, simulating shooting. Luis ignored him and they made for the trading post. Luis was more than anxious to be rid of the town, even if it meant the hostile wasteland stretching north.

Chapter 11

The rain abated as Lucas and Ruby prepared Colt to ride with his makeshift tourniquet. He gritted his teeth at the pain tracing up his leg, which he described as liquid fire in his veins. But he was still breathing, his vision was clear, and other than clammy sweat on his forehead, he seemed to be in reasonable shape, considering. He insisted on continuing their trek, reasoning that his horse hadn't been bitten and that he could sit upright in the saddle as well as he could on the ground.

Sierra dressed the wound with antibiotic ointment and placed a pressure bandage on it, which relieved at least some of the localized pain. Lucas supported him under one arm and Ruby under the other, and he hopped toward his horse with a determined expression.

The sun broke through the overcast and Colt tried a smile, which turned sickly at the end. "See? An omen. I'll be fine."

Lucas nodded in agreement, even though he didn't share the bartender's optimism. Colt's skin felt clammy to the touch, and Lucas suspected he was in low-grade shock from the bite.

They were preparing to boost Colt up into the saddle when Sierra cried out from behind them.

"Lucas!"

Lucas turned to see Sierra facing seven gunmen who'd materialized on the trail, all with assault rifles leveled at them. He cursed his M4 being slung on his shoulder and debated going for his

Kimber, but stopped when the tall man at the front of the group spoke.

"Don't move a muscle," the man ordered. He angled his head at the nearest man on his right. "Collect their weapons. Shoot them if they so much as twitch."

"Who are you?" Colt asked, his voice a rasp.

"We own this land. You're trespassing."

"You Apache?" Lucas asked.

The man nodded. "That's right. And if you know that, then you know that to ride through our land without paying the price is a death sentence."

"We...we had a guide," Colt said. "Frank."

The man's expression remained stony. "Where is he?"

"He...he's dead."

"How?"

"A fight back at Roswell," Colt managed.

"Frank? Bullshit. I knew him. He was level-headed." The man's eyes narrowed. "What did you do to him?"

"We didn't do anything. He was attacked. We were supposed to meet him at the truck stop north of town. We got there, and he was dead. Gut shot, but he took the other guy with him."

The Apache who was disarming them reached Lucas and removed his Kimber from its holster, gave it an admiring glance, and then tossed it on the ground with the rest of the weapons. Next came the M4, and he whistled when he hefted the gun.

"Serious artillery," he said. Lucas didn't comment.

When they were unarmed, the leader eyed Colt. "What's wrong with him?"

"Snakebit. Rattler," Lucas said.

"That's some bad luck."

"You have any tricks for treating a bite?"

"Tricks? Keep breathing as long as you can."

Lucas nodded. "That's what I thought."

The man studied Lucas for another moment and then looked to Colt. "You say Frank was supposed to guide you?"

"That's right."

"Did you talk to headquarters about him getting shot?"

"No. We were on our way out of town. No radio. But we already paid. Talk to your people."

"I will. Or you will." The leader looked at the sky. "Tomorrow." He turned to his men. "We'll camp here tonight. Spot's as good as any."

"No. He's been bit. We have to get him help," Sierra protested.

"We're not riding at night. Terrain's too treacherous, and it's a long way. If he's going to die, he's going to die out here. Nothing they can do for him on the reservation either." He paused. "We'll make camp. He should sleep sitting up so it slows the venom to his heart. Other than that, he's in God's hands. Welcome to Apache country."

The leader turned and strode away as his men collected the weapons and carried them to the horses. They packed them into their saddlebags and then prepared a primitive camp. They allowed Lucas to pitch tents for the women and one for himself. Lucas worked efficiently and finished by setting his saddlebags on the ground so Colt had something to lean against while he dozed.

The sun was sinking into the western mountains when the leader allowed Lucas to distribute food and water to his group. Colt waved off food until Lucas forced him to eat.

"The more you have in your system to soak up the poison, the better. Flush it out. Plenty of food and water's the best we can do for you, so take advantage of it," Lucas advised.

Colt glumly chewed his portion. Sierra slid closer to Lucas and whispered to him, "What are we going to do? Try to escape?"

Lucas shook his head. "No. Colt's people paid for safe passage. This will all get straightened out tomorrow. Don't do anything stupid, and we'll be fine."

"Are you sure?"

Lucas lowered his voice further. "Sierra, listen to me. There's no place to escape to. This is their land – there's no way we would make it far, especially with Colt. All of which assumes we could get our weapons back and overpower them, which isn't going to happen."

"I just feel so powerless."

"Sometimes you have to go with the flow, Sierra," Ruby cautioned. "Lucas is right. We need to stick together, do as they say, and figure it out at their headquarters. Anything else could get us all killed."

"I know you're right. I just don't like it."

Lucas put his arm around her and squeezed her to him. "I know. Nobody does. Just concentrate on taking care of Eve, get some sleep, and tomorrow will be a new day."

"Now I'm worried about snakes, too."

"Zip up your tent and you'll be fine," Colt said.

One of the men rose with his gun and began a slow walking patrol as darkness fell. Another sat directly across from them, the gun in his hands a reminder that they were prisoners until they accounted for themselves to the Apache leader. Lucas squeezed Sierra's arm again and she kissed his cheek before gathering Eve and escorting her to their tent.

Ruby watched them go and stood. "I'm calling it a night. Colt, holler if you need anything."

"Thanks. I will."

Lucas joined her and walked her to her tent. "Think Sierra will be okay?" he whispered.

"She's headstrong, but I think you got through to her. I'll keep an ear peeled, just in case." She paused. "Colt doesn't look so good."

"No. He doesn't," Lucas agreed. "I'll say a prayer for him tonight."

"I will too," Ruby said with a smile. "And I'll add in a request for no more snakes."

"If you're taking requests…"

"Good night, Lucas."

He took a last glance at Colt, who was shivering slightly while doing his best not to show it, and shook his head. "I hope so, Ruby."

Chapter 12

Cano adjusted his saddle straps and inspected his horse as the rest of his men did the same. They'd spent the night outside of town near the truck stop, having been delayed by their new men, who had to barter with Tucker for supplies for their trip. He'd been furious that identifying the dead men, communicating with Magnus by radio, and finding mercenaries had eaten up an entire day, keenly aware that his quarry was now two days ahead of him.

Morning had broken a half hour earlier, a distant rooster announcing sunrise, and Cano pushed the group to eat and prepare for a long slog. He didn't have much hope of picking up tracks after the storm, but he knew that if they'd hired a guide to get through Apache territory, the next outpost was Albuquerque, and they would ride as hard as they could to make up for lost time.

"I want to get sixty miles under our belts today. We'll go till dark," he announced, and the new men nodded as though the astronomical distance were reasonable. They'd been happy to get their gold the night before, with the promise of more when the job was done, and would have followed Cano into hell.

As they rode past the skeletons of looted and burned buildings, Cano wondered if that wasn't where he was leading them, the sun already blazing hot as it rose over the eastern desert. They crossed the freeway intersection, the huge overpasses a reminder of a time that seemed impossibly distant, rusting cars mute witness to their passage. Once north of the highway crossing they followed the road, sticking to the dirt shoulder for their animals' sake, where the going was relatively easy for the first few hours.

The heat of the day intensified, and they had to stop more than Cano would have liked to water the horses. At one of the pauses he overheard Luis talking to the new recruits, explaining their quest in more detail. Cano interrupted their powwow by calling to him.

"Luis, get over here. Now."

Luis stopped what he was doing and trotted to where Cano was seated. The big man glowered at him.

"What the hell do you think you're doing?" he asked.

"I was telling them what to expect and what we're after."

"Did I ask you to?"

"No, but–"

"Luis, listen closely. Don't volunteer anything. Don't tell them anything more than you have. If they ask questions, refer them to me. Clear?"

Luis struggled to maintain his composure. "I thought–"

Cano cut him off. "Don't talk to them about anything more than the weather. Period. They're not your new friends, and they aren't long-lost relatives. They're hired muscle, nothing more. So shut it."

Luis nodded slowly, his face a blank. Cano recognized the thousand-yard stare. Luis had retreated inward to a place Cano couldn't get to, and had tuned everything out. Cano had done the same many times while behind bars – it was a survival skill you learned when dealing with authority. In the joint, if you gave a hint of rebellion to the guards, they'd beat you to a pulp and you'd spend a month pissing blood. So you mastered the blank stare. Luis was getting more practice on this trip. Cano didn't care.

"Now get out of here. You're breathing my air."

Luis turned wordlessly and made his way to his horse. Cano sneered at his back, and one of the Crew gunmen saw him and smiled. They'd noted the way Cano was treating the Loco and would follow their master's lead.

Cano had already decided he would kill Luis once his usefulness had passed. The man had a rebellious streak he didn't like, and he suspected he wouldn't be a strong ally if left alone in Pecos once this episode was over. Cano would need someone more pliant, someone who didn't hold delusions of his own importance. He didn't care who, but he knew that an uppity punk like Luis was trouble waiting to happen, and could feel the hate radiating from him whenever they interacted.

Cano lurched to his feet and walked a few yards away. He unzipped his fly and urinated on the hot sand, thinking about his next move. He'd informed Magnus about their likely trajectory, with Albuquerque the next stop, but other than a dismissive assurance that Magnus would take care of things, that had been all the feedback he'd received.

Which concerned him. He knew his master, and he didn't want the same fate that had been ordered for Garret. The only reason he wasn't more worried was that he also knew that while Magnus was mercurial and volatile, he forgot quickly. A success in locating the woman and child would be all he remembered – the setbacks along the way ignored once the result had been achieved.

Cano finished his task and returned to the horses. His instinct was to push them until they dropped, but attempting to cross the desert without the animals to carry them would be a death sentence, so he had to temper his impatience so as not to drive them into the ground.

"Party time's over. Mount up," he called, listening for any signs of objection or complaint. There were none, which gladdened him. Like all leaders who ruled by force, his senses were tuned to detect even a hint of rebellion and quash it instantly. He'd learned that early in life, running his drug gang on the streets of Houston, and later, in prison. Watching Magnus had reinforced the importance of meeting any challenge with immediate, overwhelming force.

But there was none today. The men were happy for the opportunity to earn a small fortune.

"Quincy, you take point. See if you can spot anything," Cano barked, once they were all in the saddle. The big man spurred his horse forward and made for the road, where heat shimmered off the gray pavement in serpentine waves. The odds of finding anything on the endless stretch of gravel shoulder was less than zero, but Cano's order was one that must be obeyed.

Chapter 13

Lucas was roused from a surface sleep by the sound of Ruby's voice from outside his tent. He cracked one eye open and reached for the entry flap zipper. The lack of light shining through the fabric told him it was still night. He opened the flap and looked out at her.

"What is it?"

"Colt doesn't look good."

He checked the time. It would be dawn in twenty minutes. He forced himself awake, pulled on his boots, and exited the tent, hat in hand. Ruby led him to where Colt was sitting, teeth chattering.

"How you doing, partner?" Lucas asked.

"Been better."

Ruby felt Colt's forehead and looked at Lucas in alarm. "He's burning up."

"When did you last drink some water?" Lucas asked.

"Been a while."

Lucas glanced at the guard, who was watching him without interest, and moved to his saddlebags for a canteen. He held it out, a modest but vital offering, and then waited as Colt drained the container.

Lucas took it from him. "Soon as the sun's up, we'll get a peek at the bite and see if anything's changed."

"Feels pretty swollen," Colt said.

Ruby ran a hand lightly over the pressure bandage. "That's to be expected."

"Is he going to be able to ride?" Lucas asked.

"Hell yes, I will," Colt snapped. "No way you're leaving me out here."

"That wasn't what I meant. I was thinking we might have to rig something…"

"Get me into the saddle, and I'll do the rest. It'll take my mind off dying."

"If that was going to happen, it would have by now," Lucas countered.

The camp roused to life as the sun rose. When Sierra and Lucas removed the dressing, the news wasn't good. The area around the bite was purple and red, with bluish discoloration following Colt's veins. The leader of the Apaches walked over and glanced at the wound.

"You're lucky it wasn't a diamondback. You might make it."

"How do you know it wasn't?" Lucas asked.

"I've seen their bite. That looks like you didn't get a whole lot of venom, so you're lucky. Believe me, it can be a whole lot worse. I've seen skin split from the knee to the ankle and the flesh looking like someone poured acid on it. Required amputation."

"Not feeling particularly lucky," Colt said.

"You'll live," the leader said, and turned to Lucas. "Break down the tents and pack them. We mount up in ten minutes."

Once they were on the trail, Colt seemed to do better, and the time passed uneventfully as their surroundings became an inferno. Seven hours after they'd mounted up, a string of low buildings came into view, and the leader twisted toward them.

"Won't be long now."

He'd radioed ahead earlier, and a welcoming committee of several dozen armed men was waiting for their arrival. They dismounted, and three of the younger braves led the horses to a water trough in the shade of an overhang.

An older man pushed through the throng and looked down at Colt. "You the one that got bit?"

"That's right," Colt managed.

"Let's have a look at it, then."

Sierra removed the dressing, and the man knelt beside Colt and inspected the wound. He took Colt's pulse, felt his head, and then pulled a stethoscope from his satchel and listened to his heart.

Finished, he stood. "Going to need antibiotics, or you could lose the leg."

"Do you have any?" Ruby asked.

"None we can spare. But they should have some in Albuquerque."

"That's, what, a couple days' ride?" Lucas asked.

"About that."

"Will that be soon enough?"

The man looked at Colt and then at Lucas. "Sixty-forty his favor." He draped the stethoscope over his shoulder. "I'm Ben. I run this place. What happened to Frank?"

Lucas repeated Colt's story about the shooting.

Ben grunted when he was through. "Can't see someone getting the jump on Frank."

"Apparently he met his match."

"Too bad. He was one of the good ones."

"I'm sorry for your loss," Ruby said.

Ben nodded. "Now I have to figure out what to do with you."

"What do you mean? We're paid up," Colt said.

"True. But you need a guide to get the rest of the way. So you're going to have to pay for another one. Your passage is covered, not a new guide. Sorry."

"How much?"

"Thirty ounces of gold."

"What! That's outrageous!" Colt snapped.

"Frank had a wife and family. Much of that will go to support them. That's the price."

"We don't have that kind of weight on us."

"What about your boss?"

Colt blinked several times. "They'll pay. They're good for it."

"If so, we have a deal. You authorized to speak for them?"

"I am."

"Then we'll get you outfitted, give you back your weapons, and you can be on your way. Sooner the better, by the looks of that leg." Ben looked around until his eyes settled on a short, swarthy man with long hair. "Tarak, come here."

Tarak approached, and Ben had a hurried discussion with him. Tarak nodded several times during the exchange and then made for the barn to get his horse and gear.

"He'll be ready to ride within the hour. He's one of our best. He'll accompany you and bring the gold back to us."

Colt shook his head. "No. They'll never stand for it. He can wait for us in Albuquerque. I'll return with the payment. Just as someone met you here to pay."

"The condition's not negotiable. One of my men died – and he was a close friend. If you don't want to accept our terms, you're free to try your luck on your own. I won't stop you. But I'll also warn you that there are traps along the way. Tarak knows their locations. Without him, you might not make it, so think hard about your refusal. I bear you no ill will and would like to see you live, but I won't risk Frank's family going without because your people decided the price was too rich, after the fact."

"It's against the rules. They won't agree."

"Can you radio them? We have a shortwave set here."

Colt sighed. "Where?"

Twenty minutes later, after a coded discussion across five different channels, Colt got reluctant approval. Ben nodded and disappeared for a few minutes, and returned with another pressure bandage and some salve.

"This should reduce the pain some, but like I said, you're going to need antibiotics. Venom won't kill you, but the infection will. That should be your main concern in Albuquerque," he said.

"You sure you don't have any you can give him?" Lucas asked.

"We have far too little to dispense it to others. But you can take some salve. It's the best I can do."

Lucas frowned, but he understood. He couldn't blame Ben – the doses Colt might have gotten would be ones the Apaches then wouldn't have when a child sustained an ugly wound. Life in the new reality of post-collapse was one where charity could cost loved ones their lives.

"You can always buy more," Lucas tried.

"I can't take that risk," Ben said in a tone that ended further discussion.

Tarak reappeared a few minutes later with his horse, saddlebags bulging with supplies, and an AR-15 strapped to his back. Ben's men returned the guns to Lucas and his group, and then they were ready to ride, the horses fed and watered, Colt's pain somewhat eased by the goop and the bandage.

"Thanks for everything," Lucas said as they mounted up.

Ben nodded. "See to it that Tarak makes it back in one piece."

"He'll be paid, and then he's on his own. Nobody's going to babysit your man any more than you'll part with drugs for ours." Lucas took the guide's measure. "He looks like he can handle himself."

"That he can. Tarak, radio me when you have the gold."

"Will do," Tarak said, and urged his horse forward, the women trailing him and Lucas and Colt bringing up the rear.

As the reservation faded into the distance behind them, Colt spurred his horse till he was beside Lucas and muttered under his breath, "Thanks for going to bat for me."

"No problem. Sorry I couldn't convince him."

Colt shrugged. "It's in God's hands now. I'll make it."

Lucas nodded. "You better. We're screwed if you don't."

Colt grimaced and saved his energy, his message conveyed, and they continued in silence, the only sound the clip-clop of hooves and the occasional moan of the wind out of the east.

Chapter 14

Artesia's perimeter wall swam into view as Duke and Aaron pushed their horses hard, anxious to make it to the town's protection before sundown. They'd made decent time, and Duke was hoping that Lucas was still there so he could discuss setting up another trading post, perhaps with him as a partner. After all, the former lawman was honest, knew weapons, and Duke could trust him in a pinch –the most important quality in a business associate. Duke could manage the actual trading, and Lucas the logistics of operating the site. At least, that was going to be his pitch.

They slowed as they neared the guard post, which was manned by two riflemen who didn't look welcoming. They eyed Duke like he'd stolen their horses, and the larger one called out, "Town's closed down. Move on."

"I'm here to see Bruce."

"He ain't here."

"Where'd he go?"

"Beats me."

"When's he going to come back?"

"Same answer. I don't keep his schedule."

Duke's shoulders sagged, but he had a lie ready. "Bastard owes me money. I'm here to collect."

"Can't let you in."

"He's got some of my gear. I'm going to get it one way or another."

The guard exchanged a glance with the other, clearly not expecting a confrontation with Bruce's debtors. Duke sensed an opening and pressed the point.

"Look," he said. "I got no truck with you. But he has my stuff. I'm not going to just shrug and go home. I came here for my gear, and I'm going to get it. You got no right to protect the little weasel – my family's life depends on it. You try to block me, you're endangering them. I won't take kindly to that. Neither would you in my shoes."

The man looked Duke over, assessing his weathered face, and shifted to Aaron. He had a hurried discussion with his partner and then straightened as he addressed Duke.

"Don't much like being threatened."

"Didn't mean it that way. I don't want trouble, but I'm also not going away empty-handed. Rode way too long for that, and fair's fair."

"How long you reckon it'll take?"

"Not long. Although I hate to have to spend the night outside the wall if I can find an area to bunk for the night."

The man pushed the gate aside. "Bruce has a fair parcel of land. Nobody's on it. If you was to camp there, I doubt anyone would care. Long as it's only for the night."

Duke tilted his head at the guard. "Appreciate it. Where's his place at? First time I've been here."

The man stopped opening the gate. "Thought you said he had your gear."

"That's right. He came and got it. Probably because he planned to screw me out of it."

The guard considered Duke's words and then resumed sliding the gate open. "None of my business. Just don't get into any trouble, or it's my ass for letting you in."

"Don't worry. Just want what's mine."

They rode through the gap, leading their spare horses, and stopped by the guard post. The men gave them directions to Bruce's trailer, and they made their way along the perimeter road until they arrived at a broken-down single-wide mobile home sorely in need of repair. The gate to the grounds was open, and as they entered, a man watched from across the street, shotgun in hand. When they dismounted, he ambled over and nodded a greeting.

"He ain't here," the watcher said.

"Any idea where he went?"

"Scuttlebutt's that he cut out and headed north."

"To Roswell?"

"I figure." The man shifted from foot to foot and glanced at the trailer. "Ain't nuthin' worth spit in there. Been cleaned out."

"Little prick had a bunch of my gear," Duke growled. "Figures he took off without fixing it."

"Did the same to me."

"Was he alone when he left?"

"Nah. Had a couple of women with him. And some dude. Thought he was a badass. Mean-looking cuss."

"How long ago they leave?"

The man studied his boots, his face screwed tight in concentration, as though Duke had asked him to explain general relativity. Eventually he looked up at Duke with a gap-toothed grin. "Four, five days ago."

"So they're long gone."

"'Fraid so."

"Well, hell." Duke spit for emphasis. "Guess we'll spend the night and then go after him. He's not going to get away with this." Duke paused. "Anyone else been asking about him?"

"Nope. He had everyone conned."

"I'll say. And there's nothing left?"

"No. He took it all. But the well still works. You can water your horses, at least."

"That's good to know. Solves one problem."

"Name's Tom. You need anything, we got eggs and some power. We can trade. Plenty to go around."

"That's mighty neighborly, Tom. I'm Duke. This is Aaron. Might take you up on the power and eggs. Got some batteries need charging, and we haven't had a decent meal in forever."

"Long as you got some ammo, we can dicker."

"Where's your place?"

"Down this street, left-hand side, 'bout a quarter mile away. Painted blue, next to a bombed-out gas station. Can't miss it. Got lights and everything."

"We'll be along shortly. Thanks for the offer."

Tom shuffled off, leaving Duke and Aaron to their chores. They watered the horses and let them graze. Aaron swatted mosquitoes away as twilight approached and eyed Duke.

"You think he ripped the place off?"

Duke laughed. "Of course. But Bruce probably had it coming. What does that tell you?"

"He isn't going to be back."

"Right. Which means Lucas either scared the crap out of him or made him a better offer. Maybe a little of both." Duke studied the trailer. "Lucas had something up his sleeve with that woman. Bruce must have been part of the puzzle. Only thing that makes sense."

"We going to get some eggs?"

"Absolutely. Probably Bruce's chickens, too. I'd say old Tom made out like a bandit."

"I could eat."

"Let's let the horses feed and then we'll hoof it over. No point in starving to death. Tomorrow we'll ride north and see what we find."

"Four or five days is a lot of lead time."

"Yeah, but we're not looking to catch up with them on the road. Wherever they settle's fine by me."

"You haven't said why you want to find them."

"Business, of course."

Aaron raised an eyebrow, but Duke didn't elaborate. He was in charge, and Aaron had nothing better to do, anyway. Duke had treated him well at the trading post, and he had no doubt the trader would do the same wherever he wound up.

"Roswell, huh?" Aaron said. "What have you heard about it?"

"Not much. But it's a decent size, and that means opportunity.

Let's check it out. Can't hurt."

Aaron nodded. "You're the boss."

"Yup. And right now, I'm thinking about eight eggs scrambled sounds about right."

Chapter 15

Cano's men drifted along the highway in a semi-stupor as the day wore on, the swelter intolerable. While the landscape south had been brutal at times, there was little to prepare them for the inhospitable terrain as they pushed north. Quincy had found what he'd thought might be faint tracks along one of the side trails that paralleled the highway, and their party fanned out along that strip of barren trail, plodding along with the tenacity of a chain gang.

Quincy was in the lead, with Carlton a few yards from his side, their heads hanging and chins nearly to their chests, hats pulled low against the blazing sun. The horses were doing all the work, but none were moving fast, leaving their riders to doze in the worst of the heat.

Cano had insisted that they keep their breaks to only a few minutes each hour, and the animals were beginning to show the effects of fatigue. Nobody had dared counter Cano's insistence on pressing forward, and the mood among the men was glum as horse and rider alike reached the limits of their endurance.

A cry sounded from Quincy's right, and he twisted to see what had alarmed Carlton. Instead of the young trader, all he saw was a cavity in the ground. The pained scream of a horse sounded from its depths, and Cano and Quincy leapt from their mounts and ran to the edge of the hole, guns in hand.

Carlton's horse was lying at the bottom of a pit, the lower part of which skewed at an impossible angle. At least one of the beast's legs had clearly been shattered from the drop, and Carlton himself had been impaled on sharpened branches that protruded from the base of the hole. Twitching, he tried to speak, but blood gushed down his chin, and he coughed a crimson spray against the side of the pit.

Cano shook his head. "Trap."

The rest of the group gathered around Cano, who flipped his rifle safety off and aimed at the horse. The first burst of fire snuffed out the suffering animal's life, and Cano shifted his aim to Carlton, whose eyes were open, as though pleading with them to spare him.

"We need to help him," Luis said.

Cano shook his head. "Look at him. He'll never survive. He's finished."

The bark of the AK-47 ended the discussion, the rounds liquefying the young man's skull. The Rodriguez brothers watched without reaction, and Cano lowered his weapon and switched the safety back on.

"Get a rope," he called over his shoulder. "Retrieve his gold and weapons, and don't miss his water and food. We'll need as much as we can carry. No point in letting it go to waste."

The two Crew gunmen sprang into motion to obey as Cano turned to Quincy.

"Why didn't you spot the trap?" Cano growled.

"I...I was focused on the trail. Nobody told me there might be traps, or I would have."

"I thought you knew these parts."

"Never been up here. I stick close to town, mostly. Nothing up here but trouble and death."

Cano stood silently for a moment, his finger hovering over the trigger guard of his rifle, and then walked back to his horse without comment. The danger of the moment that had just passed was palpable, and Quincy snuck a glance at Luis, who shrugged and watched the pair of Crew gunmen as one braced a rope so the other could lower himself into the hole and relieve the dead horse of its burden.

Ten minutes later they were back on the trail, now in single file. Quincy searched the path in front of them for any hint of a trap, unnerved at the near miss and how quickly their expedition had claimed its first casualty.

The air had begun to cool from broiling to baking when Luis called out to Cano, "Riders hard right!"

Luis already had his Kalashnikov in play as Cano drove his horse close and pushed the barrel aside.

"What the hell are you doing?" Luis cried.

"Stand down!" Cano yelled. "No shooting. That's an order."

"But—" Luis protested.

"You heard me," Cano warned.

The men reluctantly obeyed, confusion on their faces, as a group of ten Apache gunmen cantered into view with rifles in hand. Cano held his ground, and the lead rider rode up to him.

Cano took the leader's measure, his weathered skin tanned the color of rust, the hard lines of his face all angles, his gaze unblinking.

"You're on our land," the leader said, his voice a rasp. His gunmen held their position, aiming their weapons at Cano's group.

"Yes," Cano said. "My boss was supposed to contact your people and arrange something."

"Who are you?"

"My name's Cano. I'm with the Crew."

"The Crew?"

"That's right." Cano eyed the man's radio. "Why don't you call in and talk to your headquarters?"

"Keep your hands where we can see them if you want to stay alive," the lead rider cautioned, and moved back to his men, radio raised to his lips.

A tense calm descended over the area as the radio screeched static, and then a voice answered. The leader had a terse discussion in a language Cano didn't recognize. After several minutes of back and forth, he returned, his gun now in his saddle scabbard, radio clipped to his belt.

"Your Magnus spoke to us," the leader said. "I'm to bring you to the reservation to meet with our council."

"What? No. We need a guide. You're supposed to get us someone to take us to Albuquerque. No meetings."

"Those aren't my orders. They said to escort you to see them."

"Magnus was clear–"

"All I know's what my boss told me, and that's to lead you to headquarters so you can discuss your situation."

Cano made a visible effort to control his rage, his tattoos squirming like insects on his shaved head. He drew a deep breath and nodded. "Fine. Let's go."

"It's not close. We'll ride another hour or so and make camp for the night."

"That's not acceptable," Cano growled.

"We don't ride at night. So that's how it is."

"We're in a hurry."

"Look, you don't like it, you can take it up with the chief. But he knows how we operate, and he's expecting you tomorrow. Trying to ride all night won't accomplish anything but endanger the horses, which I won't do," the leader said, his voice hard. "One misstep in the dark and I have a man without a horse. That's not going to happen, so we'll ride first thing in the morning and be there by noon."

Cano could see he was getting nowhere. "Where's your reservation?"

"North. It's in the general direction of Albuquerque, so you'll only lose the same time you would have if you'd camped out tonight anyway." The leader paused. "Judging by the look of your horses, they need rest. They probably wouldn't make it on an all-night ride even if I was willing to chance it."

Cano looked away, considering. There was no point in escalating the conflict when it was obvious the leader was intractable. "Fine. Tell your men to stand down. I don't need someone shooting me in the back by mistake."

The leader nodded and called out in Apache. There was a rustle from behind Cano as the gunmen lowered their weapons. The leader adjusted his Stetson over his brow and then pulled the reins and directed his horse to the track. "Stay single file on the trail. There are traps all around here."

Cano's lip curled. "I know. That's what the shooting was all about. We already lost a horse and rider."

The leader didn't respond, instead spurring his horse forward wordlessly. Cano debated saying something more but instead followed suit, leaving Luis and the rest to find their way into formation as their escorts brought up the rear.

Chapter 16

Cano and his men arrived at the Apache headquarters at midday after a hard night in the desert. When they neared the compound of simple buildings, they were greeted by twenty gunmen, all cut from the same bolt of threadbare cloth, their faces speaking to lives of hardship and deprivation. The patrol leader dismounted and motioned for Cano to do the same, and led him to where the head of the tribe sat in the shade with three other old men, all wearing cowboy hats.

The leader introduced Cano and left him to the council, who studied him dispassionately.

"Pull up a chair," Ben said.

"That's okay. I'll stand." Cano paused. "Why wasn't I provided a guide?"

"You mean, why didn't we anticipate that we would run into you in the middle of nowhere and have a fully provisioned guide waiting with the patrol on the off chance we did?" Ben asked, his tone flat but his words showing what he thought of Cano's question.

Cano had no rejoinder, but he silently radiated fury at the Apache. He stood silently while Ben studied him like he'd just wiped him off the sole of his boot. Ben looked to his companions, who smiled, making Cano even angrier.

Ben sat forward. "Cool your jets. We've got a man for you. He's ready to go. We had to pull him out of the field – our normal guy took off yesterday, and we lost a man down Roswell way recently, so we're a little short-handed."

"Took off?"

"Yes. Another party headed north."

Cano's eyes narrowed. "Really? Who?"

"Party of five. One of 'em Snakebit. Ugly."

"Any women?"

Ben looked him up and down. "What's it to you?"

"I'm tracking someone who stole our property. A woman. Young."

"There was an older woman. Also a younger one, with a child. Cute little thing. But at that age, they usually are."

Cano swallowed. "A child?"

"That's what I said, isn't it? Little girl."

"You had them here, and you didn't hold them?" Cano blurted.

Ben appraised him. "Why would we? They paid their way. Just like you did. We've got no beef with them."

"When did they leave?"

"Yesterday evening."

Cano did a quick calculation. "Damn. We'll never catch up. Can you radio your guide and have them delayed?"

Ben shook his head. "Our man doesn't have a radio."

"Your patrol did," Cano snapped.

"No reason to give a guide one of the few working units."

Cano softened his approach. "We would pay. A lot."

"Which would have been nice to know yesterday. But your boss never mentioned it. He just negotiated your trip. Can't read minds."

"There's nothing you can do?"

"Not now."

Cano's brow furrowed with concentration. "I need to use your radio to call Magnus. You're positive they're headed to Albuquerque?"

"Yes. Like I said, one of the men was snakebit."

"And there's only five total?" Cano asked, trying to compute how two men and a pair of women could have slaughtered his force so effectively.

"That's right."

"Where's your radio?"

"Thought you was in a big hurry. Sammy there's your guide. He's ready to roll when you are," Ben said, pointing at a thin man in his twenties.

"I need to talk to Magnus."

"Fair enough. I'll show you the way."

Ben stood slowly and led Cano into the building. An old shortwave transmitter sat on a folding table by one of the dusty windows, where a bored operator watched the scanner for signs of activity. Cano sat beside him and dialed the channel selector to the band the Crew used, and transmitted a call for Magnus. Five minutes went by, and then Snake's voice came on the air.

"He can't talk. What is it?"

"I have news." Cano relayed the information in oblique terms any eavesdropper wouldn't understand. When he was done, Snake was silent for several seconds.

"I'll relay the info. You're positive on the destination?" he asked.

"Yes. But they'll be there by tomorrow evening."

"I understand. I'll tell our friend."

"We're a day behind them."

"That's unfortunate." The rebuke was clear in Snake's tone.

"Couldn't be helped."

"So you say."

Cano terminated the transmission and pushed away from the radio. Ben stood a few yards away, his face blank, but Cano knew he'd heard the embarrassing exchange.

"We need to get out of here now. Do you have potable water?"

"Got a well. Go ahead and top off your jugs. And you're welcome on the radio."

Cano took a step toward him. "You've been paid well."

"No," Ben corrected. "We've been promised we'd be paid well and that a messenger would arrive within a week with the gold. But so far it's all talk, so I'd bear that in mind before you start assuming any entitlement."

Cano looked like he'd been slapped. "We're good for it."

"Our usual terms are cash and carry. No tickee, no laundry." Ben hesitated. "We made an exception for you, but that's unusual."

Cano frowned but nodded. "Thank you." His expression was sour; words of gratitude were unfamiliar to a man who took what he wanted and was accustomed to having his orders followed without question.

Ben adjusted his hat. "You're welcome. Let me show you to the well."

Cano and Ben continued their contentious discussion as the men filled their containers, but ultimately parted ways with a handshake and a new agreement for cooperation between the Apaches and the Crew. The price would be high, but worth it, Cano believed – he just hoped Magnus would agree when he broke the news about what he'd negotiated.

Twenty minutes later they were riding north, Sammy at the head of the procession, with brimming canteens and watered horses. Cano's mind was racing as he considered how close he'd come to catching his quarry, and he cursed the patrol's decision not to ride all night, which would have cut the woman's lead time to half a day – one that could have been covered at a gallop if the horses didn't have to go any further.

From behind, Luis called out to Cano, who'd filled them in on the near miss as well as confirming their destination. "You going to bushwhack them in Albuquerque?"

"Magnus will arrange something," replied Cano curtly.

Irritated, Luis stiffened, but he held his tongue. He filed away the dismissive snub with the litany of resentments he had accumulated, and slowed to give Cano's horse some space, cursing Cano with each hoofbeat but secretly delighted that the woman had managed to cause the bastard such distress. Luis debated twisting the knife with another remark, but thought better of it.

No, better to let it fester in Cano's guts and savor the man's visible annoyance.

Chapter 17

After thirty-six hours of hard riding with only infrequent breaks to rest, Tarak stood by his horse and pointed at the orange blaze in the near distance, where the setting sun reflected off the glass of high-rises at Albuquerque Plaza.

"There it is," Tarak said.

"We'll make camp here," Lucas said. They were on the bank of the Rio Grande, whose brown water flowed lazily south. There was plenty of grass for the horses in the deserted valley outside the city limits, and no signs of human inhabitants. Around them the ruins of homes and industrial buildings stretched as far as he could see, casualties of the collapse and the ensuing mayhem. Now the area was a ghost town, victim of countless fires that had blazed unfettered with nobody to extinguish them. The overall mood of the place was funereal, as though the spirits of the dead still lingered, reluctant to pass into the next world, their circumstance unbelievable in a former land of plenty.

Ruby helped Sierra unpack the horses while Lucas checked Colt's wound, which had grown worse on the ride. He was conscious and relatively alert, but the discoloration was ominous; his skin tone was slack and pallid, his temperature high, and his thirst constant.

"Not going to win any beauty contests, huh?" Colt said as Lucas studied the leg.

"Probably going to have to shelve the marathon, too," Lucas said. "Let's ride into town and find a medic."

"You think they'll be able to do anything for me?"

"Ben recommended antibiotics. Makes sense."

"Be dark pretty soon."

"Then we better get going. Tarak, you want to help me get him into town?"

"Sure. I need to find a radio and check in with my headquarters – let them know we got this far."

Lucas blotted sweat from his brow with a dirty bandanna and adjusted his hat. "Take one side and let's get him on his horse."

Tarak assisted, and Lucas called out to the women as he climbed into the saddle. "Keep your weapons close. Treat anything you see as a threat. I'll be back soon as I can."

Sierra approached him and took his hand. "Be careful, Lucas."

"Not like I'm going into hell, Sierra. I've been worse places."

"Still…watch your back."

Lucas nodded and pressed Tango forward. Sierra's hand slipped from his, and Colt followed with a flick of the reins, Tarak bringing up the rear.

Sierra had made a point of helping Lucas at each rest stop. She'd been overtly friendly as the trip had progressed, touching him at every opportunity to reestablish the connection they'd had when they'd kissed. Lucas couldn't say he minded, but he found it distracting; the touch of an attractive woman was unfamiliar after so many years. She was sending signals that were unmistakable, but it wasn't the time or place, which they both understood.

Still, it gave him something to think about, not all of it unpleasant.

Lucas shook off the reverie and glanced at Colt, who looked like the walking dead. "You've been to Albuquerque before, right?" he asked.

"Sure. On my way to Roswell."

"Where's the best place to find a doc?"

"I have no idea. I spent one day there bartering for supplies. Didn't have any need for one, so I never asked."

"How's security in the city?"

"Open borders. They have community policing by the militia.

Seemed okay, not great. Town's wide open, big on trading because of the river and its proximity to Colorado. Sort of a crossroads, so it's got more opportunity than most places."

"That's good. Increases our chances that someone's got meds."

"Hope so. I'm about ready to cut the damn thing off, it hurts so much."

Ben had probably been right that Colt hadn't gotten much venom, but even the little amount had worked its magic worse than Lucas had ever seen – not that he had much experience with bites, other than what his grandfather had taught him. Colt's leg looked ugly, and a part of Lucas cringed inwardly every time he inspected the wound.

Lucas addressed Tarak. "You know anyone with a radio?"

The guide nodded. "There are several who rent time."

"How long are you going to need? I hate to leave the women by themselves."

"No more than an hour, tops. Don't worry about them. I'll see they're taken care of."

"You have any ideas on where to take Colt?"

Tarak shook his head. "Never had any need to find a medicine man there. Sorry."

A half hour later they entered the city and Tarak rode off down one of the wide avenues while Lucas and Colt took a smaller street north. They hadn't gotten more than two blocks when they were stopped by a group of four gunmen in blue camouflage uniforms. Each wore a red armband and a flak jacket and carried a rifle.

"Help you find something?" one of the men asked.

"My friend's hurt. We need a doctor. Best outfitted in town."

"We got a few of them. What's wrong?"

"Snakebite."

The man looked at his companions. One of them glanced down the street. "Probably best to look for Doc Hodges, over by the old Presbyterian Hospital. He's in one of the buildings across the street. Single story, wood shingles."

"Think he'll be open after dark?" Lucas asked.

The man nodded. "That's where a lot of emergency cases in these parts wind up."

"How do we get there?"

The man gave him directions, and Lucas nodded his thanks. "Is it safe to move around at night?"

"Wouldn't recommend it if you don't have to, but doesn't seem like you got a lot of choice."

The buildings degraded as they rode along the highway, the ruins telling the same bleak story of destruction and chaos everywhere else did. If Lucas was hoping to find evidence that humanity had a running chance, he'd have to look farther than Albuquerque, which showed the effects of entropy and wanton destruction that were the collapse's legacy.

It was almost pitch black out by the time they turned off the highway, and Lucas had to use his NV monocle to navigate. They passed several groups of street dwellers gathered around fires, who watched them ride by with the fearful expressions of whipped dogs. It was amazing to Lucas that five years after the collapse so many were living day-to-day rather than having structured something more permanent. He couldn't fathom that existence; but then again, as a saddle bum without a home now, he wasn't much better.

They found the doctor's clinic on the right, across from a massive parking lot with a darkened hulk of a building at the far end. A pair of torches lit an entry, where two armed guards stood with shotguns, watching Lucas and Colt's approach. When they drew up to the entrance, Lucas called to them, "This Doc Hodges?"

"That's right. What you got?"

"Man's been snakebit. Rattler. Needs to see the doctor. He still around?"

"He is if you got ammo to trade."

"I do."

"Then tie your horses over there and come in. I'll let him know you're here."

One of the men ducked through the steel door and disappeared inside. "You have electricity?" Lucas asked the other, seeing a glow when the door opened.

"Solar. But only for a few lights at night. Batteries are for shit."

"Yeah, same story everywhere. Weakening with age."

Lucas helped Colt down and they moved to the entrance. The guard held the door open for them, and the one that had gone inside motioned to them from the end of a dimly lit hall.

"Over here."

They found a surprisingly clean room, empty except for a steel-top exam table and a single chair. A fluorescent bulb provided scant illumination, and Lucas had barely gotten Colt onto the table when a short man with white hair entered, wearing a stained lab coat.

"What have we got here?" he asked. "I'm Dr. Hodges." He named a fee for the exam, and Lucas nodded agreement. The doctor stood, waiting, and Lucas counted out ten rounds of ammo and handed them over. Hodges pocketed them and eyed Colt expectantly, a pair of scratched reading glasses with one cracked lens perched precariously on the end of his nose.

"I got bit by a rattler."

"So my man says. How long ago?"

"Two and a half days."

"Well, you're alive. Let's have a look at it."

Lucas removed the bandage and Hodges examined Colt's leg. He noted with a grunt the discoloration that had crept to the knee, and carefully probed the wound area with his fingers. Yellow pus oozed from the bite marks, and he frowned.

"It's infected. Venom's through your system by now, but there's some possible necrosis and a lot of pus. You need antibiotics."

"You have some?" Lucas asked.

"They aren't cheap."

"I'm not looking for a bargain. Are they expired?"

"Got some that are. Others that aren't. Depends on how much they're worth to you. He's going to need ten days' worth, at least."

"How much for the ones that are still good?"

Hodges thought for a minute, studying Lucas like he was something stuck to a lab slide. When he told Lucas the price, he sounded embarrassed by how high it was.

"And the others? When did they expire?" Lucas fired back.

"Three years ago. They're a lousy bet with a life-threatening infection."

"Where did you get the ones that are still good?"

"Traders from Lubbock. They make them there."

Lucas recalled Jacob's story about the lab manufacturing pharmaceuticals for trade. "You're sure they're not bogus?"

"I've treated others with them. They're the genuine article."

"I don't have that much ammo I can spare." Lucas frowned. "But I have gold."

"What kind?"

"Maple Leaf. One ounce. Way more than the medicine's worth."

"That's okay. I can make change. Let's call it a half ounce of gold for a full course, and I'll throw in the exam tonight and another in ten days."

"That's extortionate."

"Your friend's life isn't worth it? He'll die if you don't get him on meds immediately. Tell you what. I'll even prepare a solution and give him a drip with some to kick-start the treatment."

"How long will that take?"

"Ideally he'd spend the night."

Lucas looked to Colt. "You heard the man."

"I'll see you're repaid later," Colt promised.

"We'll work it out," Lucas replied.

"Are you allergic to any medications?" Hodges asked.

"No. I mean, none I'm aware of."

"Ever had penicillin before?"

"Couple times."

"All right, then. Show me the money, and we'll get this train rolling."

Lucas dug a coin from his pocket and placed it in the doctor's hand, who inspected it in the faint light and nodded. "I'll be back with your change and an IV bag." He leaned toward Colt. "And a pillow. That bed gets mighty hard overnight."

"I've slept on worse."

Lucas waited by Colt's side until the doctor returned. He handed Lucas his change in the form of a scratched, weathered half-ounce Maple Leaf, whose 9999 gold content made it so soft the slightest abrasion would mar it. Lucas glanced at the tooth marks in the surface and pocketed it as Hodges ran a line into Colt's arm and hung an IV bag on a stainless steel stand.

"Where did you get the solution?" Lucas asked.

"I make and purify it myself. It's just saline. Neutral." He held up a syringe. "I diluted some pills. This will go straight into his bloodstream and hopefully deliver a knockout punch."

Colt closed his eyes as the physician emptied the syringe into the bag and then hooked it up to the line, adjusting the drip so that it trickled a droplet every ten seconds. "This bag will drain in a couple of hours. I'll do two more over the course of the night, the second and third slightly slower. You going to camp out here?"

"I'll stick around for a while, but I have some things I need to do. I'll come back in the morning."

"Suit yourself. I lock up around midnight. Bars are closed by then, so no customers."

"You see a lot of injuries from them?"

"Sure. Always good for business. Old as the hills. Pour some booze onto a fire of frustrated men, and something's going to happen."

Lucas nodded agreement. "You'd think they'd learn."

The doctor offered a grim smile. "Be the first time in history they did."

Chapter 18

Hodges reappeared after the first bag drained and handed Lucas a bottle of pills. "He needs to take these twice a day for ten days. Can't miss any. Can't skip a dose or stop once he feels better."

Lucas nodded. "I know the drill. You think it'll work?" ·

"It'll knock out the infection. His body will have to do the rest. He's lucky there didn't turn out to be any necrosis as well. I could show you photos that would put you off your food for a month."

"That's all right." Lucas checked the time. "I'm going to head out. I'll be back at sunup. Thanks for the help."

"That's my job. Glad we got to him in time." Hodges hesitated and then remarked casually to Lucas, "If you have any more gold you want to unload, I'll give you a better exchange than anyone else in town."

"Appreciate it, but that was my last one," Lucas lied. He didn't want the doctor to think he was walking around with a small fortune.

Hodges smiled as though he'd seen through the deflection. "In case you happen across any more, then."

Hodges escorted him to the entrance, and Lucas pushed through the door and made for the horses. He'd lead Colt's stallion back to the camp and bring him back the following morning.

The hair on the back of his neck prickled as he smoothed Tango's mane with a reassuring hand, and he swept the gloomy surroundings surreptitiously. Seeing nothing, he secured Colt's horse to his saddle horn with a length of cord and retrieved the night vision monocle from his saddlebags. Lucas offered the guards a small salute and climbed into the saddle, taking care to grip the M4 in his free hand, Tango's reins in the other with the monocle.

He raised the monocle to his eye and looked around again, and spotted something across the way – a man ducking behind a tree. Could have been a vagrant looking for easy prey…or something else.

Lucas snicked from the corner of his mouth and Tango lumbered forward. They'd made it no further than a block when Lucas sensed a presence behind him. He continued on, and once he was sure that he was being followed and not ambushed, considered his options. Halfway down the block he spurred Tango to sudden speed, Colt's horse in tow, and turned down a dark street.

Lucas drove Tango to a gallop and made a left at the next intersection. A hundred yards down he stopped at a cavernous car dealership that looked like a bomb had hit it, and guided the horses inside. Once out of sight of the street, he led the horses deep into the darkness and tied them at the back of the building, and then fished his crossbow from a saddlebag.

He surveyed the interior and spotted a stairway to a second story that faced onto the showroom. He took the steps two at a time and stopped at the first office, which had a window overlooking the floor.

Lucas listened for signs of the rider but heard nothing. The interior of the building was bathed in the greenish light of the monocle, but when he looked without it he could barely make anything out. Lucas cocked the crossbow using his foot and the rope pull and, after fitting a quarrel into place, heard the unmistakable sound of horses outside.

Three riders stopped at the building and stared into it, and Lucas realized one of them had night vision equipment as well, the distinctive headgear plainly visible. He ducked down, sure he would have to engage – they would see Tango and investigate.

He heard them dismount and then broken glass crunching beneath their boots as they entered the building. Lucas waited a few seconds and then inched up into the gap and sighted on the man with the NV equipment.

The crossbow snapped like a whip, and the bolt drove through the man's chest. He gurgled and dropped his assault rifle as his companions glanced around, blind in the dark. Lucas cocked the bow again and set another bolt into place as the men scrambled for their fallen leader, and fired at the closest target.

The quarrel skewered the man through the shoulder blades, and his friend cried out.

"What the hell–"

Lucas had the bowstring drawn again and a quarrel in place in less than ten seconds as the man emptied his assault rifle into the darkness, spraying lead indiscriminately before feeling his way back toward the front of the showroom. He'd almost made it when Lucas's third bolt caught him below his collarbone, shattering his scapula and sending him facedown into the debris.

The gunman howled in pain and dropped his weapon. Lucas was already in motion, all pretense of stealth abandoned. The shots would draw a patrol, he was sure, and he needed to get out of there before one arrived.

The last man hit was moaning and clawing at the carbon fiber shaft as Lucas walked toward him. Lucas leaned and scooped up his Kalashnikov, ejected the spent magazine, and slapped the full one taped to the empty in place, reversing the mags before chambering a round.

Lucas flipped the man over so he was face up, and knelt beside him.

"Why are you following me?" he asked.

The man shook his head. Lucas pulled the shaft the remainder of the way through the man and cleaned the blood from it. The man loosed a banshee wail. When it trailed off in a moan, Lucas tried again.

"Why were you following me?"

"Reward," the man managed.

"From who?"

"The…Crew."

"How did you find me?"

"We...watching for...strangers."

"How many more of you are there?"

"Twenty...I got no beef...with you..."

Lucas's voice was expressionless. "That's good to know."

"I...I needed the...money..." His statement ended with a burble from his chest.

"Not anymore. Sounds like it got your lung there. We both know you're dead. Was it worth it?"

The man didn't answer, his face blanching as he went into shock.

Lucas removed the man's pistol from his hip holster and slid it into his vest, and then moved to the others and retrieved his arrows. When he finished, he hurried to where the horses were standing unharmed in the depth of the building and led them to the street.

Lucas climbed into the saddle and rode into the gloom. It was imperative now to get Colt and clear out of Albuquerque before he had another brush with the mercenaries the Crew had hired. The only good news for Lucas was that if they were using locals, there couldn't have been many, if any, Crew in the city.

But there would be soon. Of that he was sure.

Lucas was back at the doctor's office less than ten minutes later. The guards nodded to him as he strode toward the entry.

"Change of plans," he said. He glanced at their belts. No radios. If they were in on it, they wouldn't be able to contact anyone while he retrieved Colt.

Hodges looked surprised to see him as he made his way down the hall to the exam room.

"Thought you were gone," the doctor said.

"We're both leaving. Can you give him a shot or something, or will the pills do the trick?"

"Shot wouldn't hurt. I have one prepared for the third bag. Let me get it."

Hodges arrived at Colt's side as Lucas was helping him off the table. The doctor emptied the contents of the syringe into the IV line and then removed the cannula once the amber liquid had worked its way into Colt's vein.

"What's the rush?" Hodges asked. "He really should stay till morning."

"Emergency. Thanks for all the help," Lucas said. "Can you have your boys help him onto his horse?"

"Of course."

The guards had Colt in the saddle two minutes later. Lucas waited until they'd ridden around the corner and he was sure they weren't being followed before telling Colt what had happened. Colt's face turned mean when he heard.

"How did they know we'd show up here?"

"Fair question. But there's not a lot north of Roswell, so it wouldn't be a stretch to figure it out. Probably offered half the city a reward." Lucas looked around. "We need to get out of here and hit the trail. I hate to ride at night, but I want some distance between us and Albuquerque by morning."

"We can't. Not yet."

"We have to," Lucas growled. "Let's hope that penicillin works quickly. But you're already in better shape than when we rode in."

"No, I mean I have to get the password from our man here."

"Password?"

"The Shangri-La guards will gun us down if we don't know the password. It changes weekly."

"Every minute we stay increases our odds of getting caught."

Colt frowned. "Then we better make it quick."

Colt's contact lived on the south edge of town, a block down from a bar that was revving up as the evening progressed. Shouts and laughter echoed on the street and music drifted from the doorway – live, by the sound of it, a bluegrass fiddle and guitar feverishly wailing over the pandemonium.

"This is the place," Colt said as he stopped in front of a darkened storefront. The entry and windows were protected by steel bars, and graffiti defaced every visible surface.

"Doesn't look like anyone's home."

"Looks can be deceiving. Knock."

Lucas swung down from the saddle and moved to the doorway.

He reached between the heavy steel bars and rapped on the wood door. After thirty seconds with no response, he was reaching again when it opened with a creak and a man with a heavy beard and wild dark hair glared at him from inside.

"Go away," he said, and Lucas could make out the snout of a double-barreled shotgun pointing at his chest.

"Steven, it's Colt," said Colt from atop his horse.

Steven looked over Lucas's shoulder and then back at Lucas. "Who's this?"

"I'm his chaperone," Lucas said.

"I got bit by a snake. This is Lucas. He's helping me." Colt paused. "I need the password."

Steven shook his head and eyed Lucas. "You sure that's a good idea? Do they know he's going?"

"They know everything. Now hurry up. They're after us."

"What? How?"

"You heard him," Lucas said. "I had to kill three men to get him here."

Steven nodded slowly. "Password's Goldilocks. Good through Saturday."

"Goldilocks," Colt repeated.

"You going to be okay?" Steven asked.

Colt sighed. "Hope so."

Lucas remounted Tango and they rode away, leaving Steven to stare at their backs as they vanished into the darkness.

Forty-five minutes later, after they'd dodged two patrols, they arrived at the edge of town. Lucas swept the surroundings with his night vision scope and nodded. "I don't see anyone."

"That's a lucky break."

"It is. But we need to break camp and move." Lucas looked at Colt. "How you feeling?"

"Leg still hurts like a bitch. But I'm not as feverish."

Lucas didn't comment, though it was a good sign. "You sure about that Steven character?"

"Absolutely. He's been an asset for three years. He keeps an eye on the town and radios in any developments."

"So Shangri-La isn't far?"

"I wouldn't say that. We'll still be riding a few more days."

"You still can't tell me where it is?"

"Sorry. Not my decision to make."

Lucas rubbed a hand over the dusting of beard on his chin. "I understand. Can you at least tell me if there's water along the way?"

"We won't have any problems in that regard."

They arrived at the camp, and Lucas offered a terse report. Sierra groaned when he told everyone to pack up, but she followed his instructions, and in a quarter of an hour they were ready to ride. Colt took the lead, sticking to the bank of the Rio Grande as its muddy current rushed past.

Halfway through their trip a patrol showed itself ahead, and they spent a tense twenty minutes hunkered down in the brush as the men relieved themselves in the river and passed a bottle around. Only once the militia had moved on did Lucas dare lead them beyond that point. The sound of an occasional hoot from one of the bars along the river reached them across the water, but the only living thing they saw as they reached the northern edge of town was a single night fisherman in a wooden skiff swaying in the current, his wooden rowboat anchored as he fished.

They followed the river north past the city, and five hours later stopped for what remained of the night. The city was now only a dark blemish on the distant horizon, and the water burbled a lullaby for their few hours of restive sleep.

Chapter 19

It was late afternoon when Sammy stopped his horse and pointed out the buildings at the base of a ridge of mountains.

"Albuquerque," he announced.

Cano nodded. "If we're lucky, they'll still be here. After that many days of hard riding with an injured man, they're probably resting and restocking."

Luis held his tongue. If it were up to him, he'd have skipped the town altogether and left the snake-bit man to his fate. Why Cano believed they would take the risk of going into Albuquerque, he didn't know, but he'd been right about many things so far, so Luis didn't voice his thoughts.

"This is where I leave you," Sammy said.

Sammy spun his horse around and retraced his steps down the trail, leaving them to make their way into town by themselves. Cano led the procession, and the sun was low in the western sky by the time they entered the city limits.

"Where to?" Luis asked as they rode down a main artery.

"Magnus gave me the name of a bar. We organized a welcoming committee for our friends through the owner. He'll be able to tell us whether the trap worked."

Luis fell silent. Cano hadn't shared anything with him beyond that Magnus would hire some locals to watch for their quarry's arrival. The Crew had no reach this far from its stronghold, but it had several like-minded confederates who facilitated trade between Lubbock and

Albuquerque and who would do anything for a price. Luis had thought it a terrible idea to entrust capturing their quarry to strangers of unknown competence, but again, had said nothing – it was Cano's funeral, not his, if the group that had annihilated the Crew's force at the lake had outwitted some local yokels.

They reached the bar as purple and mauve ribboned the sky, and Cano ordered the men to wait outside while he spoke with their contact. He was gone for ten minutes, and when he returned, he looked ready to explode.

"There was a shoot-out. Three of our mercenaries were killed," he announced.

"With the woman?"

"Unknown. They were watching one of the medical clinics. Our man thinks the snakebite victim showed up there – and something went wrong."

"Obviously," Luis said, drawing a glower from Cano.

"What do we do now?" Quincy asked.

Cano thought for several beats. "I want to have a talk with the doctor. He can tell us who he treated and at least confirm it was them."

"And if it was?" Len asked.

"Then we hire a tracker and see if we can pick up their trail."

"It's a big city," Luis observed. "If they've gone to ground, it could take weeks to find them."

"I'll triple the reward and broadcast it from the tallest buildings. Someone will turn on them." Cano moved to his horse. "I already told the bar owner to tell everyone he knows that we're offering a jackpot."

Cano pulled himself up into the saddle, his overmuscled arms bulging beneath the green and blue prison ink, and rode off, leaving the rest of them to catch up. They wended through the city center until they arrived at the clinic as night fell. Cano dismounted and instructed his men to wait for him.

Cano approached the entry and called out to the guards, "Doctor here?"

"What's wrong with you?" one of the guards asked.

"Cramps. Is he here?"

The guards exchanged an uncertain glance and the nearest one nodded. "I'll tell him he's got a patient."

"Do that."

Cano held off on shooting them. He didn't want to attract the wrath of the militia, whom his contact had warned him about.

The man came back after several minutes and motioned to Cano. "He'll see you now."

The guard escorted Cano to the exam room, where Hodges waited, stethoscope draped around his neck. Cano took a seat on the table and waited until the guard left before answering the doctor's question about what was wrong.

"What's wrong, Doctor, is that I'm looking for someone who stole something very valuable from me, and I think you might have treated him."

Hodges looked confused. Cano stood, filling the space with his bulk.

"I don't know what you're talking about," Hodges stammered.

"He had a snakebite."

The doctor wasn't a poker player. He began backing toward the door. "I'm afraid I can't discuss other patients…"

"Doctor, there are two ways this can go. I can either pay well for anything you know, and then I leave and you never see me again; or I can mop the floor with you and still get the same information. You're a smart man. Educated. This isn't a tough choice."

Cano could see in the man's eyes that he believed him.

"For the sake of conversation," Hodges said, "you mention payment. What did you have in mind? Not that I know much of anything."

"Ten ounces of gold. Or all the pharmaceuticals you can carry. Whatever you want. I don't care."

Five minutes later Cano emerged from the clinic and stormed to his horse. He vaulted into the saddle and called out to the rest, "They were here. We need to find a tracker."

Quincy frowned. "How will we know where to start looking?"

Cano turned to Quincy. "The doctor recognized the mud on their boots. From the river. I'll put the word out — maybe there was a patrol or someone who saw them pass, assuming they aren't still camped out. If we don't get a lead, we'll scour the bank until we find tracks." He paused and his eyes narrowed. "One way or another, we'll get them."

Chapter 20

Lucas sat on a log by the creek with Eve by his side. Sierra watched intently as he showed the little girl how to toss a chrome spoon secured to the end of a hand line and slowly retrieve it in a manner that made it seem to swim, zigging and zagging in the current like a minnow racing for its life. Eve giggled each time he pulled the spoon out of the water and cast it downstream again, the monofilament uncoiling from the pile by his feet without tangling – a seeming miracle to her.

"Think we'll actually catch anything?" Sierra asked after another toss.

"If there's fish, we'll catch 'em," Lucas assured her.

"So jerky for dinner again?" Sierra responded.

"No. There's always the crossbow. I'm sure there are some rabbits around."

"I like bunnies," Eve said as she followed the flashes of the swimming spoon.

"Everyone likes bunnies," Sierra agreed.

"I'll leave it to your aunt to explain the food chain some other time," Lucas said, and Sierra gave him a slit-eyed look.

Following a four-hour rest, they had ridden all day once clear of Albuquerque and had clocked twenty-five grueling miles before calling it quits. They hadn't seen a soul as they traced the river's course north, easing Lucas's worry that they might leave a trail of witnesses for the Crew to follow.

When pressed by Sierra, Colt had told them that he expected to arrive at Shangri-La within another day – two, on the outside. The terrain was slowly climbing as they worked their way toward Los Alamos after giving Santa Fe a wide berth, their surroundings green from the plentiful water supplied by the Rio Grande. But the increasing altitude was slowing the animals, and Colt warned that they could expect to make worse time the following day.

Lucas looked up at the sky, only a few high cotton ball clouds drifting east, and checked the time. He sat back as he wound the line in and smiled at Sierra.

"Another ten minutes and we'll head back."

Eve looked unhappy to leave the river – she liked the cool water on her bare feet – and Lucas was framing a reassurance when Ruby's scream from their camp upstream pierced the silence. Sierra leapt to her feet, but Lucas was faster.

"Stay here with Eve. Don't follow me. I'll come back for you," he whispered, shrugging the M4's shoulder sling off.

"What do you think it is?" she asked. "Another snake?"

"I'll be back," Lucas said, and took off toward a game trail that ran along the water, the firing selector of his rifle already switched to three-round burst.

His boots pounded on the dirt as he pushed himself to run faster, and his lungs burned from the lack of oxygen at the higher altitude. The trail branched off and he took the left fork, slowing as he neared the campsite so his footfalls wouldn't alert whatever had caused Ruby's alarm.

A shot rang out from the camp and he winced – that would draw anyone within five miles. He crept the final twenty yards to the clearing with the tents and stopped when he saw Colt propped against his saddlebags, holding a pistol; two strangers lay on the ground near Ruby, both clearly dead.

"What happened?" Lucas demanded.

Ruby looked to him with frightened eyes. "I was at the river, getting some water, and heard something in the brush. They must have followed me up."

Colt took over the narrative, his voice low. "I was dozing, and this pair showed up with guns."

Ruby pointed at one of the men. "They had Colt and me covered, so we couldn't draw our weapons, but Tarak was in the bushes."

"Nature called," Tarak interjected.

"They were getting ready to shoot us when Tarak's knife came flying and took that one down," Colt said, gesturing at one of the corpses.

Lucas walked to the man and turned him over. A hunting knife, its bone handle smeared with crimson, was lodged to the hilt in the base of his throat.

"That bought me a chance to get my pistol out, and you can see the rest," Colt said.

"Any idea who they were?" Ruby asked.

Lucas examined the men's weapons, both battered AK-47s that looked like they hadn't been cleaned in a lifetime, and removed revolvers from their hip holsters – .38-caliber service pistols that were sixty years old if a day.

"Scavengers, by the looks of them. They look half-starved, and their gear's crap."

"You think there are more?" Colt asked.

"If there are, they're on their way here. We need to get moving again."

Tarak reached to his knife jutting from the dead man's throat and pulled it free. He inspected the handle with a look of distaste and shook his head. "I'll be back. Need to rinse this clean."

Lucas turned his back on the dead men and addressed Ruby. "Break down the tents while I get Sierra and Eve. Colt, keep an eye peeled for company."

He didn't wait for a response, but spun on his heel and jogged back along the trail, his muscles protesting the exertion after twelve hours in the saddle. When he arrived at the river, Sierra was hugging Eve, smoothing her hair and whispering to her. She looked up at Lucas's approach.

"What was it?" she asked.

"Couple of dirtbags. We need to clear out. That shot will bring more cockroaches out of the woodwork."

"Was anyone hurt?"

"Just them. Come on. Time's a-wasting."

Sierra struggled to her feet, a look of resignation on her face. Lucas moved to the water's edge and gathered his fishing gear. He slid it into a pouch that he slipped into his flak jacket.

Sierra shook her head. "It never ends, does it?"

Lucas didn't answer.

"I'm so sick of riding…"

"I know the feeling. But we need to put some miles between us and the camp, or we're asking for it."

She sighed. "I know. I'm just whining."

"We're all at the end of our ropes. You've earned the right. But whine while we ride."

Chapter 21

Cano watched as the tracker they'd hired in Albuquerque squinted at the trail while Quincy stood by his side. They'd been contacted by a fisherman the prior morning who had told them he had been on the river the night before and seen a group headed north. The man had nothing more to add, other than his approximate position when he'd spotted them, but that had been enough. Cano had him lead them to the spot, and the tracker had quickly found evidence of the group's passing and led them north.

They had spent the day following the tracks and made camp when it had grown too dark to distinguish them any longer. Up at dawn the following day, they'd continued along the river's course until mid-afternoon, when the tracker had begun having problems.

"Too rocky," he'd said, the going painful as he roamed ahead and then retraced his path in case he'd missed something. Hours of that had led them to this point, and Cano waited for the man's verdict with a sinking stomach.

The tracker straightened and consulted with Quincy in a low voice. After a minute, Cano interrupted their discussion with an impatient tone. "Well?"

Quincy looked around and then shrugged. "We lost the trail. Ground's too hard."

"What about broken branches or something?" Cano asked. "Isn't that how trackers are supposed to follow people?"

"They're being careful. Sticking to the bank or trails. They aren't breaking anything; not that there's much around here to break anyway. But it's amateurs that do that sort of thing. These people know what they're doing." The tracker shook his head. "Cain't follow a trail where there ain't none."

"You're being paid a lot, old man. Too much for failure," Cano warned.

"I done what you asked. But this is as far as I go." The man spread his hands before him in a reasoning gesture. "Sorry."

"So do you only get part of the fee?"

"That ain't how it works."

Cano snorted dismissively. "I don't pay for best efforts. You told us you could track them, what was it, 'to the end of the earth'?" Cano looked around. "I don't see any end here, do you?"

"I done my job. Earned my money fair and square."

"You didn't finish the job."

The man turned away and made for his horse. "This is bullshit. You're a cheat. Find your own way back. I'm out of here."

Cano's pupils shrank to pinpoints and his hand flew to his pistol. He whipped it out and fired three times in rapid succession. The tracker screamed and pitched forward, all three shots grouped in the center of his back, and hit the ground hard, where he convulsed and stilled.

Cano dropped from the saddle and walked to where the man lay facedown. He looked around at his men, whose faces were blank, and kicked the tracker in the head with a sickening thwack.

"You're going to call me a cheat and walk away? How did that work for you, you dumb prick? You roasting in hell now? Save a spot for me."

The men looked away as Cano unzipped his jeans and urinated on the dead man, a grin revealing yellowing incisors. When he finished, he seized his horse's bridle and faced his men.

"Anyone else want to call it quits? I still have plenty of rounds for your severance pay," Cano said.

None of the men spoke. Cano nodded. "That's what I thought. Now get that garbage out of my sight. We'll make camp here. I have a good feeling about this place," he said.

Luis waited until Cano had calmed down before approaching him. "Maybe we should head back to town and get some dogs or something," he suggested.

"No, we'll stay put."

Luis considered pressing the point, but a glance at Cano's face made him think better of it. "Okay, then. Anything you want me to do?"

"Keep the new guys in line."

"If you don't mind my asking, what are we waiting for here? I mean, I'm fine with it, but what should I tell them?"

Cano's voice dropped to a raspy growl. "Tell them that they're to follow orders and not pester me with stupid questions, or they'll join the tracker in a ditch."

Luis nodded at the nonanswer. "Sure."

Cano fixed Luis with a hard stare. "You're getting on my nerves with your questions and your attitude. You got a problem? Because I have bigger fish to fry than whether you approve of my decisions or not."

"It's not that. I just want to make sure—"

"Luis, you're not here to think or second-guess. You want to be in the Crew, you play by our rules – and that means you do as ordered, with no backtalk or attitude. This is your last warning. I'm not going to say it again."

Luis bit back his response and managed a tight nod. He crossed over to where the men were assembling their tents and set to driving tent pegs into the hard ground, using the back of his camp hatchet, his temples pounding. In his mind's eye, he flung the hatchet with deadly accuracy and it cleaved Cano's forehead in two.

Len looked at him strangely. "What's the joke?"

Luis realized that he'd allowed himself a smile, and he grew serious as he finished his work. "Nothing. Just remembering a time when I hacked a guy to pieces with this thing."

That chilled any further appetite for conversation, and Luis stood and made his way to his horse to get his bedroll, reminding himself that he couldn't let down his guard. It was obvious to him that Cano had it in for him, but he wasn't going to give him any excuses to take him on.

Luis glanced at the hatchet on the ground beside his tent and forced himself not to smile again.

Chapter 22

"How's the leg?" Lucas asked as Colt drove his horse up the steep incline toward the deserted remnants of Los Alamos.

"Pills are doing their job."

It was late morning the second day after the attack by the river, and Colt had announced that they were close – they would arrive at Shangri-La before nightfall. The mood had been excited as the women broke camp, in anticipation of their brutal trek drawing to a close. Earlier that morning they'd negotiated a trail across Diablo Canyon and ridden to the highway bridge that crossed the Rio Grande, and were now entering the town that had been built around the lab that birthed the atomic bomb.

Around them the ruins of Los Alamos stood like cemetery headstones, the remains of the hamlet a mausoleum for a past that would never return. Fire had ravaged the area, burning many of the wood structures to the foundations, and the only buildings left standing were the old steel-sided government apartments left over from World War II days and the sturdier of the adobe buildings in the center of town. In the distance stood the Los Alamos National Laboratory grounds, and Lucas called out to Colt as he led them toward the facility.

"Government didn't try to put up a last-ditch effort to keep the Lab guarded?"

"Sure, but eventually the food ran out, and the flu got most that starvation didn't," Colt explained. "That was the problem the military had – they couldn't convince soldiers to stay on duty when their families were being slaughtered back home, particularly when the money they were being paid wasn't worth anything. When the supply lines failed, there was no way to hold the ranks. Some stayed out of a sense of patriotic duty, but they died when they discovered ideology didn't fill your stomach."

"Weird that a top secret security area like this is abandoned."

"Not that odd. How would they find people to man it, and how would they feed and pay them? And who's *they*? Remember that the idea of a government is a group that provides the population services, which it bills for via taxes. But if everyone's dead or destitute and the currency is worth nothing, how do you collect anything, or even find anyone to collect it for you?"

Rather than taking them along the road that led up past the Lab into the forested hills, Colt veered off down a steep path that Lucas hadn't even noticed from the road. When the rocky way turned a corner and broadened so they could ride two abreast again, Colt continued his sermon.

"Governments are faceless bureaucrats who took jobs where they got paid more than they were worth for working as little as possible. The faith that people had that they would do something ignored how badly they performed in the regional disasters. Remember that big hurricane in Louisiana? That was a train wreck. Why anyone believed the same morons would manage anything better in a real national emergency beats the hell out of me."

Lucas recalled how torn he'd been when he'd abandoned his job in El Paso, but he understood Colt's sentiment. When the chain of command had broken down, it had become clear that it was every man for himself. In that scenario, staying out of loyalty merely got you killed, because there was nobody watching your back or making sure you were fed or had ammo. He'd felt terrible when he'd packed up his truck and headed for his grandfather's ranch, but with civilization collapsing around him, there had been no choice but the stark one of life or death.

"You've heard the rumors of underground bases back east and on the west coast?"

"I've heard a million rumors. But nobody's actually seen one. It's always the same: they know someone who told them they had, or who knew someone who knew someone." Colt paused. "I think the biggest shock to the survivors was how much of a con job the semblance of order actually was. The government pretended it had the people's interests in mind, but it really was all about protecting its cronies while they fleeced the population. That's why nothing worked the way it should have – not that it would have made much difference."

"What do you mean?" Lucas asked.

"Nobody was actually concerned with doing anything remotely about saving people – it was all about how to suppress rioting and rebellion. They declared martial law, which just made things worse, but they didn't declare it because it was the right thing to do. They did it because they wanted to protect themselves while they got out of Dodge and to protect their interests. And because everyone was pretending to do their job instead of actually designing responses that would work, none of them actually did work when put to the test."

Lucas remembered well the truth of Colt's observation. It had been almost comedic how disorganized and ineffectual the government had been when the country fell into crisis, how the central management attempts had been horribly conceived and done more harm than good. When faith in the currency disintegrated after the country had been plunged back into the Dark Ages by the flu, the government's authority had collapsed with it. Most measures had been designed to protect the banks and the elites, and that had become increasingly obvious as forces were deployed to keep mobs from overrunning financial institutions or to cordon off privileged enclaves in D.C. and New York while people died by the millions around them.

But the flu hadn't played favorites, bringing down the mighty with the same relentlessness that it felled the poor. Even with the best care, there had been no way to reverse the immunological response that turned a victim's immune system against the host, and even the richest victims died the same agonizing death.

"Yeah," Lucas said. "I've always thought the 'survivor cities' were BS."

"It's human nature to want to believe somewhere, order was maintained and the trains run on time."

"Which is why I'm skeptical about your Shangri-La."

"Oh, it's got its problems. Just like everywhere. Anytime you get a large group together, there are going to be differences of opinion on how to do things. But we've been able to get along and build a better world, at least better than other places. It's not unicorns and marshmallow clouds, but there's power and water and food, the place is clean and safe, and it's well supplied."

"How is it supplied at all?"

"Most of it's self-sufficient. A lot of the equipment came from Los Alamos, so we can make limited quantities of simple drugs like antibiotics. We have gardens and indoor growing areas for the winter months. Because we've got power, we can pump water for irrigation and sanitation." Colt paused. "You'll see."

"How much further?"

"A ways."

"Cat's sort of out of the bag now that it's in the mountains near here, or we won't be able to get there today," Sierra said from behind Lucas.

"Then why ask?" Colt fired back.

Sierra frowned at Colt's testiness, but held off on any further questions. After all, the man had been through hell with the snakebite and probably was feeling lousy; his leg was still visibly swollen, albeit less discolored now.

They entered the canyon, its sides towering on either side, and the rocky terrain steepened as the temperature dropped. Aspen trees climbed the sides of the visible slopes above the canyon top, rising into a sky so blue it seemed painted.

They continued for an hour and then turned into an even deeper canyon, and stopped to rest at a small lake with shimmering azure water, the air crisp and cool. Ruby helped Lucas with the pressure bandage and inspected Colt's wound, which was now no longer seeping pus, and they concluded that the infection had diminished to something manageable.

"They named it Shangri-La partly because of the location," Colt offered as they patched him up. "The approach from the east is a series of canyons that are easily defendable and that connect together in a sort of natural labyrinth. It would be almost impossible to stumble across it by accident – there are no roads that lead to it, and in the winter it's completely buried in snow."

"What do people do then?" Ruby asked.

"Stay inside, for the most part. There are some buildings they built out of cinder block, and there's an underground area and a bunch of caves. The scientist who founded it thought it through pretty well – it can support three hundred people, which is about what we have."

"You mentioned power? From solar?" Lucas asked.

"That and a dam."

"A dam?" Ruby said.

"Yes. Abiquiu Dam. North of here at the base of the mountains. We've kept it operating, but just barely. It provides more than enough for our needs."

"I would have thought that would be difficult."

"We got lucky. One of the survivors was an engineer there. He knew everything there was to know about it. He can repair anything, and our machine shop can create new parts if necessary."

"Machine shop?"

"Sure. There are a lot of skills in our little group. Doctors, scientists, engineers, tradespeople, mechanics. We've been pretty selective about who makes the cut." Colt glanced at his bandage. "Am I going to live another day?"

"You better. We aren't there yet," Lucas said.

They resumed their journey and further along the long canyon turned up another. The afternoon was growing late when Colt held up a hand and then pointed at the crest on their left.

"What?" Lucas asked.

"We're here. First line of defense. There are four snipers up there who can split a hair at six hundred yards."

Lucas squinted against the sunlight and raised a hand to adjust his hat. Colt shook his head.

"Keep your hands where they can be seen, and don't make any sudden moves. That goes for the rest of you." Colt cupped his hands around his mouth and yelled out, "Permission to enter!"

His voice echoed off the sheer stone canyon walls, reverberating until the sound faded to nothingness.

A voice answered from above. "Password?"

"Goldilocks."

Silence greeted Colt's cry, and then the voice answered, "You can pass. They're waiting for you." A figure rose from the crest, dressed in camouflage that blended with the surrounding foliage, and waved. Colt waved back and spurred his horse forward.

"Won't be long now," he called over his shoulder. Lucas and Sierra exchanged a glance and followed, Tarak and Ruby trailing them with Jax in tow.

Colt led them up a steep trail carved into the side of the canyon, the path no more than three feet wide, and then they emerged onto a rise with green aspen shimmering in the wind. They stopped beside Colt and took in the sight below them – a long valley that stretched at least ten miles, narrowing in places like a voluptuous woman's waist. Beyond the farthest gap was a compound of white buildings in a valley with a creek running through it, with fields of tall grass on either side, a windmill spinning dizzily atop a steel tower beside the largest building, and well-trodden paths leading everywhere with scores of people on them, no bigger than ants from their high vantage point.

Sierra pressed closer to Tango and Lucas, and when she spoke, her voice was barely a whisper. "Is that–"

The peal of a bell reached them from across the five or six miles between the gap and their position, and a half dozen riders emerged from a structure and galloped toward them, tiny as miniature toy soldiers in the distance.

Colt grinned and turned to the women, a triumphant expression on his face.

"Looks like they radioed ahead. This is a big day for everyone involved – and it's been a long time coming. Everybody...welcome to Shangri-La."

Chapter 23

The riders met the newcomers halfway across the first stretch of valley, the creek burbling blue down the middle. Colt waved as they drew near, and the lead rider waved back. As he approached, they could see he had white hair worn longish around his ears beneath a leather cowboy hat, and a neatly trimmed silver beard. He pulled up beside Colt and offered his hand.

"Congratulations, my friend. A job well done," he said in a refined voice. Lucas caught a slight British accent beneath his crisp diction.

Colt flushed at the praise and then turned to the group. "Everyone, this is the founder of Shangri-La and the reason we're all here: Dr. Elliot Barnes."

Elliot grimaced at the introduction. "Sounds far more grandiose than it is. Chief bottle washer's more like it."

The doctor greeted each member of the party with a nod, but the entire time he remained focused on Eve. He smiled at the little girl, his blue eyes twinkling above ruddy cheeks.

"Ah, and this must be Eve," he said. "A veritable angel."

"That she is," Sierra assured him.

He tore his attention from Eve and looked Sierra over. "You must be her caregiver; Sierra, is that right? Jacob's description of you hardly did you justice."

Sierra nodded, a smile lighting her face. Elliot held out a hand to Lucas next. "You're Lucas, I do believe? We owe you a considerable debt for rescuing them and keeping them safe. Eddie told us your story before he…before he went dark."

It was Lucas's turn to deflect compliments. "Somebody had to do it."

Elliot nodded, taking Lucas's measure. "Yes, well, *you* did, and that's what counts." He looked at Ruby. "And you, gentle woman, were also instrumental, I assume by your presence in this rarified group?"

"I did what I could."

Colt nodded. "Her name's Ruby. She's a computer wiz and a healer with herbs."

"Computers, eh? Well, we have more than a few of those."

"You do?" Ruby exclaimed.

"Oh, of course. Hard to do complex work without them, you know." Elliot shifted his scrutiny to Tarak. "And this is the representative of the Apache nation?" he said, more a statement than question.

"Tarak," Colt confirmed.

Elliot eyed the guide. "We're readying your payment. You are our honored guest this evening and are invited to our celebratory feast. When you get back to your territory, be sure to thank your council for their cooperation in this matter. I'm sorry you lost a man. It's never easy."

Tarak nodded wordlessly.

Elliot twisted to his fellow riders. "I'm sorry. In my excitement I neglected to introduce my colleagues." He indicated the man to his right. "This is Arnold Sheer. He's our head of security. And this is Michael Bailey, my second-in-command." The pair tipped the brims of their hats in unison. "Beside them are Toby, Ken, and Richard, our operations directors – they're actually the ones who keep things running, not me."

"Pleased to meet you," Toby said, and the others nodded.

"Let's get you to the compound so you can get oriented and then rest. This must have been grueling. I can only imagine how hard it's been."

"If you have hot water, I'd sell my soul for a bath," Ruby said.

"Of course we do. Solar heaters, courtesy of Los Alamos. I think we can arrange something bearable."

Lucas shifted in his saddle. "You're a medical doctor?" he asked.

"Well, yes, but mainly research. Been quite some time since I saw patients. Why?"

"Your man here got bit by a rattler, and his leg's something of a mess. Got him on antibiotics, but he needs a checkup."

"Good Lord. That's right. Our fellow in Albuquerque mentioned something about that."

"It's getting better," Colt said.

"Sarah will look you over first thing."

Colt made a face. "Sarah's the camp doc. The butcher, they call her."

"Nonsense. The woman's a national treasure."

"Not really generous with the pain meds, is she?" Colt countered.

"I'll ensure she's less parsimonious in your case," said Elliot, with another infectious grin. "Now come. Everyone's anxious to meet you."

They followed the riders across the grass-covered expanse through a gap between a pair of small peaks. When they arrived at the compound, a crowd had already formed: healthy-looking men and women, their skin bronzed from the sun, most Lucas's age or younger. Lucas's party dismounted, and several young men approached and took their reins.

"See to it that these animals receive our platinum treatment," Elliot instructed. "They've done a noble job." He turned to the assembly and executed a small bow. "Ladies and gentlemen, our covenant to make the world livable again is nearly a reality. Our prayers have been answered, and our hope for the future has been delivered to us by these fine men and women." Elliot introduced Lucas, Sierra, and Ruby. "They've ridden countless miles and been through the mill, so they're to be afforded every courtesy." Elliot turned to them next. "We'll show you to your quarters, and someone will explain how everything works. Get cleaned up, and then eat your fill and catch up on your rest. I imagine you're knackered, as they used to say in the old country."

Lucas nodded. "I'll want my saddlebags."

"They're safe with us," Arnold said.

"No doubt. I'd still like them with me."

"I'll have someone bring them to your room."

"Barn's right over there. I can get them myself."

Arnold's expression hardened, but he merely nodded. "Sure thing. I'll give you a hand."

Lucas followed the security head to the massive barn and noted dozens of horses. "This all your animals?" he asked.

"No. We have three other holding areas."

"What about in winter? You keep them here?"

Arnold nodded. "The barns have heat. And we built them with insulation. Same with all the buildings, although it can get hairy with a big snowfall. Lot of shoveling."

"Why did you choose this location?"

"I didn't. The Doc did. I joined up after they were already established."

"Huh. What's your background?"

"Marines. Captain. Three tours of combat." Arnold studied Lucas's face. "You?"

"Texas Ranger."

"That's a relief."

"Why?" Lucas asked as he retrieved his saddlebags from where one of the youths had placed them with his saddle.

"I'll be honest. When I heard Colt was bringing a mess of people with him, I wasn't thrilled. We got plenty of mouths to feed already, and some of them don't know a whole lot about guns and the like." Arnold noted Lucas's M4. "I'm guessing you're not one of those."

Lucas nodded. He could understand the man's concerns. "I can handle myself."

"What about the rest?"

"Sierra's coming along. So's Ruby." He gave Arnold a brief rundown of their battles with the Crew. "Neither of them is dead weight."

"I don't like that the Apache knows our location."

Lucas nodded. "Neither do I. But it wasn't my call."

Arnold moved a step closer. "Need some help?"

"No. I got it." Lucas looked at where a youth was brushing Tango. "Horse could use some food and water."

"He'll probably get a massage, too. We'll take good care of him."

They exited the barn and Lucas walked to where Sierra was waiting with Eve, speaking to Tarak. Colt and Ruby were nowhere to be seen. Sierra spotted Lucas and her face lit up, even though it was obvious she was tired. Lucas's heart beat faster at the sight. Arnold leaned a little closer. "Fine-looking woman."

"That she is," Lucas agreed.

"Judging by the way she's eyeing you, you're a lucky man."

Lucas remained silent, the only sound his boots on the dirt path.

Elliot came out of one of the long, low buildings with Michael as Lucas approached Sierra. "There you are. Good. I'll show you to your rooms. Eve, you get your own. Will that be acceptable?"

Eve nodded and smiled at the idea.

"Of course, you all will as well," Elliot added as he registered the fatigue on Lucas's face. "My apologies. We've taken up far too much of your time. It's just that this is an exciting moment for us."

"Where's Ruby?" Lucas asked.

"Your friend got a head start on you."

"And Colt?" Lucas asked.

"Sarah whisked him away. Didn't like the way he looks."

"We did what we could."

"Oh, you undoubtedly saved his life. He mentioned that we owe you some gold, as well."

"You can put it against my bill."

Elliot laughed at that. "I think you underestimate our gratitude for all you've done. You'll be able to drink out on your good deeds for the duration, I assure you." Elliot motioned to the second building to their left. "These will be your sleeping quarters until we can arrange something more permanent. And we'll see if we can find you some clean things to wear. I imagine you're tired of those after weeks on the road."

"Did the job," Lucas said.

"That will be wonderful. Thank you, Doctor," Sierra said.

"Please – Elliot to you."

Sierra held out her hand to Eve, who took it. "Well, Elliot, let's get this youngster scrubbed off and see if she has an appetite, shall we?"

"Indeed," Elliot agreed.

She threw a thousand-watt smile at Lucas, which wasn't lost on Arnold or Elliot. "Lead the way."

Chapter 24

The sleeping quarters were snug – Lucas's room was a twelve-by-ten box with an efficiency bathroom attached, but to his eye it was a suite at the Ritz. He set his saddlebags down by the door, sat on the bed to remove his boots, and nearly fainted at the feel of a real mattress. He'd almost forgotten what a bed felt like after so many nights on the road, and it was all he could do to resist lying down, but the coating of road dust on him was the deciding factor.

The gravity-fed shower provided enough warm water to last fifteen wondrous minutes, and the unfamiliar luxury of soap and shampoo was almost too much for his senses. When the water finally cooled, he stepped from the stall and studied his face in the mirror: the dark lines beneath his eyes provided mute testament to the ordeal they'd been through.

Five minutes later he was outside in the sunshine, wearing his last clean shirt and jeans; earlier a young man had appeared at his door and taken his soiled clothes to wash them. Sierra appeared moments later and his breath caught in his throat at the sight of her in a simple white summer dress, Eve in a miniature long-sleeved version by her side.

"I could get used to this," she said as she joined him and tiptoed to kiss his cheek.

"Me too," Lucas said, taking her hand and trying not to fixate on the tattoo of the eye of Providence on her bare arm.

"They took my clothes," Eve said.

"Probably needed a cleaning," Lucas replied.

"Hope they bring them back."

Sierra smiled down at the little girl. "If all their clothes are as pretty as your dress, maybe we can trade them for our old stuff."

Elliot reappeared from the larger building, trailed by Arnold and Michael. The two subordinates couldn't have been more different in appearance – Arnold a hardened veteran with the lean, no-nonsense physique and features of a professional combatant, Michael a slender younger man with birdlike features and quick eyes. Elliot moved toward them just as Ruby emerged from the sleeping quarters, her hair brushed, also wearing a white dress.

"I hope everything fit," Elliot said. "We only have so much fabric, but what we have is white, as you no doubt surmised."

"It's lovely," Ruby said. "You make these here?"

"Yes, but only recently. It's one of the additional products we've found we can trade."

"Where do you barter?" Lucas asked.

"Santa Fe's the closest outpost. But of course nobody knows it's us. We do only small lots through different people to keep from leaving a trail. Not that anyone suspects a thing. We've been very careful to keep our presence a secret, as you probably know. We used to have our own trading post, but we shut it down a couple years ago so we wouldn't draw too much interest."

Ruby nodded. "Smart. You'd be overrun if people suspected how nice this is."

"Yes, a regrettable byproduct of the crisis. One would hope that civilization would return, but it's showing great reluctance. And now, with the threat of a new virus…well, let's just say Mother Nature's won every round so far."

"But you believe you can create a working vaccine?" Ruby asked.

"That's the hope. Which reminds me – do you have the USB drive with young Eve's information?" Michael said, stepping into the conversation before Elliot could reply.

Lucas fished it out of the front pocket of his jeans and handed it to Michael. "That's it."

"Brilliant," Elliot said. "Thank God for small miracles – or in this case, big ones." He crouched down and smiled at Eve. "Want to look around at all the cool stuff?"

Eve nodded shyly, and Elliot chuckled as he straightened. "We can start with the layout, and then I'll show you the growing areas and the underground bunkers."

"Colt mentioned you have gardens," Ruby said.

"That's right. Over on the far side of the valley, where the sun's optimal. Tomatoes, carrots, other vegetables, some fruits and herbs…"

"I'd love to see them. I have somewhat of a green thumb."

"Marvelous. A woman after my own heart."

The tour lasted an hour and ended at what was obviously Elliot's pride and joy as well as his lair: the laboratory that he'd built in a subterranean bunker, connected to the other storage bunkers and equipment rooms by a series of passages. Elliot's living quarters were adjacent to the lab, which he explained was at his orders so he could work odd hours whenever an idea sprang to mind.

"I came up with the concept the second year here – something that would stay constant temperature year round with minimal heat or cooling, wouldn't be affected by unusually heavy snowfall, and would be defendable if attacked. There's no sign of it from above, and the only entrance is through the cave we passed through," Elliot said. "We've since created a whole complex of subterranean dorms for winter. Came in handy last year, which was especially brutal."

"Don't you have a problem living underground?" Sierra asked. "I couldn't do it."

"Like everything, one adapts. It's not so bad. I'm not a mole or anything, and I tend to work best at night, so often it's dark out when I'm in here anyway."

"The Doc is one of those rare birds who only needs four or five hours of sleep," Michael added.

"One of the benefits of old age," Elliot said.

"Ruby used to live in a bunker too," Sierra said. "Isn't that right?"

"Did you really?" Elliot exclaimed.

"Yes, well, it did the job." Ruby told him about her bunker. When she was finished, Elliot was frowning.

"What a tragedy that you lost it," he said. "We owe you so much."

"Spilt milk," Ruby said with a shrug, although her eyes were moist.

Elliot showed them around the laboratory, explaining the different pieces of equipment, including a level 4 clean room setup where he could work with pathogens like the virus. Lucas was uncomfortable being in the same area with something so virulent and deadly, but Elliot assured them that it was perfectly safe.

"Another reason I stuck this under a mountain – very little chance of anything damaging the vault and letting our bug escape. We poured three feet of high-density concrete in the floors, walls, and ceilings of the lab to ensure nothing nature threw at us would cause a problem."

"It's very impressive. But why not use the facilities at Los Alamos?" Ruby asked.

"Too obvious and out in the open. And too many ghosts," Elliot said with a shudder. "Or rather, bad memories."

Ruby let the subject drop, as Elliot was obviously agitated by the question.

"There's much more to show you. The computer area, for one. Ruby, I think you'll approve. Then the communications room, the mess facility…"

Arnold nodded. "Speaking of which, it's way beyond lunchtime. Let's go grab something to eat."

"That sounds great," Lucas said.

The dining area was in one of the aboveground buildings, large enough to seat a hundred and fifty at the long bench tables in one sitting. Elliot led them past a few scattered groups of late diners to the service counter, where they scooped out helpings of chicken stew and rice with vegetables. A woman brought them pitchers of freshly made fruit punch, and they sat at the nearest table and dug in.

The food tasted like ambrosia, and they all overate, Elliot's appetite nearly equal to theirs. When they were done, he sat back and rubbed his ample belly. "That hit the spot, don't you think?"

"It was wonderful," Sierra said.

Elliot glanced at Eve. "Somebody looks sleepy. I don't blame her. Perhaps a siesta? We really have nothing for you to do until the celebration tonight."

"Is a celebration really necessary?" Sierra asked.

"Of course it is! Your arrival is the biggest event of the year. We've made some hard cider, dressed venison, and everyone's looking forward to the feast. Get some rest, because it will probably go late."

"No point in arguing," Michael said. "We never turn down an excuse for a party."

"I like this place already," Ruby said, and everyone laughed.

They made their way back to their rooms, and Lucas was asleep within a minute of his head hitting the pillow. The last image in his mind was Sierra in her white dress, her tanned arms glowing in the sun, and the tattooed eye staring at him like a fury.

Chapter 25

Elliot hadn't been kidding about the enthusiasm of the Shangri-La residents for a blowout, and the mess hall, as well as the outdoor area around it, was packed. A four-piece acoustic band played folk and country music outside, where tables had been set on the freshly trimmed grass.

Lucas sat between Colt and Sierra, with Eve next to her aunt and Ruby and Elliot across from them. Elliot entertained them throughout the meal with stories of developing Shangri-La into a refuge for civilized living, as well as his plans to develop a vaccine that would save mankind.

"The vaccine idea came later, honestly," Elliot explained, finishing his monologue. "I originally conceived of the place as a refuge from the madness out in the world, and wanted a lab to develop medicine to save people. I knew early on that existing stocks would expire in a few years, and figured there would be a thriving market for antibiotics, blood pressure meds, a few other things."

"He was right about that," Michael interjected from Elliot's left.

Arnold held up a cup of cider, his face flushed from the alcohol. "As he usually is!"

Everyone toasted for the umpteenth time, and Sierra leaned closer to Lucas and gave his cup an extra clink. Lucas, ordinarily no drinker, felt light as air from the booze and the altitude; his head swam slightly, and he made a mental note for the third time that this was his last cup of cider of the night.

Sierra had looked ravishing when he'd seen her at dusk, her dress now decorated with several wildflowers, her slim form silhouetted by the torches that encircled the dining area. Eve had been playing with a group of six other children, laughing with the innocence of youth at some simple game, and Lucas had stood frozen at the sight of Sierra as the warm evening breeze stirred her hair, her long, lean legs finishing with the combat boots that were her only shoes.

She'd drifted to him like a wraith and planted a soft, lingering kiss on his lips, and the moment had seemed to last forever, time suspended for a beat that was a small eternity. When she'd pulled away, her eyes had been bright and penetrating, and Lucas had felt a thrill run up his spine. She'd taken his hand and led him to the table, where he'd spent the last two hours trying not to think about her naked form with only scant millimeters of fabric covering it.

Ruby was engrossed in a conversation with a reed-thin man with salt-and-pepper hair and three days' growth of beard, whom Elliot had introduced as Terry, one of their mechanical specialists as well as a pilot. Apparently Terry was also funny, because Ruby had spent much of the evening laughing at his observations between sips of cider.

"So, a pilot, huh? Where's your plane?" she asked when the music quieted during a slow song.

"Over on the other end of the valley. Just a single-engine Cessna, but it does the job."

"Which is?"

"Flying to the dam, mainly. And anything the Doc wants me to do."

"What do you run it on?"

"Ethanol. I detuned it so the compression will handle it, and replaced all the seals. Runs like a champ. I'll take you up sometime if you like."

"As long as you have a parachute for me. Just in case."

Terry leaned into her and murmured something in her ear. Ruby blushed and laughed like a schoolgirl. Lucas and Sierra shared a sidelong glance – it appeared their travel companion had made a new friend.

Elliot called out when the band took a break, and then delivered a ten-minute oration that was both florid in its praise of the newcomers and endearing in the heartfelt gratitude it expressed. When he took his seat again, Michael stood and gave his own, shorter speech, welcoming them to the enclave and thanking Providence for their safe arrival. Much toasting ensued, and in spite of his resolve, Lucas's cup seemed to empty itself yet again before another pour from the never-ending procession of pitchers magically filled it.

Sierra was laughing at something he'd said, but he didn't remember what, her eyes flashing in the torchlight. Lucas steadied himself and pushed his drink away, wary of the home-brewed concoction, and blinked away the slight wave of weightlessness that passed through his body.

"What's that?" he asked, suddenly aware that Elliot had said something to him.

"I said there's plenty more where that came from. The night is young, even if I'm not." Elliot waved his goblet and winked at Lucas, and the scene suddenly seemed surreal, a fête in a secluded glen as distant from the dangers of the trail as anything he could imagine.

The band returned and struck up a ballad Lucas recognized from pre-collapse days. Sierra leaned her head against his shoulder and squeezed his hand.

"Come on. Dance with me."

Lucas frowned. "Not much of a dancer."

"Prove it."

She was standing and pulling him to his feet before he could protest, and then they were in the crush of bodies, the alcohol swimming in his head as he held her close, her curves sculpted to his like they'd been made that way. The smell of her skin and her hair in the soft moonlight was as intoxicating as the cider.

They swayed together, the singer crooning a lament about never-ending love over the strumming guitars and the melody of a mandolin, and then they were kissing again. The world around them faded to a blur, their tongues darting and lips crushing in a hunger that was all-consuming.

Lucas didn't know how they wound up in his room, how Sierra was lifting her dress over her head, her body a miracle in the faint starlight filtering through the gauze curtains. All he knew was that she was with him, tearing at his shirt, and then they were naked, falling together onto the bed, all hot skin and steaming breath and soft lips and entwined limbs and a sensation like sinking into a warm ocean whose surf broke against the shore again and again until they both lay panting, their passion and energy, for the moment, spent.

Chapter 26

Dust motes drifted lazily in the sunlight streaming through the curtains as Lucas rolled over and opened his eyes. He squinted against the glare and raised a hand to his head, which was throbbing like he'd gone ten rounds with a bear. He rubbed his face and patted the bed beside him with his other hand, and then sat up.

The bed was empty.

He remembered Sierra sleeping beside him, the sound of her soft breathing, the look of her face, childlike and peaceful in slumber, and smiled. He could still taste her lips on his as vividly as he could feel the soreness in his muscles from the night's demands.

Lucas shook his head and immediately regretted the movement. So much for taking things slowly once they arrived at Shangri-La and figuring out their relationship. Part of him felt guilty, but he knew it was irrational – his wife had been gone for five years, and he'd mourned her passing every one of them, but he was only human, and at some point it was reasonable that he'd be interested in someone new.

That the someone was a woman he'd rescued, about whom he knew almost nothing, was par for the course in the chaotic new reality that was his life. And it wasn't like he'd coerced her into bed – they'd both been willing participants, so there was nothing to be guilty about.

"You're in the swamp now," he muttered, Sierra's scent still on the sheets.

Lucas swung his legs off the bed and stood. He padded to the bathroom, twisted on the shower, and luxuriated in the soft spray of hot water that washed over him. When he was done, he toweled off, ran his fingers through thick hair, and donned his clothes. A glance at his watch told him that he'd slept far later than normal – it was coming up on eleven, and he was usually awake with the rising sun.

When he stepped outside, he winced at how bright it seemed. He made his way over to the mess building and found a quiet corner to wolf down some eggs prepared by a stern woman wearing a blue apron and matching hat.

Arnold entered halfway through Lucas's breakfast and nodded to him before loading a plate with food. He sat across from Lucas and offered a hushed greeting before digging into his meal. When he finished, he sat back and gave Lucas a bleary stare, his eyes red and puffy.

"Quite a shindig, huh?" Arnold said.

"Yeah. That cider's a killer."

The security chief nodded agreement. "Got to pay the toll for the fun. Nothing's for free."

"Don't need to ask how you feel."

"That obvious?"

Lucas didn't answer, preferring to wait while a wave of dizziness passed.

Arnold cleared his throat. "What do you have planned for the day?"

"Nothing much."

"I can take you around and show you the rest of the place, if you like."

"I'd appreciate that. Be interesting to see how you organized things to support three hundred people. Especially when you're buried in snow half the year."

"It isn't that bad. More like three or four months." Arnold shrugged. "At least in winter we don't have to worry about anyone discovering us."

"You're about as remote as I can imagine. How far's the nearest town?"

"Santa Fe's a long day's ride downhill, two back."

"You ever have anyone stumble across you?"

Arnold frowned. "Not yet. But there's always a first time."

"Seems like you've got some natural defenses with the canyons. No roads leading anywhere nearby, are there?" Lucas asked.

"No. We destroyed all the roads to the west and engineered a few rock slides to seal off those approaches. Only way in is the canyon."

"Then it's perfect."

"Nothing is, but this is close," Arnold acceded.

"How long you been here?"

"Coming up on four years."

Lucas nodded. "How did you find out about it?"

"The Doc recruited me out of Santa Fe."

"What were you doing there?"

Arnold looked away. "Little of this and that. Trading. Trying to stay alive. You know what it was like the year after the flu hit."

"I remember well."

"I had a few men I'd organized for mutual defense, but things were touch and go. Santa Fe was getting raided almost monthly by one group or another. When I was offered a job here, I jumped at it. Brought my men, and haven't left since except for a few trading runs to town and some expeditions to get weapons or supplies."

"Where did you go for weapons?"

"National Guard armory down in La Cienega. Same in Albuquerque. Back in the early days they hadn't been completely looted and stripped, at least not the good stuff. Now they're empty buildings."

"Get anything good?"

"Three .50-caliber Brownings. Twenty thousand rounds. Some mortars, a few AT4s, frag grenades, M4s and M16s. Much as we could carry without attracting too much attention."

"No missile systems?" Lucas joked.

Arnold laughed. "Don't think I didn't try. They put me in charge of security, and I took the job seriously."

"I bet."

They rose and carried their trays to the kitchen before making for the entrance. Lucas almost ran Ruby down as she stepped through the door with Terry behind her.

"Well, good morning," Ruby said.

"Morning. You just get up?"

"Oh, no. We've been awake for hours. Just came in looking for you," Ruby said.

Lucas caught the *we*, but didn't comment. "Yeah?"

"I wanted to see if you were interested in seeing Terry's plane."

Lucas looked to Arnold, who rolled his eyes. "Sure," he said. "But I wanted to check on Colt."

"Already did. He's stable. The doctor's keeping him for a few days while he mends."

"Not surprised."

Terry rubbed his hands together. "Well, then, let's go. It's quite a walk. Might want to take our horses." He glanced at Arnold. "You going to tag along?"

"I've got to make the rounds. Lucas, look me up when you're done. I'll probably be around the lab entrance."

"Sure thing."

Terry led them to the stable. Tango whickered to see Lucas, and he gave his steed a few pats and checked his legs for any signs of inflammation or soreness. Noting none, he saddled up with the rest of the party, and they rode west for several miles, following the creek until they could cross at a shallow stretch. They approached a building, the exterior raw cinderblock, and Terry dismounted.

"The hangar," he proclaimed. Ruby and Lucas followed him off their horses as he strode to a roll-up door and raised it with a clatter. "Got this from town," he said. "Loading dock wasn't using it anymore."

They peered inside the dark space and saw the dark form of a small prop plane. Terry walked to it and tapped the fuselage. "Cessna U206A. Runs like a top, if not all that quickly. But it's not like I'm in a hurry to get anywhere."

"You take it up often?" Lucas asked.

"Not as often as I'd like. Don't want to attract attention, so mostly at night."

Terry gave them a tour of the plane and rattled off a host of technical specs, smiling as he spoke. When he concluded the presentation, he waited for questions like a high school teacher at the end of a lecture. Lucas obliged with some about the engine, which he fielded with enthusiasm, obviously passionate about his baby.

They waited by the horses as he closed the hangar, and Lucas murmured to Ruby, "You see Sierra around this morning?"

Ruby regarded him for a moment. "No. Why?"

"Nothing. It's just…she wasn't with me when I woke up."

Ruby restrained the smile that flitted across her face. "You two were heating up the dance floor last night, that's for sure. Can't say as I'm surprised, given how she looks at you."

Lucas shrugged, not wanting to explain. "Just thought she'd stick around some."

Ruby shook her head. "Not necessarily. Never assume you know what's running through a woman's head."

"I learned that lesson a long time ago."

"She'll show up again when she's ready."

"I figure."

Terry guided them back to the complex, recounting his background as they rode. He'd been a master mechanic in the Navy and then earned his pilot's license in his thirties, caught by the flying bug after a few trips with a friend. He'd saved carefully most of his life, and when his wife had passed away ten years before the flu, he'd bought the Cessna at auction and rebuilt it from the ground up. The project had clearly consumed him as he approached retirement from the auto repair shop he'd founded.

They strolled back to the barn and handed the horses over to stable hands, and Lucas went in search of Arnold, watching for Sierra as he walked to the caves. Arnold was speaking with one of his men when Lucas arrived at the lab entry. He quickly ended the conversation and moved to Lucas.

"I thought you might be interested in the layout of the place. The Doc only showed you a small part of the compound. There's a lot more to see."

"Love to."

"Want to grab lunch first, or head straight to the armory and the dorms?"

"I'm going to skip the food. Stomach's a little rough."

"Probably smart."

The afternoon went by quickly, and by the time dusk was falling, Lucas felt like he knew the place as well as he'd known Loving. The level of sophistication of the systems was remarkable, and he had to hand it to Elliot – everyone he'd recruited had been an asset, and all had contributed materially to creating an enviable sanctuary.

Back in the sleeping quarters, he knocked on Sierra's door, but nobody answered. He debated going in, but opted instead to nap until dinnertime, given that his head still ached from the prior night's excesses. After two hours of sleep he felt better, and he took time to shave with his straight razor, touching his neck where Sierra's pendant had hung before he'd returned it to her the night before. She'd been fingering it as they'd basked in the afterglow of lovemaking, and he'd slipped it off and lowered it over her head with the solemnity of a head of state awarding a medal. She'd laughed at his expression and kissed him hard, and then the world had faded and it had been only them.

He made his way to the mess hall and spotted Ruby sitting with Terry and Eve at one end of the crowded tables. Lucas helped himself to a rich brown stew and joined them. Elliot was sitting one table over with Michael and Arnold, and the hearty scientist waved.

Lucas smiled as he took a seat.

"How'd your day go?" he asked Eve.

"Good. I met a pig! Her name's Ellie."

"A pig?"

Ruby nodded. "A piglet. Cute little thing. Eve fell in love."

"That's wonderful," Lucas said. "What else did you do?"

"Played. Made new friends."

"There are a bunch of kids here," Ruby said.

"Yes, we have twenty-three, fourteen of which are Eve's age or younger," Terry said.

"Your Aunt Sierra have fun with you?" Lucas asked, feeling sneaky at the loaded question.

Eve studied her knees beneath the table but didn't respond.

Ruby frowned. "What is it, Eve?"

The girl shook her head and remained silent, her mouth a stubborn line.

"Is it about Sierra, Eve?" Lucas tried.

"Can't talk about it."

Lucas eyed Ruby and bent down to the little girl. "Who told you not to talk about it?"

"Aunt Sierra."

"It's okay, Eve," Ruby said. "Sometimes grown-ups play jokes on each other. To be funny. One of the ways they do that is to ask people to keep secrets they know they can't keep."

Eve frowned. "Why's that funny?"

"To see how long they can hold out." Ruby paused. "It's a grown-up thing. I don't think it's funny."

"Neither do I," Lucas said. "So you can tell us. You won't get into trouble."

"She made me swear."

Ruby smiled. "Then it has to be a joke. Nobody would make a little angel like you swear unless it was a joke."

Eve brightened. "Really?"

"Of course."

Eve looked away. "I miss her."

Lucas swallowed hard. "Where did she go, Eve?"

"She didn't say that. Just she has to leave, and that she really loves me." Eve blinked, and a tear trickled down her cheek.

"I'm sure of that," Ruby said, struggling to maintain her composure.

"When did she tell you that?" Lucas asked.

"Early. She woke me. It was dark." She looked up at Lucas. "She'll be back, right?"

Lucas shoved his plate away and rose. "Better believe it."

Ruby was right behind him when he pushed outside and stood glowering at the darkness. "You can't do this tonight, Lucas."

"I can, and will."

"You're just going to wind up with a lame horse, and we both know it. Not with this terrain. Wait until morning."

Lucas looked at Ruby, and she could see pain in his eyes. "Why do you think she left?" he asked.

"I don't know. But she's always had her own agenda. I told you that before."

He nodded. "You were right. But then why…why last night?"

Ruby had no answer.

Lucas looked around the valley, the stars so close at the high altitude he felt like he could touch them, and exhaled a long hiss of breath. "Be foolish to put Tango at risk on that trail tonight."

"You're better on a horse than she is. You'll catch up to her."

"Well, there's only one way out. I'll talk to Arnold and find out who was on guard duty this morning." Lucas shook his head and his voice softened. "I don't get it. I really don't."

"You'll figure it out, Lucas. You always do."

Lucas didn't respond and instead trudged slowly back to the bunkhouse, his shoulders slumped like a defeated man.

Chapter 27

Duke and Aaron ambled up the main street in Roswell, leading their horses on foot. Their trip from Artesia had proved a grueling one and had taken three times longer than they'd expected due to flash floods. They'd barely left the town in pursuit of Lucas when the heavens opened up again, turning the trail into an impassible nightmare. They had made camp and waited it out. After a long day the rain had finally stopped, and they'd decided to spend the night where they were.

When they finally reached Roswell, they'd been stopped by guards and given the first degree, the sentries openly hostile until Duke had been able to reassure them that he was there to see his acquaintance, who owned the trading post in town.

It had been too late that evening to see Tucker, so they'd rented a room for the night in a sprawling Victorian house two blocks off the main drag and had their first hot meal in almost a week at an outdoor grill that boasted fish, rabbit, and dove.

After a solid night's sleep, they'd gone in search of Tucker's Trading and were making their way up the street on their horses when a man called out to them at the main square.

"You two. Hold up!"

A rugged man in a ten-gallon hat with a semiautomatic pistol in a hip holster walked toward them from the far sidewalk. Duke spotted the badge pinned to his vest and nudged Aaron. "Looks like the local lawman wants a word."

"We haven't done anything."

"Then we've got nothing to worry about."

The sheriff neared and stopped a few yards from them, taking their measure, a look of disapproval on his face. "Where are you boys headed?"

"Up to Tucker's," Duke said, his voice neutral.

"You got business there?"

Duke nodded. "Yes. He's a friend of mine."

The sheriff stared up at Aaron for a long beat and then shifted his gaze back to Duke. "That right? Where you boys from?"

"Down south," Duke said, wanting to keep it vague.

"Look like you've been through it."

"Got caught in the storm. You know how it is."

"Right. Well, I figured I'd introduce myself and lay out the town rules. We don't like trouble. Which means we tend to keep to our own kind and mind our business," the sheriff said, looking to Aaron again.

"Your own kind?" Aaron asked.

"That's right. Locals tend to like other locals, if you catch my drift."

Duke nodded, trying to diffuse the tension that was building from nowhere. "We're just here to check in with Tucker."

"Best to keep it to that."

Both Aaron and Duke nodded, and the sheriff moved away. Duke shook his head and gave Aaron a sidelong glance, and the younger man rolled his eyes.

They arrived at Tucker's and tied their horses outside. When they entered, Tucker looked up from the ammo he was counting and nodded a greeting. "That really you, Duke?"

"One and the same."

"Off the beaten path, aren't you? What are you doing slumming in these parts?"

"Closed down my place. Not much happening since Loving got destroyed."

"Heard about that." Tucker held his hand out to shake. "Nice to see you."

Duke clasped his hand. "Likewise. This here's Aaron."

"Pleasure." Tucker raised an eyebrow. "What brings you to beautiful Roswell?"

"Thinking about opening a new place around here."

Tucker's face clouded. "Yeah?"

"But before I did, I wanted to check in with you and see if you need any help with yours. Be a lot easier to partner up than start from scratch."

Tucker regarded Duke for a long moment. "What do you bring to the table?"

"Besides my charming disposition and gift of gab? Well, I have Aaron here and a bag of working capital." Duke leaned into Tucker and whispered softly. Tucker's eyes widened as Duke described his gold and silver holdings.

"Crap, buddy, you could just buy the place for that," Tucker said.

"Nah. I'm looking to build something, not buy it." Duke looked around. "There enough trading to support growth?"

Tucker nodded. "Sure. I mean, it's steady, but there are only so many hours in a day."

"Maybe we can help out and I can throw my back into it some. Pay you a commission for every deal I do? Or split our hours...and the take?"

"You serious?"

"As a heart attack."

Tucker rubbed the graying stubble on his chin. "I'm short-handed right now, so the truth is I could use some help. One of my guys took off the other day. Said he'd be back in a few weeks, but you never know." Tucker told him about losing Carlton to the big tattooed thug. When he was finished, Duke was frowning.

"This fella have a tattoo of an eye in the middle of his forehead?"

"That's right. How'd you know?"

"He gets around. Stopped at my place and made a bunch of threats."

"Long way from home to be throwing shade."

135

Duke nodded. "Guy's seriously bad news. He say what he was doing here?"

"Looking for somebody."

"Same as at my place. Must not be having any luck."

"No. Bunch of his boys got shot up pretty good over at the lake." Tucker told Duke about the battle.

Duke whistled softly when he was done. "Sounds like he bit off more than he could chew."

"Yep."

Tucker and Duke dickered for a half hour over how they could do business together, and finally agreed on an equitable split. Duke and Aaron would work half days and pocket the profits after paying a slice for the use of the store. Anything in their inventory would be stored in a separate locked area, and if they sold something out of Tucker's, they'd get a small commission for their trouble, whereas if they bought or sold anything for themselves, they paid the fee and that was it.

Duke led Aaron from the shop, a smile on his face. "That wasn't so hard, was it?"

"I don't know. It isn't like you to partner up."

"Only for a while."

"Really?"

"Nothing lasts forever, but at least this way we're earning our keep rather than depleting our savings. Paying as we go. Long as we make enough to cover our nut, it's a win. If we don't like the town, we move on, and in the meantime we develop relationships and a reputation we can take with us if we decide to set up shop permanently."

Aaron nodded. "Smart."

"Even a broken clock's right twice a day."

Chapter 28

Lucas was up and dressed by the time dawn broke. His clothes had been cleaned, folded, and brought back the day before while he was out, and he'd packed his saddlebags before turning in. In the cold early light, he shouldered his M4, slid his Kimber into its hip holster, and hoisted the saddlebags before making for the door.

A skin of fog hung over the valley like fresh snow, stirring as he strode to the barn, and the air bit at his lungs with each breath. At the stable door the attendant watched him groggily while he hurried to Tango's stall. The space next to the big stallion was empty, confirming what he already knew – Sierra had taken Nugget before the camp had awakened the prior morning.

Lucas checked the Remington 700 sniper rifle in the saddle scabbard to verify it was still ready for duty, fitted the bags and saddle into place, and led Tango from the barn into the field of white.

They approached the main building, where Arnold was waiting with one of the guards from the previous morning. Arnold nodded to Lucas and introduced Lyle, a man in his late twenties with a military bearing and hair cropped close to his skull.

"He saw them leave yesterday," Arnold said.

"Them?" Lucas asked.

Lyle cleared his throat. "Yes, sir. First the Apache. An hour or so later, the woman."

Lucas's expression darkened. "Why didn't you stop them?"

"The guide had clearance to leave."

"And the woman?" Lucas demanded.

"She said he'd forgotten something important and she had to give it to him. Said she'd return shortly."

"But she didn't," Arnold muttered.

"I was off duty at nine in the morning. I wouldn't know."

"You believed her?" Lucas asked. "Why?"

"I had no reason not to, did I?" Lyle fired back. "We've been ordered to treat you as honored guests. That didn't include assuming everything we were told was a lie."

Arnold took Lucas aside. "It's not his fault. He was just doing his job."

"Way he describes things, the guide was in on it."

"Sounds like he was. But to what end?"

Lucas's expression hardened. "That's what I'm going to find out."

"Need some company?"

Lucas shook his head. "No. This is my problem."

"Might be our problem if it's a security breach."

"You'll be the first to know if it is."

Arnold took in Lucas's grim expression and nodded. "I believe it."

Lucas swung up into the saddle and directed Tango to the trail that led to the canyon entry, his mind racing at the implication that Sierra had somehow conspired with the Apache to leave Shangri-La the day after she'd arrived. It made no sense to him after all she'd been through to get there.

He tried not to take it as a rejection, his logical mind telling him that if she'd planned it in advance with Tarak, it had nothing to do with him, but it was difficult to separate emotion from fact.

But then why? Why abandon Eve — and him — when they'd succeeded?

A dark suspicion formed in his mind as he recalled Arnold's words. Had she been a turncoat all along, chartered with learning the location and reporting back to Magnus? Had her time with Lucas been nothing more than an act to lull him into trusting her? Had it meant nothing?

The thought twisted in his guts like a knife. If true, he had brought calamity to three hundred good people, and their very existences were now in jeopardy.

Eve's face flashed through Lucas's mind.

The idea was monstrous. But he couldn't discount it. What did he really know about Sierra, anyway? Just what she'd told him, which he now realized could have all been lies – a cover story artfully crafted to fool him.

But what about Jacob? He'd been convinced she was genuine.

Which made it even worse. Perhaps she'd been planted all along and had used her charms to gain Jacob's trust, just as she'd done with Lucas.

He banished the thoughts as he entered the first branch of the ravine, aware that he was being watched through sniper scopes from the caves at the canyon lip, the crosshairs tracing over his back as he wended his way along the dry wash.

The trip down the mountain went far faster than the climb up, and he was in Los Alamos little more than two hours later. He guided Tango along the main road, scanning it for tracks, and found what he was looking for as he neared the bridge over the Rio Grande. She was retracing her steps, either with the guide or close behind him. In the end it didn't matter. She'd left under her own steam, nobody coercing her.

Lucas straightened in the saddle, grinding his teeth as he rode, digesting the unpleasant implications, and then forced the speculations from his mind. They had a day on him, so how to narrow the lead? Judging by the tracks, they were moving at a walk, which made sense if they expected their horses to have to travel many miles – like back to Albuquerque and then on to Houston or Lubbock.

Lucas had an advantage, because he could drive Tango hard and cut their lead down by continuing after dark, thus overtaking them, with any luck, by late that night or tomorrow. They would probably expect pursuit, though, so he couldn't be reckless.

He calculated the math. They might make thirty to thirty-five miles per day, best case, on these trails. Tango could cover that in about six hours in judicious sprints, but he'd be blown out afterward and would be hard pressed to manage much more than a slow walk.

Which was fine. It meant by afternoon he'd have covered the distance they would have made their first day, and the rest would be keeping pace with them. He would close the final gap after dark, and they'd get the surprise of their lives in the wee hours.

He deliberately avoided thinking about what he would do when he caught up to them. There was no point in making his already miserable trip worse with trying to predict the future. All he knew was that there would be no more assumptions, no further benefits of the doubt given to Sierra.

Once across the river he urged Tango to a trot, somewhere around eight miles per hour, a loping speed the stallion could keep up for a half hour at a time. At a gallop he could hit over thirty, but he couldn't sustain it, and even a canter would wear him out quickly. But a trot was manageable and the timing would work.

Lucas would be confronting Sierra some time that night.

And then he'd learn the truth.

One way or the other.

Chapter 29

Ruby heard Elliot's distinctive voice before she saw him. He rounded the corner of the sleeping quarters from the trail that led to the lab, in a heated discussion with Michael and Arnold. Eve was playing with three of the local children, Ellie the piglet running alongside her as she hopped on one leg and made horse noises, their game punctuated by loud peals of laughter when one or the other caught up to the lead pretend rider. Ruby looked up from the kids as Elliot neared, and he drew up short when he spotted her.

"Ruby, dear woman. Good morning to you," he said.

"Dr. Barnes," she said with a nod.

"Please. Elliot."

"Elliot," she said. "What can I do for you?"

"I need to take some blood from young Eve here so I can begin working on the vaccine. I have considerable sense of urgency in light of the recent developments."

"Yes, I can imagine. Troubling."

"I'm glad you understand. It's the last thing any of us were expecting under the circumstances…"

"Agreed. But Lucas will sort it out. I have a lot of faith in him. He's faced down armies and lived to tell the story. He'll get to the bottom of it in short order."

Arnold frowned. "You don't think his relationship with the woman could affect his judgment?"

Ruby's expression was stony. "You don't know Lucas."

"I know human nature," Arnold replied.

"Lucas was as surprised as any of us."

Arnold regarded her skeptically. "That's the story, anyway."

Ruby stood. "What's that supposed to mean?"

Michael touched Arnold's arm, but he shrugged it off and took a step closer to Ruby. "It means that you two weren't part of the deal when Jacob arranged this, and now we have a security breach that could result in disaster. No offense, but you're both unknown quantities, and by inviting you in we've put ourselves at risk."

Elliot scowled. "Arnold, really, I don't think…"

"No, Dr. Bar…I mean, Elliot, he's right," Ruby said. "You don't know anything about us except what we've told you. That is, except that we've put ourselves in harm's way multiple times, crossed the state to reach you, and been almost killed in the process of delivering Eve to you."

Arnold's stare was glacial. "So you say."

"Maybe you should talk to Colt," Ruby snapped. "He watched Lucas kill several dozen Crew fighters single-handedly so we could escape. Or you can ask Eve. She was there when we all ambushed another Crew war party down by the Texas border." Ruby fought to control her fury, and her tone softened. "It must be lost on you that I didn't ride off in the dark, and neither did Lucas. It was Sierra, who *your* Jacob vouched for and sent with Eve. We're just the poor slobs who did your people's job for them. If it wasn't for us, there would be no Eve, and your entire reason for existing would be gone, wouldn't it?"

Arnold had no comeback. Elliot stepped between them. "Arnold, take some time to cool down. She's right. She came here in good faith and has done nothing wrong. You're out of line."

"Out of line?" the security chief demanded angrily.

"Yes, Arnold, out of line. You're insulting our guest. I understand your frustration; we all share it. But lashing out at Ruby accomplishes nothing. The problem still remains."

"Fine. Handle this however you like. But don't ask me to be happy about it."

Arnold stormed off, trailed by Ruby's dark stare. Elliot shook his head and sighed. "I'm sorry, Ruby. Tensions are obviously high, and Arnold's responsible for security. He takes his job personally."

"Sometimes too personally," Michael said, pursing his lips in disapproval.

Eve continued racing after the other children, who were now chasing a butterfly, its bright yellow wings flapping above their heads as they jumped with outstretched arms. Elliot couldn't help but smile at the sight, and when he turned back to Ruby, his eyes were sparkling with his usual good humor. "Ah, to be young again, eh?"

"It goes by fast," Ruby agreed.

"That it does, dear lady, that it does. Can I presume upon you to help me with Eve? She'll probably be frightened having her blood drawn."

"I imagine she's suffered through worse," Ruby countered. "But sure, I'll help." She cupped her hands around her mouth and called out, "Eve! Come here, please."

Eve gave her a long-suffering look and disengaged from her companions, panting as she ran to Ruby, her eyes dancing with joy, Ellie scampering behind her.

"Is Auntie back?" Eve asked.

"Not yet. But Dr. Barnes needs to check you to make sure you're healthy."

"I feel fine."

Elliot smiled. "I'm quite sure you do, my young friend. Purely a formality. Won't take more than a minute or two."

Eve looked to Ruby, who nodded. "It's no big deal, Eve. You'll be back playing in no time," she said, holding out her hand.

"Can Ellie come?"

Elliot and Ruby exchanged a glance, and he nodded gravely. "Normally we don't allow swine in the lab, but I think we can make an exception in this case."

Eve looked uncertain. Ruby clarified for her. "You can bring Ellie. I can carry her if you like."

"I'll do it," Eve said, and scooped up the animal, which squealed before settling into her arms. They followed Elliot and Michael to the cave and then down the steps carved into the stone to the steel blast door of the lab.

Inside, every light was illuminated, and it was nearly as bright as outside. Elliot escorted them to the sterilized area of the laboratory and moved to a rack of equipment. He selected a butterfly needle in a sealed packet and a bottle of alcohol, and placed a plastic vial holder filled with glass tubes on the table beside him.

"Sit down here, young lady, and we'll get this taken care of." He laid a hand on Ruby's shoulder. "Would you see to our piglet while I do the honors?"

Ruby nodded, and Eve reluctantly handed over Ellie.

"Put your arm on this pad, please," Elliot said to the little girl.

Eve did as instructed, her face suddenly slack. Ruby glanced at Elliot, who nodded once – he'd caught the change in her demeanor too. He pretended not to notice and swabbed her arm with alcohol before cinching a length of rubber surgical tube around her bicep and studying the veins in the crook of her arm. Satisfied, he had her make a fist.

"Why, you're going to be an easy one," he declared jovially, and removed the needle from the package. He offered another smile and lowered his voice. "You should look over at Ruby. This might sting just a little."

Eve leveled a stare at Elliot that chilled him for its dead quality. When she spoke, her voice was no longer that of an innocent child. "I'm used to it."

Elliot nodded and slipped the tiny needle into the vein. Eve didn't blink. The narrow plastic tube that hung from the needle went crimson with blood, and he snapped the first of three vials into place.

True to his promise, he was finished in little more than two minutes, and Eve was holding a cotton ball against the needle mark, her arm folded. Michael brought a glass of fruit punch and offered it to her. "Drink this. You'll feel better."

She took it with numb fingers and nodded mutely. Ruby watched as she drained the glass and set it down carefully on the table beside her, and then looked at them with the same blank expression that had settled over her when she'd sat. "Done?" she asked.

Ruby looked to Elliot, who was sliding the vials into another tray. "Yes, yes. For the time being, anyway. You're a very brave little girl, Eve. Remarkable."

"Can we go?" Eve asked.

Ruby nodded and held out her hand, the piglet squirming in her other. "Let's."

Elliot watched as the woman led the child out the door and frowned at Michael, his eyes troubled.

Michael shook his head. "Poor thing."

"Yes. She's obviously been traumatized." Elliot finished his task and placed the used needle into a glass tray and immersed it in alcohol – supplies being far too valuable to throw anything away.

"Animals."

"Yes, Michael, they are. Now you get a sense of what we're dealing with. If they have their way, we'll all be their slaves, and the world will be a dark place indeed."

"That won't happen. You'll be successful. You always are."

Elliot regarded the test tubes full of the most precious blood on the planet and nodded thoughtfully. "I hope you're right. For all our sakes."

Chapter 30

Sierra followed Tarak along the trail that paralleled the Rio Grande, her cowboy hat pulled low on her brow against the afternoon heat. The Apache was clearly annoyed by their slow pace, but Nugget couldn't manage any more than she was giving, still not a hundred percent after the grueling march north.

Tarak had waited for Sierra in Los Alamos, as she'd arranged with him the day before she'd slipped away from Lucas at five a.m. He'd had no problem with her accompanying him after she'd paid him a hundred rounds of ammo, which left her with only sixty for her rifle – he was headed back south anyway. But his disposition had turned sour at the pace of her horse, and they'd ridden all day without a word, which was fine by her, given everything else on her mind.

She'd improvised a story when challenged by the sentries and for a nervous moment had feared that her trip would be over before it started, but to her relief they'd let her pass. That had been the big hurdle, and the rest was now downhill – literally.

A dove cooed from a tree by the river, its call plaintive and sad, and she urged Nugget faster as Tarak's horse soldiered on with the determination of a bulldozer. The trail had transitioned from hard stone to shale, and her horse was having difficulty with the surface.

"Come on, Nugget. You can do it. Once we're in Albuquerque, you can take a break. Just a little further," she coaxed, her voice low.

If Nugget was swayed by her words, she didn't show it; she

maintained her plodding gait, barely above the speed Sierra could manage on foot.

The river curved left and they followed the trail along the gentle bend, where the land turned lush and green. Farmland that some enterprising grower had leveled and plowed had been reclaimed by wild vegetation, and some of the chaotic sprawl of plants stood taller than a man. A branch brushed at her face, and she pushed it aside. Tarak pulled even further away from her as Nugget slowed.

"Tarak, wait up," she called, and dug her heels into Nugget's flank. Sierra rounded another, sharper bend, and almost ran headlong into Tarak, who'd stopped in the middle of the trail.

"What is it?" Sierra asked.

Tarak turned his head partially toward her, his eyes remaining on the trail. "No sudden moves."

"What? What's wrong?" she asked, and then her words froze in her throat as a mountain of a man covered in tattoos, whose black leather vest and eye of Providence on his forehead announced him as Crew, stepped into view, assault rifle trained on them.

"That's far enough," the big man said. "Get off your horses. Now. Reach for your gun and that'll be the last thing you ever do."

Two more men emerged from the brush, also covered in prison ink, pointing the menacing snouts of their AKs at Sierra. With a glance over his shoulder at her, Tarak shrugged and dismounted, landing on the bank with the lightness of a cat.

Sierra moved more slowly, calculating her chances of escaping or shooting it out – neither of which were realistic, she concluded by the wary anticipation on the faces of the gunmen. She lowered herself and stood with her hands raised as one of the pair made his way to her and disarmed her.

The big man stepped closer to Tarak and nodded. "Took you long enough."

"It's a couple of days away."

"You map it out?"

"No need. I can give you clear directions. You can easily find it on a map."

Sierra's eyes narrowed and she gasped. "You're working with them!"

Cano moved toward her and backhanded her across the face, knocking her head to the side. She staggered but didn't go down.

Cano grinned, the effect more chilling than if he'd hit her again. "You're a regular genius, aren't you?"

Sierra gaped at Tarak. "How could you? Why?"

Tarak's face was untroubled. "Orders. This isn't our fight."

"They'll destroy everything."

"Kind of like the white man did to my people? You'll get over it."

"You're no better than they are," Sierra spat.

"Whatever." Tarak shrugged and informed Cano, "They're up past Los Alamos. In the mountains to the west. Probably about, oh, nine or ten miles up the canyon. I'll give you directions – it's a little tricky, but not if you know the way. Oh, and they have snipers guarding it, so you'll need to deal with them."

"They paid you to stay silent," Sierra hissed.

"No, they paid me to guide them through our territory, which is what I did. I don't decide this – my superiors do, and they worked a deal that's to their advantage. They told me when I radioed from Los Alamos."

"Enough with the questions," Cano snapped.

"What are you going to do to me?" Sierra demanded.

"Anything I want. You're lucky I like 'em with more meat on their bones."

"I'd rather die."

Cano smiled. "That can be arranged. But I think Magnus will want to decide that, not you."

"Magnus…" she whispered.

"That's right." Cano turned to his men. "Take her. Tie her up." He waited until they'd grabbed her arms before bellowing at the top of his lungs. "Luis!"

Sierra struggled, but a painful squeeze from one of her captors convinced her to think better of it. She licked away a trickle of blood from the corner of her mouth and probed her cheek with her tongue, where the flesh was already swelling from the blow. The men led her into a small clearing by the river where four others were waiting, guns at the ready. All focused on her as one of the men approached with a length of yellow nylon cord, smirking at her predicament, his eyes taking in every inch of her with a lascivious intensity that left little to her imagination.

Chapter 31

Arnold pulled the door closed behind him and strode into the room where his six most loyal men were already waiting, troubled expressions mirroring their demeanors. Arnold sat heavily at a round table and poured himself a cup of water from a steel pitcher.

"It's not good," he announced.

"Tell me about it," Toby grumbled.

"What we know so far is nothing. The woman took off after the guide. And this Lucas character left in search of her. At least, that's what they would have us believe. I'm not so sure."

"You think it's a con?" Toby asked.

"Could be. The old woman swears it isn't, but they could have tricked her, too."

"I talked to her some. She seems straight," Ken said.

"She probably is. But the rest of them – who knows?"

"Maybe it's exactly what it looks like? The woman bolted for unknown reasons. The way she was going at it with Lucas that night, maybe she had second thoughts?"

"No way of knowing. It's all speculation until he finds her. Assuming he does."

"None of this makes any sense," Toby said. "They crossed hell and back to deliver the girl. Why would they do so if they weren't on the level?"

"To find us," Arnold said softly.

Ken cleared his throat. "It's pretty frigging hard to keep the compound safe if the Doc's bringing in unvetted strangers."

"I'll second that," Toby said.

"I think we have to assume the worst," Arnold said. "That we've been compromised." He looked around the room. "Which means we either need to prepare for an attack or pack up and move."

"Be pretty hard to move three hundred people without leaving a trace."

"True," Arnold acceded. "That leaves us with defense."

"Not like we haven't run scenarios for the last four years. It would be pretty hard to attack us successfully," Ken said.

"Maybe. Depends on what they throw at us," Toby said.

"Don't you think we're getting a little ahead of ourselves? All that's happened so far is a woman decided she didn't want to stay. Could be a million reasons. Maybe she didn't like it here. Or maybe Lucas rubbed her the wrong way."

The men chuckled, but the sound was like boys laughing hollowly as they passed a graveyard.

"We need to have a meeting with the Doc and Michael," Toby said. "They have to be brought up to speed."

"I already spoke with Elliot. He thinks I'm overreacting," Arnold said.

"He doesn't have any kind of tactical background, so his opinion's meaningless when it comes to defense," Toby countered.

"No, it isn't. He'll listen to reason if we have a strong case. It's Michael I'm more worried about."

Arnold and Michael had a long-running rivalry. Michael was educated and dismissive of Arnold's ideas, whereas Arnold viewed him as a suck-up, a yes-man who played to Elliot's ego. That Elliot often deferred to Michael for operational decisions stuck in Arnold's craw, but when he'd brought it up, Elliot had assured Arnold that he was in no way playing favorites – that Michael simply had more depth in some things than Arnold by virtue of his scientific background.

By 'depth,' Arnold understood the doctor to mean that Michael was smarter. Which might have been true academically, but not operationally, and certainly not tactically. Arnold had lived through combat under the harshest conditions before the collapse and had proven himself time and time again in the ugly new world of anarchy that was their everyday reality. Michael, on the other hand, had spent too much time in the safety of Shangri-La and had forgotten the snake pit that was the world outside the canyon walls.

"What are we going to do?" Toby asked.

Arnold took a long sip of water and stared into space. "Let's assume a worst-case scenario. I think we have to. I want to review our inventories of ammo, explosives, everything, and put together a trading team to go into Santa Fe in the next twenty-four hours and buy every piece of gear we can get our hands on. If there's a siege, there will be no such thing as enough ammunition or food."

"We can do that," Ken agreed. "But without knowing what we're defending against, we're spinning our wheels."

Arnold nodded as he stood. He finished his drink and set the cup down on the table. "Spinning our wheels is our job. We get paid to be paranoid. We're the first – and last – line of defense, and it's up to us to imagine the unthinkable and prepare for it." Arnold strode to the door. "Toby, have that inventory for me by tonight. Anything that looks borderline needs to be replaced. I want a complete list of all raw material we can commit to bolstering our defenses."

"I have schematics of some antipersonnel devices we could make in the machine shop if we shunted off all other projects," Ken volunteered.

"Make a list of what you need, and I'll meet with the Doc tomorrow and get it approved."

Toby followed Arnold to the door and stepped outside with him. When they were out of earshot, he murmured to Arnold while looking around to confirm they wouldn't be overheard. "You really think this is the big one?"

As the force chartered with Shangri-La's defenses, they'd often discussed their nightmare scenario – a full mobilization of a hostile force against them, rather than opportunistic scavengers. It had been considered by Michael and Elliot as a distant likelihood, given the security safeguards they had in place, which had withstood years of testing with flying colors, but Arnold had always believed they were living on borrowed time.

He met Toby's stare without blinking. "We're going to find out. And that should scare the crap out of everyone, because most of these people have never been in an all-out war. I have." He swallowed away his frustration and lowered his voice. "Pencil out an evacuation scenario, too. I want all options on the table once we know what we're dealing with."

Toby nodded. "Hope she was just pissed at him. Lovers' quarrel or something."

Arnold looked away. "Hope's a lousy defense. Get to work."

Toby returned to the room, leaving Arnold to his thoughts. The security chief made his way toward the lab, a coil of anxiety tightening in his stomach with every step.

Chapter 32

Night had fallen hours earlier, but the temperature was still broiling, and the heat radiating from the hard-packed dirt sapped Lucas of energy with every mile. Tango had performed valiantly, but Lucas had wrung about as much out of the stallion as he dared, and had slowed to a leisurely clip as the sun had crested and begun its steady descent. He estimated he'd covered fifty-five miles, though couldn't confirm his impression, there being no obvious landmarks.

He was using the night vision monocle as he rode; the light from the stars was dim, a high striation of clouds blurring their glow and making their faint illumination untrustworthy for navigation. By his reckoning, he would come across Sierra and the guide at any moment, and in spite of his fatigue, a buzz of adrenaline coursed through his veins at the thought.

Lucas hadn't arrived at any monumental conclusions as to how he'd handle Sierra when he found her, but he figured that the likeliest straight answer he would get would be from Tarak, who'd performed as requested at every step of their journey and would have no reason to mislead him. That he couldn't trust Sierra wore at him, but he was an adult, and in his line of work he'd seen everything, so he was no stranger to dishonesty. That he had to be on the defense against someone for whom he had feelings was immaterial.

A hint of wood smoke wafted on the breeze from the south, and he slowed to a crawl. He sniffed the air like a tracking dog and, when he was sure he hadn't imagined the odor, drew Tango to a halt and dismounted.

He listened with his head cocked, ears straining for the slightest sound, but could make out nothing but the rush of the river and the occasional low whistle of the faint wind through desiccated branches. After several minutes of standing motionless, he tied Tango to one of the stunted trees and crept along the trail, staying away from the river in the hopes that he could surprise Tarak and Sierra.

When he arrived at a thicket of tall bushes, he blinked at the sight of a small fire flickering near the river. His heart skipped when he spotted a collection of sleeping forms around it – six that he could make out. He swept the area with the monocle and froze at the sight of Sierra, sitting up, back to a log, eyes closed. Lucas squinted through the scope but couldn't make out enough detail to identify who the men surrounding her were, or why she wasn't also lying on her bedroll.

He set the monocle down and lifted his M4 to his shoulder, the high-power NV scope on, and peered at Sierra. In its high magnification he could make out the odd angle of her arms and realized that they were tied behind her back. The crosshairs drifted down to her legs, and he spotted rope binding her ankles, confirming his deduction.

Lucas eyed the sleeping forms, noting their weapons lying where they could get to them in an instant. In the scope's higher resolution he recognized Tarak, his distinctive hat tilted over his face, covering his eyes.

Movement in the periphery of the scope stopped him dead, and he adjusted until he found its source: a gunman with an AK hanging from a shoulder sling, relieving himself near some bushes. Lucas frowned at the logistics he was facing – a total of six hostiles, counting the lookout, heavily armed. His chances of taking them all out before one could return fire were slim no matter how precise his aim.

He watched the sentry return to where he was stationed near a tree. The man took a seat, unslung his rifle, and laid it across his lap, sitting Indian-style. Lucas waited ten minutes to see whether anyone else appeared and, when nobody did, made his careful way back to Tango. He patted the horse and then lifted the leather flap of one of the saddlebags and retrieved the crossbow and quiver, cocking it silently before fitting a quarrel into the firing slot.

His trip back on the trail was soundless; the artificial light of the monocle enabled him to pick the most solid sections so he didn't inadvertently kick any loose rocks or, worse, stumble. Moments later he was closing on the guard from his flank, reducing the distance until it would be almost impossible to miss him.

The bow discharged with a loud snap and the bolt drove through the sentry's temple – a tricky shot from any distance. He winced at the sound and listened for any sounds of life from the fire, but heard nothing.

The guard died instantly, as Lucas had hoped. If he could eliminate one more man with the bow and then bring the M4 to bear in three-round burst mode, he might be able to neutralize them all without getting killed.

Lucas cocked and loaded the crossbow again and made his way toward the fire. He was almost in range when he stopped – one of the sleeping men was no longer there.

Heavy footsteps crunched on dry twigs from his right. One of the men had awakened and was moving toward the dead guard, forcing Lucas's hand.

Lucas spotted a huddle of dark forms near a stand of trees well away from the fire and moved toward the group's horses, an idea forming. When he was close to the first animal, he untied it and led it in the direction of the sentry, hoping an improvised distraction would buy him the few seconds he would need.

Lucas broke into a trot with the horse, keeping its body between him and the dead lookout, and saw a surprised bearded face looking up at him from the edge of the scrub, no more than ten yards from the sentry's body.

Lucas released the reins and the horse continued on, leaving himself exposed, bow at the ready. He squeezed the trigger and sent the arrow flying; and then he was in motion, dropping the bow and running at the man, Bowie knife unsheathed. The bolt struck the gunman in the chest with an audible thwack, and Lucas was on him as he went down. He drove the knife through the man's eye as he tried to bring his weapon around, ending the fight with a violent shudder.

"Quincy?" a voice called from the fire, and Lucas ran in a crouch toward the dense brush that bordered the clearing, stealth abandoned now that others were up. He reached the bushes and raised his rifle to see one of the men standing, gun in hand, and two of the other sleeping forms stirring.

The M4 barked three rounds and the man's chest fountained blood. The others rolled toward their weapons and Lucas fired at the nearest, two of his rounds shredding through the target's torso as he screamed in anguish. He adjusted his aim at the next man but missed as the gunman threw himself to the side, hoping to use the fire pit as cover. Another burst from the M4 stopped the man cold as he returned fire at Lucas, and took half the shooter's skull off as he crumpled in a heap.

Lucas searched the area for the last gunman but came up empty. He swore under his breath and then rounds snapped past his head – Tarak was firing at him. Lucas couldn't scream at the Apache for fear of drawing the missing man's fire, leaving him little choice. He grimaced as he drew a bead on the guide and stitched him with a burst, knocking him backward, and his gun fell by his side as his arms windmilled.

Shots erupted from Lucas's right and he dove for the ground. An AK on full-auto hammered the brush with a sustained burst. Lucas waited for it to end with a telltale snap as the shooter ejected the spent mag, and then fired at where the muzzle flashes had lit the night twenty-five yards along the bank.

Answering fire dashed any hope that he'd scored a lucky hit, so he rolled left and dog-crawled to a different spot as the shooter rattled another half a magazine at him. Forcing himself to remain calm, Lucas peered through the scope for a glimpse of the shooter and waited in tense silence for the man to make a mistake.

Seconds ticked by, and then one of the bushes directly ahead moved. He fired two bursts and was rewarded with a volley from the ground beneath it – the shooter had done the same as Lucas, hugging the dirt to minimize his profile as a target.

What he hadn't banked on was the night vision.

Lucas saw a flash of faint reflection in the scope and realized it was a man's bald head. He fired four bursts, grouping the rounds within a two-foot area, and then ejected the magazine and slammed another home by feel, his eye never leaving the scope's glowing field.

His pulse thudded in his chest and a bead of sweat trickled down the side of his face. He ignored the itch caused by its passage and continued to sight on the target's last position. After a good five minutes, Lucas rose slowly and ran low to the ground toward the gunman. When he reached the bushes, he found a powerfully muscled figure lying face down in a coagulating pool of blood. Lucas toed an AK-47 away from him and checked his torso for any evidence he was still breathing. Seeing nothing, he stepped away and put a final burst into the man's head for good measure, and then made his way to the fire to confirm all threats were neutralized.

Sierra's jaw dropped when she saw him materialize from the darkness, and she uttered a strangled cry.

"Lucas!"

He ignored her and moved to Tarak, whose eyes were staring into the eternity of the night sky. Lucas took cautious steps to each fallen form, leading with the M4, and verified that the men were all dead before slowly turning to Sierra with an unreadable expression.

"Lucas," she tried again. "Thank God."

His boots crunched on the gravel bank as he neared. She looked up into his steel gray eyes and her face fell at what she saw in them.

"Please. Untie me," she pleaded.

"Hello, Sierra," Lucas said, his voice a rasp. "Fancy meeting you here."

"Lucas, I can explain. Untie me – I can't feel my hands."

Lucas nodded and unsheathed the bloody blade of his Bowie

knife. He studied it in the firelight before kneeling by her side, his movements mechanical and a bitter frown twisting his features. He hesitated at the rope and glanced at the dead men.

"You're going to tell me everything, Sierra. Everything, or so help me God, you'll be joining this bunch in hell."

Chapter 33

"Lucas, I'm sorry. I know…I know how this looks." Sierra hung her head as Lucas severed the cord on her wrists and then went to work on her ankles.

"You mean where you snuck out of my room and left with Tarak in the middle of the night?" he spat. "I'm sure there are a dozen plausible reasons."

"Nothing I say is going to change that." Tears streamed down her face as she slowly flexed her fingers to get the blood flowing. "But this isn't about you, Lucas."

"Of course not. How about we skip past all the drama and you tell me how you wound up with a bunch of Crew gunmen, for starters?"

Sierra sighed. "I want you to know that our night together meant a lot, Lucas. That was real. It was."

"Sure," Lucas said, his voice tight. His expression hardened. "No more stalling. Why did you leave?"

"I'd fulfilled my obligation. I got Eve to Shangri-La safely."

"Right. And I risked everything to get you there. So did Ruby. So did a lot of people. And then you snuck out under cover of night."

"I had to, Lucas."

"Sierra, I'm losing patience. Give me some hard answers and stop talking in riddles."

"I was heading back to Texas."

"Why?"

"Unfinished business."

"That's a bullshit answer. Why were you going back to Texas?"

Sierra looked away. "My son."

"Your son's dead. You told me so yourself."

She nodded. "I thought so."

"But now he isn't?" Lucas demanded skeptically.

"When Garret took me captive, he told me that my son was still alive. That he'd survived."

Lucas studied her face, trying to decide whether she was telling the truth. He gave up after a few moments. He couldn't read her. "And you believed him?"

"Why would he lie?"

"Let me guess – he was interrogating you when he popped out with that?"

Sierra closed her eyes. When she opened them again, she looked lost. "Does it matter? If there's a chance that he's alive, I have to find him. You're not a parent, Lucas. You don't know what it's like. For a mother, especially. There's nothing more precious than your child." She drew a ragged breath. "Nothing."

"He used that to break you down, Sierra. It's predictable. The job of an interrogator is to do whatever he has to in order to get answers. Lie, misrepresent, threaten, cajole – anything. And you fell for it."

"You're guessing. Neither of us knows." She paused. "And I need to know."

"Because nobody tells you what to do, right? You just get an idea into your head, and it's damn the torpedoes. And every time it results in disaster – but you don't learn a thing." Lucas shook his head. "So that's why you left? I'm amazed."

"I don't care whether you approve or not, Lucas. This isn't any of your business. It's mine. You don't own me. We had an amazing night together, but I'm not some schoolgirl to be scolded because you disapprove of my choices."

Lucas sighed. "Choices that had you a captive of the Crew within forty-eight hours. Way to go, Sierra. Why listen to anything I have to say when you're doing so well?"

Sierra pursed her lips. "Thank you for saving my life. Again. Sorry

I'm such a burden." She forced herself to her feet and walked over to Tarak's inert form. "But we've got a bigger problem than you being pissed because I left."

"Which is?"

"Him," she said, pointing to the dead guide. "He told them where Shangri-La is."

"Doesn't matter. Dead men tell no tales."

"No. You don't understand. The big one, Cano, sent a pair of riders to Albuquerque to radio Magnus with the location."

Lucas scowled. "When?"

"In the late afternoon."

Lucas checked his watch and swore. He'd never be able to catch up to them – it would be physically impossible.

Sierra turned to him. "So for all your anger over me leaving, the real problem is that our guide here sold Shangri-La out. Which would have happened whether I'd left or not. In a way, we only know about it because I *did* leave, so maybe everything happened for a reason."

Lucas moved to Tarak and searched him. He retrieved the heavy suede pouch with the gold in it and slipped it inside his vest pocket. Sierra stood uncomfortably close, but he forced himself to ignore her presence.

"We have to warn them," he said.

"Obviously. You can go back and save the day. I'm headed to Texas."

"Did you overhear anything that we can use?"

"Just that Magnus would pull out all the stops once he knew where it was."

"Any idea of what that means?"

"Cano bragged that he'd send a thousand men."

Lucas's frown deepened. "Was he serious?"

"He sounded like it."

"It would take weeks to get a force that large from Texas to Los Alamos."

She shook her head. "No, it wouldn't."

"Do the math, Sierra. Figure twenty-five miles a day. It's got to be a thousand miles. And you'd have to supply all those men and horses."

"That's not what he thought. He figured a week."

"There's no way."

"You're underestimating Magnus. He's got vehicles. And fuel. He'll be in a hurry to take down Shangri-La, so he'll throw everything he's got at this. Cano was confident enough to wait for him here. That's not the actions of a man who expects it to take a month."

Lucas hadn't considered the possibility of a motorized force. But it made sense that if Magnus controlled so much territory, he would have access to resources beyond the norm.

The thought chilled him. What Sierra had described was a modern army headed their way, and only three hundred denizens of Shangri-La to defend themselves against it.

The outcome wasn't hard to predict.

He turned to her. "First things first. You're not going back to Texas."

"You don't tell me what to do."

"I'm doing exactly that, and for once you're going to listen. You almost got yourself killed here. Is that your plan? To just ride south until you're captured by any number of miscreants and get your throat slit after they're tired of gang raping you? Think, Sierra. Use your head. You have less than zero chance, and that's even if Magnus wasn't mobilizing."

She threw him a defiant stare, but her lower lip trembled. "I'm not abandoning my son."

"Right. So it's better to get killed than to have a workable plan. Good thinking."

"You made it into Lubbock and back. It can be done."

"I'm not going to argue with you, Sierra. Promise me that you won't try any more idiocy, or I'm going to hog-tie you again, and you'll go back to Shangri-La a prisoner."

"Who do you think you are, Lucas? You can't do that."

"Right. Just like Cano couldn't." He paused. "Those are your options. Either you do this my way, or I force you." Lucas was out of patience. He squared his shoulders. "At this point I don't much care which it is, because we need to get out of here. The gunfire will draw any predators around here, so we've already outstayed our welcome."

"This isn't over, Lucas. If he was your son, you wouldn't quit until you found him."

"Sierra, I'm going to say this with all possible kindness, and then we're done discussing it. Garret lied to screw with your head. He told you a story to confuse you, to break down your resolve. I'm sorry, but your son isn't alive. It's a fiction. I watched the same technique used over and over in interrogations back when I was a Ranger. You were fooled. End of story."

"I need to be sure."

"What you need to do is recognize the disastrous consequences of your impulsive behavior and think about the number of times you would have been killed if I hadn't saved your bacon, not to mention all the other people you've endangered. Now are you going to come willingly, or do we do this the hard way?"

She stepped toward him and touched his arm. "Lucas..."

He shrugged off her hand. "Promise me, Sierra."

Sierra blinked away tears and sighed. "Fine, Lucas. I promise. Happy now?"

He shook his head. When he looked at her, his eyes were pained. "Wouldn't use that word, but it'll do." He angled his head, listening, and then began walking back toward where he'd tied Tango. "Gather up a weapon and some magazines and get your horse, Sierra. I want to be on the trail in two minutes."

He stalked off, hating that he had to doubt every word out of her mouth, looking for the lie. The only reason he didn't believe she was a threat was because she'd been the Crew's prisoner. Otherwise he would have thought she'd been in it with them. But the ropes proved that wasn't the case. As to the rest, he could understand why she'd left – the guide could ensure her safe passage, or so she'd thought, and she'd never get another chance like it.

That she believed the story about her son he didn't dwell on. People believed all sorts of incredible stuff, and Garret had chosen her one weak link and worked a blade through it with considerable skill. Of course she'd believe what her heart wanted to think was true – even though Lucas didn't have children, he could understand a mother's love.

Whether she had any intention of honoring her promise to him remained to be seen. She didn't have a choice for now, but he suspected he hadn't seen the last of her attempts – he had to hand it to her for persistence, if nothing else.

He despised himself for the stirring he felt when he gazed into her eyes, and wanted to maintain his fury at her, but it was already being replaced by concern over her story about Magnus and compassion at the grief that she must be feeling at the idea her son was still alive.

What he couldn't forgive her for was abandoning him without telling him. It was childish, he knew, but there it was. She'd chosen to sneak away rather than sharing her problem, and there was no way to pretend that hadn't harmed any chance they had together.

Tango shook his head at Lucas as he neared, and Lucas pushed the thoughts from his mind. He needed to get clear of the camp and ride all night; the clock was ticking ominously, the damage by the treasonous guide already done.

Chapter 34

Luis and one of the Crew gunmen – a particularly nasty piece of work named Ross – rode all night and arrived in Albuquerque two hours after sunup, their horses exhausted. Once in the city, they plodded along a main street until they found a promising area with several watering holes and numerous trading posts.

Nothing was open yet but a greasy spoon in the middle of the block, so they parked themselves at a sidewalk table and ordered breakfast. Ross was uncertain about eating before he found a radio, but Luis assured him that it was fine – not much would be open at that hour, and they might as well maintain their strength.

Cano had ordered Luis into town with Ross because he considered the Loco expendable, which he as much as told Luis. Luis had offered no reaction, understanding Cano's attempt to bait him. Their final confrontation would happen on Luis's terms, not Cano's, he was determined, and he took pleasure in giving the Crew boss his best stone-faced nod of acquiescence.

Ross was a serious lowlife, even by prison standards. Violent and fearless, he had the cunning of a rat. On the ride south he'd regaled Luis with stories of brutality that were typical for hard cases. He'd been locked up for multiple life sentences following his arrest for a string of particularly vicious home invasions, where he'd pistol-whipped geriatrics for the thrill of it, costing one an eye and another her hearing. The public defender had argued that Ross was mentally ill, positing that nobody sane would rape an octogenarian while filming it on his phone, but the jury had disagreed, as had the judge, who'd thrown the book at him.

Of course to hear him tell it, he was a victim, unable to get a job due to his lack of education, forced into selling drugs on the street, and then later moving up to violent crimes to support his habit. Luis had heard variations of the same story hundreds of times and had tuned the man out; there was nothing new under the sun once you'd done as much time in lockup as Luis had.

The eggs were delicious, and a full stomach diminished the throbbing in Luis's temples to a manageable ache. The cook didn't know where they could find a radio, so they sat in the shade and waited for the trading post to open. Twenty minutes later a scruffy man arrived with a pair of menacing-looking sidekicks, and Luis told Ross to stay put while he got directions to the nearest shortwave transmitter.

Luis returned after a brief discussion with the trader, and they rode into the center of town, ignoring the glowers of the residents. Six blocks up, near a square with a century-old church, they tied up outside of a barber shop with a towering antenna rising from its flat roof.

The owner of the establishment wasn't thrilled by their looks or smell, but seemed happy enough when Ross counted out several fistfuls of rounds for ten minutes of airtime. Luis distracted the man with questions while Ross raised the Crew operator in Houston and delivered the coded message that Cano had scrawled on a scrap of paper. Cano's fear was that Shangri-La would intercept the transmission, so he'd created a three-part message, sent over several frequencies, lingering on none for longer than twenty seconds.

It seemed hyper-paranoid to Luis, but he played along, congratulating Ross on a job well done when they exited the shop. The owner had offered them a bath and a shave for a few more rounds, but neither of them took him up on it, preferring to spend their barter elsewhere.

Luis was the one who suggested finding a whorehouse, and Ross had enthusiastically seconded the idea until doubts had surfaced over how Cano would react. Luis assured him that he wouldn't tell Cano and that it could stay between them. When Ross agreed, Luis smiled inwardly, the move a calculated one to earn the dolt's trust and give Luis leverage over him.

They made for a brothel that stayed open round the clock. They were stopped by a patrol on the way, but when they told the men their destination, all had laughed and wished them luck.

Chapter 35

Magnus stood with Snake and the rest of his inner circle, watching the preparations for his battle force to roll. Twenty diesel buses had been fueled in the parking lot of the church he used as his headquarters, and he waited as his men loaded the cargo holds with weapons and supplies. A row of semi-rigs with livestock carriers were lined at the front, and still more Crew members led horses aboard, the front sections containing bales of feed stacked to the ceiling. Nearby, a procession of Humvees was being readied; crews checked their oil and tires as his technical team hooked trailers to them for ammunition and supplies.

Four olive green M777 Howitzers were grouped near the parking lot entry, where hundreds of shells rested in crates, waiting to be loaded onto a tractor trailer. The artillery and ammunition had been looted from an abandoned armory – the only four that hadn't been disabled by the staff. Whitely had managed to make them operational using parts filched from other big guns, the computer systems being the touchiest parts.

Magnus strode to his senior general with Snake in tow. "Jude, what's our departure time?" he barked.

"Another hour, at least. Lot to onload."

"How many men, total?"

"Nine hundred and seventy of our best."

"How long do you estimate it'll take to get there?"

"Three days if we run round the clock."

"Which we will. How are we set for spare parts?"

"We'll have two trucks with tires, repair kits, belts, oil, the usual. I'd like to have twice as many, but we'll make do."

"Cano's driver said the road to Pecos is relatively clear."

"Yes. It's the highway north that's the unknown. We can assume we'll have to remove vehicles along the way. That's why we're bringing three tow trucks." Jude paused. "My biggest concern is supply lines. We'll need to have plenty of food and water, and trying to carry enough to last us over a week will use more fuel than we can spare. As it is, we probably won't be able to make it all the way back. Not enough diesel for a round trip with a force this size."

"We've been over this already. I don't care. We'll worry about getting back once we've destroyed their base. Worst case, we can ride cross country to Lubbock and use some of their vehicles."

"They have almost no fuel left."

Magnus waved the statement away. "Where do you plan to commandeer supplies en route?"

"Roswell, and then Albuquerque. From there we should be fine. If this goes more than ten days, we can hit Santa Fe, too."

Magnus nodded. "Then you've thought everything through?"

"Yes. As much as we could in the time we had." He paused. "I've mapped out the best route – fortunately, there's a highway all the way to Los Alamos, so we'll never be off the pavement. We should be able to make good progress."

"According to Cano, they're only three hundred strong. If your men can't grind them into hamburger in short order, you have no right to call yourselves Crew."

Jude frowned but said nothing. He knew as well as anyone that you contradicted Magnus at your peril. Once he had an idea in his head, he didn't want to hear anything that wasn't in line with his assumptions. Privately, Jude wasn't as glib as his master, as he'd had actual combat experience in the Middle East. He'd seen tribesmen inflict horrendous casualties on the best armed, best trained forces on the planet, and understood that, absent aerial and satellite support, nothing was a given, no matter how determined Magnus might be.

"Very well," Magnus continued, turning to his inner circle. "Snake will be in provisional charge during my absence. You're to follow his orders as though I was here. Is that clear?"

The men nodded with expressions ranging from neutral to displeased. Snake had his rivals among the group, where Magnus's favor was the only currency that mattered, and they constantly worked to undermine each other in his eyes. Snake's appointment as their surrogate master hadn't sat well with some, but they'd held their tongues, wary of provoking Magnus.

"Don't worry. There shouldn't be any surprises," Snake said.

Magnus acknowledged him and then moved to the artillery. "We know these work?" he demanded.

"Whitely assured us they do." Jude hesitated. "I wish we had time to get him down here from Lubbock."

"Well, we don't," Magnus snapped. He watched as a group of his fighters checked their weapons near one of the buses, donning plate carriers and loading magazines, some practicing fieldstripping their rifles under the watchful eyes of their squad leaders, and then nodded.

"Call me when we're ready to roll. I have some last minute items to attend to."

Magnus hurried back to the church, where he had a radio transmission scheduled with the Apaches to negotiate a price for his army to cross their territory. Whether he would actually pay it or simply wipe them out, he hadn't decided yet, but he was leaning toward killing them – after all, he was a conquering head of state. Why would he pay for what he could take for free? He had more than enough firepower, and it would be good practice for his men – whet their appetite for blood.

But he would make that determination once he saw what he was up against. With almost a thousand fighters, he was mounting the largest fighting force he'd ever heard of post-collapse, and the sight and sound of a motorized army bearing down at high speed would cow anyone planning on challenging him. Like his idols Genghis Khan and Attila the Hun, he would sweep across the land like a plague, destroying everything in his way.

The thought made him grin. Finally, he was fulfilling his destiny, preparing for the final battle that would decide who ruled the world – a battle he would not lose.

Chapter 36

After a grueling day's ride to Los Alamos, the final approach through the canyons draining what resources Tango and Nugget had left, the sentries held Lucas and Sierra at gunpoint until Arnold could be reached on the radio to confirm that they were to be admitted. As the light went out of the western sky, their approach to the compound was notably less celebratory than their first. No bands of joyous riders greeted them, no crowd of well-wishers waited to make them feel like honored guests.

Arnold, Michael, and Elliot stood by the main building with a small group of men as Lucas guided Sierra and two of the Crew's horses loaded with their weapons and ammo toward the entrance. They dismounted, and four stable boys came at a run to take the animals. Elliot cleared his throat and motioned to them to follow him inside.

"Come. We have a lot to discuss," he said, none of his usual good humor in evidence.

Sierra looked down at her dusty pants and hands. "Lucas knows everything that I do. If you don't mind, after two days with no sleep, I'll sit this one out."

Lucas glanced briefly at the men and then nodded. "No reason for you to be there. Get some rest."

"I want to see Eve first. Is she in there?" she asked, motioning to the sleeping quarters.

Arnold nodded. "She's with your friend Ruby."

"I'm sorry I caused you any trouble," Sierra said, her tone contrite. "I didn't mean to."

Elliot didn't speak. Arnold snapped his fingers, and one of the men moved toward the bunk hall, the unspoken message clear as a bell: she would be watched around the clock. The man sat by the front door after Sierra disappeared inside, and Lucas shook his head. "Probably don't need to do that. Just let the sentries know that nobody's to leave."

Arnold gave him a hard look. "Appreciate the advice, but our sandbox, our rules."

"Suit yourself."

"This way," Elliot said, and led them into the building, where they sat at a rough-hewn wood table. Toby, Ken, and Richard joined them from outside, and Arnold leaned forward with a dour expression on his face.

"Your radio report was rather cryptic," he started. Lucas had transmitted from Los Alamos to indicate he was on final approach, and had requested an immediate gathering of everyone concerned with security.

"That was deliberate," Lucas said. "I figured you wouldn't want the whole camp to hear what I have to say."

"Well, we're all here now. Spill the beans."

Lucas gave them a terse report about his attack on Cano's camp, Tarak's death, and Sierra's news that the Crew had been told Shangri-La's location. When he was done, the men's complexions were pale – all except Arnold, who was flushed with anger.

"I told you it was mistake to allow strangers here," he snapped, pounding his fist on the table.

"Yes, you did. And I overruled you," Elliot said. "Which, believe me, I now regret." The patriarch queried Lucas, "How large a force did she say again?"

"A thousand men. Motorized, so here within a week. Certainly no more."

Michael frowned. "A week? Then we need to get busy."

Arnold snorted. "Get busy? Against a thousand men? How?

There's no way we can repel that many attackers. They'll overwhelm us."

"What are you saying?" Elliot asked softly.

"We need to leave."

Michael shook his head. "Out of the question. We've always known there might come a time when we were attacked. That was part of the logic in choosing this location – we can hold out indefinitely. We have water, food, power…worst case, we can wait for winter to do our work for us. Any attacking force has the problem of supply lines and then the snowstorms and freezing cold. We're used to it, and we're prepared. They would be at nature's mercy."

"You're dreaming," Arnold said. "They'd just take cover in Los Alamos. Plenty of the buildings there are serviceable."

"Then that's one of the first things we need to do – destroy anything that could provide shelter. Scorched earth," Michael countered.

Lucas watched the exchange without comment. Elliot noted his silence and sat back with a hard stare. "What do you think, Lucas?"

"Who cares what he thinks?" Arnold snapped. "Who's responsible for security here, anyway? Me or him? Or Michael?"

"I care, Arnold," Elliot said. "I don't undervalue your perspective, but I want to hear everyone's before making any decisions."

Arnold's frown creased his face into a death mask. Lucas inhaled slowly, and when he spoke, his tone was soft.

"Seems like you have natural defenses. If it was me, I'd plant charges at key spots in the canyon and use landslides against any riders. That's an easy one – it blocks the route with rubble and takes a bunch of them off the board." He let the idea sink in before continuing. "I'd also look at antipersonnel weapons. Claymores. Land mines. Anything that can inflict damage without risking anyone's life from here. Mine the entire canyon if you can. And blow the bridge that crosses the river. Make them fight and claw for every inch."

Arnold nodded in spite of his anger. "Not bad," he conceded. "Probably doable. We have some mines, and we could make more.

For the record, I drew up a plan to mine the approaches a few years back, so we're on the same page."

Lucas shifted in his seat. "Shall I go on?"

"Please," Elliot said.

"If you have any grenade launchers or rockets, save those for after you've used all the mines and landslides." He paused. "My grandfather gave me some advice a long time ago, and it makes a lot of sense now. The question was, how do you eat an elephant? The answer: one bite at a time. If you know there's going to be a big force coming at you, you need to break the attack down into a series of manageable battles where you can take five or ten of them for every one of you. So if I was running the show, I'd stage things so that instead of a siege, you draw them into a slew of skirmishes where you can even the odds through attrition. That means guerilla warfare. Snipers. Mines. Sneak attacks. Blowing bridges, dropping bombs. Anything that can compensate for your smaller numbers."

"Man's got a point," Michael said.

"How many able-bodied fighters do you have? I know you said three hundred live here, but I've seen a bunch of kids and some older folks…"

"About two hundred and fifty, give or take," Michael said, looking to Arnold.

"That's right," Arnold said. "But back up a second. You said drop bombs?"

Lucas nodded. "Sure. You have a plane. That's an air force. If you can figure out how to make some homemade napalm, that would cause some damage. Make it as ugly to take you on as possible. If the cost is high enough, they might lose the stomach for the fight. Although from what I've heard, Magnus won't quit."

They went back and forth for two hours, arguing the finer points of mounting a coherent defense. After the meeting, Arnold pulled Lucas aside as he was leaving, the deep discoloration beneath his eyes telling the story of his exhaustion.

"I wanted to say that was pretty impressive for a civilian," Arnold began.

"I just threw some crap at the wall to see what sticks. You had most of that covered. My ideas were icing."

"Not true. Sometimes it's important for the Doc to hear different voices. He places a lot of faith in Michael, but Michael doesn't have a background in this sort of thing."

Lucas shrugged. "I don't want to get involved in any power struggles."

"No, that's not it. I guess what I'm saying is that we need every resource we can leverage, and you even managed to convince me that we might stand a chance defending the valley. And I walked in saying we needed to leave." Arnold studied Lucas. "That's a hell of a hat trick."

"Never got good at running," Lucas said. "It's easy to start, but then it becomes a habit. You got enough ammo and explosives here – don't see why you couldn't take them on."

"What if they order up reinforcements?"

"After losing a thousand men? Not sure I'd sign up for round two if I was the cannon fodder."

"Only thing I disagree with is taking the fight to them. We don't have enough competent people to dilute our efforts like that."

"Again, none of my business. Do whatever you think is right. I just spitballed some stuff." Lucas yawned. "Look, Arnold, I'm dead on my feet. I need some sleep. Let's talk about this tomorrow, okay?"

Arnold nodded. "Yeah. Sure. Anyway, I just wanted to say that maybe I was wrong about all strangers being a bad idea."

Lucas exhaled and adjusted his hat. "In this case, you were right about the guide. Sierra wasn't trying to sell you out. He was, and he did a good job of it."

"Water under the bridge."

"Yep. Which reminds me. If you have any demolitions experts, I'd get to that bridge sooner than later, and I'd also look at alternative approaches and fortify those. Remind me again – you got any big machine guns?"

"Three Browning .50s."

"That's a decent start, depending on how you deploy them. Good thing you have NV gear. Because they'll come at night once they start losing men. That's how I'd do it."

Arnold watched Lucas make his way to the sleeping quarters with a pensive expression. The former Texas Ranger had demonstrated why the organization had been one of the most respected law enforcement groups in the country – and he'd done so after being sleep deprived and shell-shocked from a gun battle that had been seven against one.

Chapter 37

The Crew army had crossed almost two hundred miles of highway by the time the sun had risen. The column of overloaded vehicles stretched a half mile long, led by the tow trucks whose hoods had been equipped with heavy iron pipes filled with cement for battering ram bumpers that made short work of the odd car the larger buses and semi-rigs couldn't get past.

So far they'd lost three tires – two on the buses, one on a horse trailer. The problem was the age of the rubber, which had degraded with time and sun exposure. Even though the procession was crawling along, the weight was considerable, and it had become obvious within the first twelve hours that Magnus's hope of a rapid trip was overoptimistic.

The fighters slept in their seats as the buses growled down the highway, and Magnus dozed in the rear of one of the Humvees that had been customized as his command vehicle with a bed in the back, as well as steel plating on the doors and run-flat tires in case of attack. The force stopped every eight hours to refuel; the process took several hours, further slowing their progress and increasing Magnus's frustration with each delay.

He could taste victory now that his nemesis had been located. While he would like to take the girl alive – he knew from the Apaches that the travelers had a female child with them – if he had to kill her, he would. The rush to develop the vaccine would be over once the parallel effort of Shangri-La had been eliminated, and his technicians had assured him that even without her they would have it in a matter of months.

The Humvee lurched to a halt with a squeak of brakes, and Magnus sat up and called out to the driver, "What is it now?"

The radio in the cab crackled and a voice screeched from the speaker. The driver yelled back to Magnus, "One of the horse transports lost a radiator hose."

"Damn. Let me have the radio," Magnus ordered.

The driver handed it to him through a sliding window and Magnus growled into it.

"This is Magnus. Can you repair the truck and have it catch up with us if we keep moving?"

A long pause ensued as static crackled over the airwaves. A voice answered just as Magnus was losing patience.

"Negative. No way of knowing whether the engine's damaged. We lost all the coolant, for starters."

"I thought these rigs were in good shape."

"They are, but the hoses and belts are all at least five or six years old. Some of them are going to give. No way around it with the loads we're pulling."

"How long will it take to get it up and running again?"

"We're going through the parts right now. Changing a hose won't take much time, assuming we have one that will fit. Should know more in half an hour."

Magnus twisted the radio volume down and handed it back to his driver. He lay back in the cool from the AC vents and cursed their luck so far. He'd known there would be setbacks, of course, but it seemed that his confidence in the integrity of the vehicles had been misplaced. And he was learning the bad news firsthand as the temperature climbed into the red outside, making for a miserable wait.

Time ticked by at a glacial pace, and eventually Magnus threw open the door and barked at the driver, "I'll be back. I want to see what the hell's taking so long."

He marched to where the repair crew was huddled around the

open engine compartment of a massive Peterbilt rig, a toolbox open beside it. One of the repairmen uttered an oath and stepped back to wipe sweat from his face, and froze when he saw Magnus watching him.

"Well?" Magnus demanded.

"This is the third hose we're trying."

"What happened to the other two?"

"They disintegrated once we tightened them down."

"So what's the solution, other than continuing to do what isn't working?"

"This third one's looking promising. I should know in a few more minutes."

"Then we can get under way?"

"Shortly. We have to refill the cooling system and check for leaks. The engine spiked well into the red, so we also need to make sure nothing's been damaged. But if everything's okay, sure, we can get rolling in a few."

"A few," Magnus echoed.

"Sorry I can't narrow it down. It's the parts that are the problem. I told my boss before we left, but he ignored me."

"Your boss is Woody?" Magnus asked, naming the head of the mechanics in Houston.

"Yeah."

Magnus nodded. "Do the best you can."

When he returned to the Humvee, Magnus got on the radio again, this time to Houston. The radio operator responded in seconds, and Magnus demanded to speak to Snake.

Five minutes later Snake's distinctive voice emanated from the speaker.

"This is Snake."

"Snake, Magnus."

"Is there a problem?"

"Our spare parts are failing. The crew leader here says he warned Woody about the parts, but he ignored him."

Snake grunted but didn't say anything, waiting for what came next.

Magnus's voice lowered to an ominous volume. "I want you to strip him of his rank and flog the skin off his back until he's half dead. Leave the other half for when I get back."

"I'll take care of it immediately."

"Do so. And see if you can raise Whitely in Lubbock. He might have some ideas on workarounds for the parts that are bad. Tell him it's the rubber that's the problem. Hoses, tires, seals."

"Will do. Is there anything else?"

"Make the flogging a public spectacle, and make sure everyone knows why it's being done."

"Of course. I'll add it to tonight's executions."

Magnus signed off and tossed the driver the radio before climbing back into the climate-controlled interior, the vehicle's diesel engine clattering reassuringly in the oppressive swelter.

If the vehicles continued to break down as they had so far, the cross-country run would be more like a death march, he knew. His only hope was that the run of failures in the first part of the trip was infant mortality of the weakest vehicles, and once those questionable parts were replaced, the rest would continue to run well.

Magnus refused to consider the alternatives. His fate was to destroy Shangri-La and dominate the country, and he would not be refused. If he had to walk all the way there, pushing his men at gunpoint, then he would.

The one thing he'd learned was that perseverance and the willingness to do whatever it took were the keys to leadership, whether it was a prison crew or a massive multistate criminal empire. Sheer force of will had enabled him to achieve the unthinkable so far, and he would continue to be an irresistible force of nature. His future was written in the stars.

And nothing would stop him from fulfilling his destiny.

Even if every one of his men had to die trying.

Chapter 38

Ross was in the lead as Luis tailed him along the trail. The going was slow. They'd camped overnight along the river, where they'd been eaten alive by mosquitoes, and Luis was in a foul mood at the daunting prospect of subjecting himself to more of Cano's abuse. The clopping of the horses' hooves on the dirt was the only sound as they drove north. Ross at least was in better spirits after having rewarded himself with two meth-addled skanks who'd been missing most of their teeth.

Luis recognized one of the rock formations near where Cano had made camp, and his shoulders sagged as they neared the flat clearing by the Rio Grande.

Ross stopped abruptly and unslung his AK. Luis slowed and called out to him, "What is it?"

The Crew gunman didn't respond, instead dropping from the saddle and moving cautiously down the trail. Luis couldn't see what had spooked the man, but followed his lead and dismounted, gun in hand. He crept after Ross, heart hammering in his chest, and then froze at the sight of the corpses near the water's edge.

Hundreds of flies buzzed around the scattering of bodies. Ross held a finger to his lips and edged into the clearing, leading with his assault rifle, his expression agitated. Luis maintained his position, uninterested in learning whether whoever had killed everyone was still around. He busied himself with counting the bodies while Ross moved toward the dead, and came up four short – the woman and three men weren't there.

Ross toed one of the corpses and recoiled at the mound of insects that had consumed most of its face. He moved to the next and found the same, and did a quick inspection of the area before returning to Luis, his skin gray beneath the veneer of prison ink that covered his face.

"Missing four," Luis whispered.

"Yeah. They been dead a while. Least a day. Maybe more. Stink something fierce, and they're bloated like balloons."

"Cano one of them?"

Ross shook his head. "Don't see his vest."

Great, Luis thought. The one he'd been praying would choke on a chicken bone had survived.

"You sure?"

"Yeah."

"We should spread out and search the perimeter. Could be more there."

Ross nodded and nodded to his left. "I'll go that way." He stopped after a few steps. "No sign of their horses. Or their guns."

"Raiding party?"

"Don't know. But someone cleaned them out."

Luis ascended to the rise where the lookout had been stationed and stopped near the tree. He called to Ross in a tight voice, and the Crew gunman came at a run.

"What is it?" he asked.

Luis pointed at the bodies. "The rest. All dead. Whoever got them did it silently."

"How do you know?"

"Because the ones around the fire died where they lay. If they'd had any warning, they would have taken up better defensive positions."

Ross looked over the bodies. "No Cano."

"Not yet," Luis agreed.

They continued searching until Ross gave a yell. Luis followed his voice until they were both standing over what had until recently been the bane of Luis's existence. Ross's expression was grave.

"That's everyone." He looked around. "I wonder who got them?"

Luis shrugged. "Doesn't really matter much. We need to get out of here, though, in case they come back."

Ross shook his head. "No. Our orders were to stay put and wait for Magnus."

"Those were Cano's instructions. And they didn't work out so well for him, did they?"

"Doesn't matter. He was the top Crew boss here, and that's what he wanted."

"Well, I'm now the top Crew dog, and I'm saying we go back to Albuquerque and wait for Magnus to arrive."

Ross sneered. "You're not Crew. I am, which makes me the boss."

"You seem to be confused. The Locos are part of the Crew. That was the deal. I'm the head of the Locos. That means what I say goes."

Ross shook his head. "I don't know anything about that deal, but Cano wanted us to wait here, Magnus is expecting to meet us here, and nothing you say changes that. So I say we stay and wait for Magnus."

As Luis had feared, Cano's disrespect of Luis had infected his men, and now this foot soldier believed himself to be Luis's equal, if not his superior. Luis couldn't allow that to stand, and as Ross turned dismissively, Luis pulled his H&K 9mm from its holster and fired two rounds into the back of Ross's head. The Crew thug tumbled forward and Luis sprang into motion, resigned to dragging Ross to the river and disposing of his body so there was no evidence of the execution.

Luis would concoct a story for Magnus, assuming he even missed Ross, which was unlikely if he was heading up an army. But in the event he did, Luis would tell a tale of having gone back into town for supplies at Cano's orders and, upon his return, finding the camp slaughtered.

A thought occurred to Luis as he neared the camp area with Ross.

He hastily removed the Crew gunman's flak jacket and leather vest and carried it to Tarak's deteriorating remains. Luis held his breath as he stripped Tarak's shirt from his maggot-infested carcass and pulled Ross's gear onto the Apache. When he was finished, he stepped back and inspected his work.

By the time Magnus made it there, all the bodies would be skeletons. One would look the same as the other, and only the clothes would identify which piles of bones were Crew and which were hired hands.

Luis dragged Ross's body into the shallows and pushed him into the current, where the body bobbed as it turned over and drifted down the muddy current.

He collected Ross's weapons and carried them to his horse, and was riding back to Albuquerque minutes later with Ross's steed in tow; his animal and ammunition would provide sufficient barter to maintain a high lifestyle until Magnus arrived. Whoever had killed Cano had done Luis a favor – now Luis was once again the head of the Locos and, as far as Magnus was concerned, a valued ally.

Chapter 39

Arnold inspected one of the twenty bounding mines his trading team had bartered for in Santa Fe – stolen from an armory, they were complete and appeared to be in good shape. The foray had been a worthwhile exercise, and they had increased their stores of weapons significantly, along with some rare finds like the mines, which were deadly up to a hundred yards.

"These look like they'll do the job," he said, nodding. "What about explosives?"

"We scored a few hundred pounds of TNT from a mining warehouse. Some of it was useless. We only bought the stuff that had been well taken care of," Toby said. "It also had thirty kilos of RDX we took for land mines and avalanches."

"Good. We'll deploy those mines in the canyon." Arnold gave Toby a grim smile. "Wouldn't want to be on the receiving end of one of those."

Toby nodded. A bounding mine would launch three to five feet into the air before detonating, spraying shrapnel and ball bearings in all directions.

"We also bought a gross of blasting caps. Scavengers pulled them out of steering wheels. You know the story."

Blasting caps were used to inflate air bags.

"Sounds like we're set on that front," Arnold said.

"How's the napalm going?" Toby asked.

"Good. We figure we can have fifty gallons of it ready. We found some gas that's still good enough for that and plenty of candle wax. And we finally have a good use for all the milk jugs we were saving for a rainy day." Arnold paused. "I warned everyone about handling them, of course."

"You sure about the Armstrong's mix for the detonator?" Armstrong's mixture was a combination of ground match heads and small amounts of the strike faces from match books. It was highly explosive, but unstable. They'd discussed taping pouches of it to the milk cartons – when the containers were dropped from the plane, the pouches would explode and the homemade napalm would catch, showering anyone within range with liquid fire. It was crude, but would be lethal on troops in the open.

"Sure. It's a homemade blasting cap that'll detonate on impact and ignite the napalm. It's either that or use up some of the caps you got. But I don't want to waste them if we don't have to."

"Any idea where you want to plant the anti-vehicle mines?"

"Lucas suggested the approach to the bridge, which we're going to blow tomorrow. And we'll string a bunch on the secondary approach to the valley, just in case. We can't rule out that they'll try to mount a pincer attack once they see how tough the going is through the canyons."

"I gather you have a contingency to move most of the defense force to that area if they do."

"Of course, but we'll see how it works in practice." Arnold frowned. "Lucas is advocating hitting them fairly far from home so they've already taken heavy casualties before they get here for the main show."

"Makes sense."

"Sure, and with unlimited personnel and ammo, I'd be all over it. But we've only got a couple hundred capable adults and, of those, fewer than a hundred that have any real experience. I think it's a bad idea to risk any – especially the most capable, which is who we'd want to send."

"No word yet on how big the attack force actually is?"

"Nope. We won't know for sure until they hit Albuquerque. But we have to assume the worst."

"You really think a thousand men can make it from Houston?"

"If they have fuel, sure. At any rate, I'm handling preparations like they will. So's everyone else."

Toby shook his head. "Four to one. Miserable odds."

"No question. Our only advantage is it's our home turf, so we can prep for an ugly welcome."

"Ken and Richard going to handle the bridge?"

"Yeah. We keep going back and forth on that with Michael and Elliot."

"What's to disagree about?"

"They want to wait and blow it when the Crew's on it; my vote is to do it in advance. We have a meeting later, and I'm going to put my foot down. Michael's exerting way too much influence over these decisions. He's going to get a lot of people killed if I don't rein him in."

"I can see the point about blowing it while they're on it. More casualties, and the psychological effect would be incredible."

"No question. It all sounds good. Until something goes wrong. Like a blasting cap doesn't trigger. Something fizzles out. They spot our men. Then they have unrestricted road all the way to the canyon. If we do it my way, we forego the shock and awe, but we stop them fifteen miles away and force them to schlep in on foot or horseback. And any heavy gear they've brought will be stopped at the bridge."

Toby's eyes widened. "You think they'll have armor or something? Tanks?"

"Probably not tanks. They're a bitch to maintain. But I could be wrong."

"So what's the plan?"

"We'll meet this evening. I've drawn up a map for the minefields so we'll remember where we planted them once this is over. Now that I know how much explosive we have to work with, I can do some calculations to determine how many anti-vehicle mines we can make, and how much we'll need for the bridge. That's going to be harder than it sounds, but the RDX will inflict some damage."

"When do we deploy?"

"Depending on what's decided tonight, I'll assemble a crew to mine the roads first. Then we'll do the closer work – the bridge and the canyons. The mines will be hands off, which I like." Arnold sighed. "What I wouldn't give for a half dozen helicopters and some sidewinders. Those would make short work out of a column."

"Or some drones. Why not dream big?"

Arnold smiled ruefully. "Yeah. As it is, we're better than catapults and swords, but not very. Anyone we don't stop with the fireworks is where it's going to get snotty. Then we're in a straight firefight, and you know as well as I do how unpredictable those can be."

Both men had seen their share of combat before the collapse and after. One truism was that no matter how dependable someone was, until they'd been tested under fire, there were no guarantees how they would perform. It was a coin toss how much of their defense force would actually be lethal and how many would be disasters waiting to happen. With limited ammunition and a large attacking force, if many of the defenders panicked or were inept, their paradise would be overrun.

"Sounds like we need to do most of the damage before they make it through the canyon."

"That's the plan." Arnold exhaled noisily. "Elliot has a dozen people working on manufacturing a crap ton of black powder, too. I suggested that to keep them busy. We can use it for the secondary approaches."

"Good idea." Toby thought for a moment. "What do you make of Lucas?"

"He's dangerous, but quiet. No bluster to him. Unlike Michael, he knows what it's like to be in the shit, and everything he's suggested has been practical and valid. I'm warming up to him."

"Good. We need every able-bodied man we can get."

"No kidding. Here's hoping this meeting goes well."

"Just you, Michael, and the Doc?" Toby asked.

"And Lucas. Elliot likes him. I don't mind – he's a good counterbalance to Michael."

Toby made a face. "Enjoy yourself. Sounds like a hoot."

"Yeah. Thanks."

Chapter 40

Duke heard an approaching roar from the south before he saw anything – the sound of dozens of big engines belching exhaust, the motors deafening after five years of silence. Everyone in the trading post stopped what they were doing. Tucker had dropped by to shoot the breeze, as he did many mornings, and he, Duke, and Aaron swung their heads toward the entrance at the same time. Aaron rose from where he was seated behind the counter, his AR-15 in hand as a deterrent against would-be thieves.

"What the hell is that?" Tucker exclaimed, moving to the doors.

They stepped out into the sunlight and watched as a motorcade rolled down the main street, led by a dozen Humvees equipped with .50-caliber machine guns manned by tattooed Crew gunmen. The convoy stopped in front of the trading post, and a powerfully muscled man climbed from the lead vehicle, followed by six gunmen, all armed to the teeth. Duke and Tucker took in the leader's elaborately inked head and exchanged a quick glance as he approached.

"You the traders?" Magnus demanded.

Tucker nodded. "That's right. What can I do for you fellas?"

"I need everything you got. Your entire inventory. Weapons, ammo, explosives, the works. And I'll also need all the horses you can round up, as well as food and water for my men."

Tucker took in the endless column of trucks and buses. "How many men?"

"A thousand."

Tucker nodded as though he received that sort of request every day. "How you paying?"

"We're good for it," Magnus snapped. "I'm the leader of the Crew. Out of Houston. Magnus. You've heard of me?"

Tucker looked Magnus up and down. "Our policy's no credit. Sorry. Can't give you my entire inventory based on a bet you'll pay later. It would clean me out, and I have to eat in the meantime." Tucker glanced at the Humvees. "Seems to me you must have some barterable goods. Ammo. Guns."

Magnus took an intimidating step closer to the trader. "I control three states. Most of Texas. If I say I'm good for it, I am."

Tucker didn't back down. "That may be, but you're in New Mexico, not Texas. And here it's cash and carry. Sorry – nothing personal."

Duke edged closer to Tucker to warn him not to bait the Crew warlord, but Magnus was too fast. He reached out with both hands, the muscles in his arms bulging, twisted Tucker's head, and snapped his neck like a twig. Duke looked away, but not before he saw the black of the abyss in Magnus's eyes.

Magnus released the trader and he crumpled into a heap. The Crew boss next regarded Duke. "You the number two boy?" he asked.

"Just one of the traders," Duke said. "Came to pick up my stuff, that's all."

"You don't work for this piece of garbage?" Magnus demanded, indicating Tucker's inert form.

"No. Just trade." Duke stepped closer to Magnus as he saw the sheriff approaching from down the sidewalk. "But I can help you get anything you need. I know everyone for five hundred miles."

"That right?"

Duke nodded. Aaron appeared at the door with his rifle, and Duke motioned for him to lower the gun. Aaron complied, and Duke angled his head and lowered his voice further. "Don't look now, but the local law's making for you."

Magnus slowly turned as the sheriff neared, the lawman's hand on his pistol. The sheriff stopped a few yards from Magnus and eyed Tucker's form before speaking.

"What happened here?"

"Man went crazy on me. Came at me like a nut, trying for my throat. I defended myself. I think he may have got hurt," Magnus said.

The sheriff leaned down and felt Tucker's neck for a pulse, and then stood, his expression wooden. "He's dead."

"Yeah? Shouldn'ta tried anything."

The sheriff looked to Duke. "You see this?"

Duke shook his head. "Sorry, Sheriff."

"I got about a thousand witnesses seen the whole thing," Magnus said, gesturing at his vehicles.

The sheriff looked around the area for any other locals, but they'd made themselves scarce at the sight of an army rolling into town. Magnus raised an eyebrow as the sheriff glared holes through him.

"I don't believe you. Tucker was a good man. No way he'd do what you said."

"Yeah, well, he did." Magnus paused. "Now, sheriff, here's how this is gonna work. You're going to get your ass out of here, or you're going to keep annoying me, and I'm going to cut you down like a dog, burn the town to the ground and rape all the females, and kill everyone. I'd do it anyway just for fun, but I'm on a schedule. So, you want to die today, along with everyone here, or you going to get out of my way?"

The sheriff blinked but didn't show any emotion. "I have a dozen deputies with rifles trained on you, tough guy. You so much as sneeze, you're dead," he said.

"See those guns on the Hummers? .50-caliber Browning M2s. How long you think it would take to gun down everyone in this shithole? About as long as it takes me to fart. I've got a dozen of them, cocked and ready. Want me to give the signal so you can see what they can do? Because you're about three seconds from getting a bird's-eye view. Final warning." Magnus grinned. "Never liked cops much, so I'm really hoping you make the wrong choice."

The sheriff shook his head. "Did you not get that if you try anything, you're the first to die?"

"You must be hard of hearing, because you'll be dead before I hit the ground, and then the entire town will be massacred." Magnus shrugged. "Man's got to die sometime. Today's as good as any for me. How about you, sheriff? You want to see sundown, or you ready to meet your maker?"

Duke cleared his throat. "Sheriff, no disrespect, but I've heard of this gentleman. He'll do exactly as he says, so if you decide to push it, you're signing my death warrant along with that of everyone in Roswell. I'd appreciate it if you didn't play fast and loose with my life, even if you don't much care about yours."

The sheriff twisted toward Duke and snarled at him. "Stay out of this."

Duke nodded. "Magnus, for the record, I know your reputation, and if this idiot makes the wrong choice, leave me out of the bloodbath. I'd put a bullet in his fool head myself if you wanted me to."

Magnus nodded. "Either way he'll be just as dead."

The sheriff saw the intent in the Crew warlord's eyes and slowly backed away. His small-town bravado had failed, and now that he'd been shamed in front of everyone, he'd lost any authority he'd had. He turned to Duke, hatred radiating from his face.

"You better be gone by sundown, or I'm coming for you, you scum. Put a bullet in me, will you? I'll make you eat those words."

Duke's expression didn't change. "I was just leaving. Aaron, grab our stuff and let's hit it."

The sheriff stormed off, and Magnus grinned. "Looks like you have to find someplace new to trade. I could use someone who can source whatever I need. You want a job?" he asked Duke.

Duke considered the offer and then glanced at the trading post. "Me and Aaron are a team. You got to take him on, too."

"Fine."

"What's the pay?"

"I'll make you rich."

Duke nodded. "I hear you got quite a spread down Houston way. Be nice to have a place of my own where nobody will bug me."

"Consider it done."

Duke regarded the buses. "Lot of men there. What's your final stop?"

"Los Alamos."

Aaron reappeared with Duke's cash bag and an armful of ammo satchels and assault rifles. Duke eyed them calculatingly. "That everything?"

"Yeah."

Duke nodded to Magnus. "I'll see if I can round up some horses for you. The locals might not want to let 'em go on just your say-so."

"Then tell them I'll kill anyone who resists."

"That should do the trick."

Aaron and Duke walked off to where their animals were tethered, and Aaron whispered, "You're seriously going to work for them?"

"We don't have a choice. They're just going to take whatever they want by force, which will leave us broke, and nobody with anything to trade. So we either join the winning team, or we'll wind up losers."

"But Tucker…"

"Damn shame about the man, but he called that one wrong. So now he's dead, and there isn't anything we can do to bring him back. You don't want to work with these bastards, that's fine, but I don't have anything better going, and I don't want to be in the crosshairs if that psycho decides to kill everyone – do you?"

Aaron frowned. "Put that way…"

"Exactly."

Chapter 41

The Crew convoy left Roswell shell-shocked at the confiscation of most of its inhabitants' valuables – horses, food stores, ammunition, and weapons. Duke had done his best to soften the news that the town was facing an invading army, but some of the more stubborn had resisted. That hadn't ended well, as the Crew fighters had delighted in destroying all in their path, and Duke had been left to wonder how the town would have fared if Magnus hadn't been in such a hurry. Duke had heard stories about Dallas and Houston – the satanic rituals, the pedophilia, the wholesale raping and pillaging – but seeing what the Crew was capable of in person shocked even him.

The highway transitioned into a wide-open stretch and the column picked up the pace, which lasted only a few hours before more mechanical failures grounded it for the night. The Crew fighters bivouacked in tents around the buses. The desert air was still hot even after the sun had set, and their cooking fires glowed along the road as they roasted the animals they'd confiscated from Roswell for food.

Duke and Aaron kept to themselves. The Crew were hardened criminals to a man, best avoided as far as possible, and neither had much to say to each other as they ate their rations quietly at the periphery of the camp. Aaron was clearly uncomfortable with the circumstances, and most of their hushed discussion involved how best to stay alive by being useful to Magnus.

They spent an uneasy night under the stars, and the next morning the procession got under way again, the repair crews having worked until dawn, readying the vehicles for another two-hundred-mile leg. Duke and Aaron rode in one of the tow trucks with a driver who was long on curses and short on patience, their horses in a trailer behind it. They'd noted the howitzers being pulled by the semi-rigs, confirming their impression that Magnus intended to crush anything in his way.

By noon they'd lost six more tires to the sweltering pavement, and Magnus was visibly agitated at the constant interruptions. He was pacing near his Humvee when a lookout radioed on his handheld – a party of riders was approaching.

The Apaches neared, taking in the size of the force, and conferred among themselves before their leader swung from his saddle and walked to where Magnus was waiting.

"I see you made it," the Apache said.

"Of course. You're here to guide us?"

"Yes. But we need to stop at our headquarters so you can speak with our council."

"Why?"

"This is a lot of men. We were expecting half as many."

"I was clear that it was going to be a thousand men."

"Yes, well, I'm just delivering the message."

Magnus frowned, the tattoos on his face writhing like live snakes beneath a sheen of sweat. "Deliver one to your council: I will not be delayed. I have no problem talking to them, but if it will slow us down, it's not an option. We can talk on the radio."

"It's just off the highway – about two hours' ride from here. I'll let them know you're en route."

Magnus watched the man mount his horse and ride back to his fellows with a clouded expression. He'd negotiated a fair price, but he'd done enough horse trading to see a curveball coming and silently debated how he would deal with it. The patrol retraced its steps, and Magnus ordered his column procession forward.

The Apache patrol must have ridden hard, because it was waiting for the Crew convoy when it appeared from over a rise, the afternoon sun having already begun its slow descent. The lead rider motioned to Magnus in the point Humvee. On Magnus's orders, the buses remained on the highway, and only the Humvees followed the horsemen down the gravel road to the Apache headquarters.

Ben was waiting for their arrival surrounded by his council, projecting authority with at least a hundred Apache fighters by the buildings, all armed and staring at the vehicles bouncing toward them. When the Humvees pulled to a stop, Ben eyed the Browning machine guns and then turned to confront Magnus, who'd swung his door open and stepped onto the gravel, his heavy black boots coated with road dust.

"You Ben?" Magnus asked curtly.

Ben nodded. "That's right. You must be Magnus."

Magnus motioned to the Humvees. "We brought your payment. As agreed."

"We need to discuss that."

"There's nothing to discuss. We had a deal."

"We lost a guide getting you the information you requested, which we did without question. Since then, he's gone dark. We have to presume the worst."

"I don't have time for this. How much more are we talking?"

Ben threw out a price in gold, at which Magnus laughed harshly. "You're dreaming."

"It's a fair price."

Magnus waved dismissively. "I'm willing to pay more, but nothing like that." He countered with a considerably smaller increase.

Ben scowled. "I need to talk to my council."

"Me too."

Magnus stalked back to his Humvee and climbed in. He snapped his fingers and the driver handed him the radio.

The Brownings opened fire on the buildings, cutting down the Apache gunmen where they stood. The heavy rounds shredded Ben and the council members, spackling the wall behind them with blood and bone.

The shooting lasted less than a minute, and when the guns fell silent, Magnus stepped from his vehicle again and inspected the scene. Nobody was left alive that he could see, and he didn't want to waste the time to do a search of the buildings. He turned to the Humvees and called out to the drivers, "Turn it around. These clowns aren't going to be a problem."

Magnus strode back to his vehicle. He was a conqueror. He would take what he wanted and make no excuses. Magnus had gotten what he needed from the Apaches, and they'd overestimated their importance and paid the price.

He wasn't worried about traps they might have laid or any attacks. Only fools would take on a heavily armed force like his, and he'd put some men out front on horses to verify the road was clear. For the amount of gold he'd saved, he could afford to lose a few men to traps. And if any of the natives decided to play hero, they'd die like rats, just as their lofty council had, bleeding out on the worthless land they treasured.

Chapter 42

Arnold stood beside the Shangri-La radio operator as Elliot and Michael listened to the report from Steven, their contact in Albuquerque who'd given Colt the password. Elliot seemed to have aged ten years in the last few days; his eyes were bloodshot from lack of sleep and his sagging skin had a sallow cast. The broadcast had come in while they'd been at dinner, and they'd raced for the radio to hear the report.

Steven's voice faded in and out over the communication channel they used. Elliot had his hands in the pockets of his loose pants, staring at the radio with an intensity that could have powered the compound.

"Are you sure about the count? Over," Elliot asked for the third time.

"Yes," Steven assured him. "Based on the number of buses, you're looking at somewhere around a thousand men. But the worst news is the four heavy artillery guns – howitzers that can lob shells fifteen to twenty miles. They can bombard you for a week before ever mounting an attack. Over."

"The lab and the winter quarters are all underground and reinforced," Michael said.

"Unless they were designed to withstand direct hits, I don't like the odds. Sorry," Arnold replied.

Michael leaned toward the transmitter. "How soon will they be here? Over."

"They're pulling out tonight or tomorrow morning, depending on how their vehicle repairs go, so figure fifteen hours from when I call in again. Over."

"Very well. Keep us appraised," Elliot said, his tone resigned. "Over and out."

The men stared at each other, each waiting for the other to speak. Eventually Elliot motioned them to his office area and they took seats at a small table. Elliot sighed heavily and stared at the men for a few moments before speaking.

"Well, we knew it would eventually happen. And here it is," he said.

"We never expected howitzers. That changes everything," Arnold said.

"Maybe," Michael began. "Unless we can disable them before they're in range. That underscores the wisdom of the plan I've been advocating. Like it or not, we need to take the battle to them before they get here. Send sniper teams out to hit them on the road. We've already laid the mines, so hopefully some of those will disable them and slow them down. They should. Then we can hit them when they're stopped. One of the big Brownings would make short work of a camp."

Arnold shook his head. "Again, that would involve dividing our focus and risking the lives of some of our most capable men, as well as one of our few big guns. It would be suicide against a force that size. Even if we were able to eliminate some of the Crew, our people would be wiped out eventually." Arnold stared hard at Elliot. "Look, I know you love this place, but against a sustained shelling we have no chance. Staying is suicide."

"Which is why we need to stop the artillery before they reach us," Michael pressed.

Arnold ignored the younger man. "Doc, you need to issue the evacuation order, or you're going to lose everyone. Michael here has never been under artillery fire. I have. I never want to repeat it."

Elliot nodded. "It doesn't sound pleasant. But the lab and winter quarters have the protection of the mountains above."

"After days of shelling, none of that will matter. Trying to stop the guns en route is madness, which leaves us sitting ducks against a force of hardened fighters that outnumber us four to one." Arnold shook his head. "Doc..." He paused, clearly struggling to put his argument most convincingly. "Elliot, what we should do is mine the way in, launch a few guerrilla attacks to slow them down and buy us time to evacuate someplace safe. We'll have at least a day's head start, plus another for them to make it through the canyon, at best. That's two days. We can be a long ways away in two days." Arnold swallowed back his frustration. "You have to give the evacuation order. There's no other way."

Michael snorted in disgust. "Of course there is. You just don't agree with it. I think we can stop them on the road and take out the artillery, and that leaves them having to go through the canyon, which is booby-trapped to the teeth."

Arnold frowned at Michael. "Spoken as a wire-head with exactly zero combat experience."

"I'm sorry I've been skilled enough to avoid being shot at my entire life. That's called being smart. I don't expect you'd understand it."

Temper flaring, Arnold stood. "I'm in charge of security here, and I'm telling you that you can't defend this place against artillery, and your boy here has come up with a plan that will divide your resources and get everyone killed."

"No," Michael retorted. "I've just come up with a better plan than yours, and your ego can't handle it." Michael paused. "Yours is basically to run away. Mine is to take preemptive action and surgically eliminate the threats before they arrive."

"Yours is idiocy, which you'll only learn once you've lost your men." Arnold slammed his fist on the table. "I'm done with this discussion. Elliot, if you're going to listen to this moron, you're risking everyone's lives on someone with zero experience. If that's how it's going to be, I'm tendering my resignation, effective immediately, and getting the hell out of here."

Elliot's expression hardened. "Arnold, there's no need for

melodrama. I understand you disagree…"

"I don't 'disagree.' I refuse to lead everyone to the slaughter out of some crazy sense of power. Staying and fighting is certain death, with big guns and a thousand men coming at us. I won't go to my grave on somebody else's mistaken whim. And that's what staying is." Arnold frowned at Michael and then straightened as he faced Elliot. "No disrespect, Doctor, but it's suicide, and I'll have no part of it."

"So you're going to cut and run when we need you most?" Michael snapped.

"I'm going to survive, you fool. You'll learn I was right, but you'll be dying by the time it sinks in. We have exactly zero chance with a clown like you calling the shots. I'll say a prayer for you, but it'll be a prayer for the dead, because that's how you and everyone that stays will wind up. Sorry. That's how it'll go down."

"Arnold, please. We have to work together," Elliot implored.

"Either I lead everyone to safety, or you can make this your Alamo and die to the last man. Those are your choices."

"Just get out of here, you coward. We don't need you. I always thought you were all talk, and this proves it. First sign of trouble and you turn tail. Don't let the door hit you on the way out," Michael snapped.

Arnold barely controlled his impulse to lunge across the table at Michael and instead shook his head. "I'm talking to a ghost. Enjoy your remaining hours," he said. "You too, Doc. You're making a big mistake, but it's yours to make. I'll tell my men my decision, and any of them that want to stay are welcome to. Most probably will, which is sad, but they're more loyal to the idea of Shangri-La than they are realistic."

"Great. So now you're going to cause a mutiny because you didn't get your way," Michael said.

Arnold stopped at the door and leveled a flat stare at Michael. "One more word out of you and you'll be swallowing teeth. Don't tempt me, because there's nothing I'd rather do than knock you senseless. You're going to get everyone butchered with your little power grab."

Michael held his tongue, and Arnold left. When he was gone, Michael shook his head.

"We don't need him. The mines are laid. All we need to do is blow the bridge and assemble some volunteers to run guerilla raids between here and Albuquerque. Maybe Lucas can help."

Elliot stared at his hands as though he didn't recognize them. "Maybe he's right."

"He's not. He's just not willing to consider anyone's perspective but his own. That's why he was a soldier instead of a general."

Elliot exhaled and closed his eyes. When he opened them, he nodded. "Let's get a sniper detail formed and assign a crew to blow the bridge. The charges are in place, right?"

"Correct. Arnold's men set them yesterday. Hopefully correctly."

Elliot regarded Michael dispassionately. "Michael, Arnold is many things, but incompetent isn't one of them; nor is he a coward. We have to respect his decision, whether we agree with it or not. Don't dismiss him so lightly – he's done a fine job for years here, and we'll be the poorer for his loss."

"At the worst possible moment. Don't forget he's choosing to abandon us, not the other way around," Michael spat, his tone bitter.

"We don't have time to dwell on it. Come. Let's break the news to the assembly and hand out assignments. We don't have a moment to lose."

Chapter 43

Lucas stood beside Sierra near the back of the gathering. On her other side Eve held her hand tightly, Ellie the piglet nuzzling the little girl's ankle as Ruby looked on with concern. Michael had called an emergency assembly twenty minutes earlier, attendance mandatory. Terry waited next to Ruby, his long face furrowed with doubt but his gaze determined as Elliot emerged from the main building and faced the crowd, Michael behind him.

"Thank you for coming so quickly," Elliot began. "We've just received word that the Crew is on its way and will probably be here at some point tomorrow."

A collective gasp went up from the group. Elliot held up a hand for silence before continuing. "Our man in Albuquerque says it's a big force. He estimates around a thousand strong, in a motorized convoy towing horse trailers…and four howitzers."

Another gasp was quickly followed by alarmed murmurs. Elliot allowed the unrest to continue for a half minute before signaling again for silence.

A voice called out from near the front, "How are we supposed to defend against howitzers, much less a thousand fighters?"

Elliot nodded. "A fair question. We've anticipated a large force, and as many of you know, we've already mined the highway approach and set charges on the bridge across the Rio Grande to stop the vehicles well away from here. But now that we have a definitive on the number of men, we've decided that it makes the most sense to conduct guerilla raids en route as well and to mine further away. They won't be expecting it, and it should have a profound psychological effect on their fighters."

"But you said they'll be here tomorrow," another man argued from the front of the throng.

"I said probably. But if the mines do their job, we can slow them considerably, which is where the guerilla raids will come in. Our strategy will be to send out a group of skilled snipers with night vision equipment, high-powered rifles, and AT4s, and hit them while they're stopped at the minefields."

Lucas frowned. "If they're that well equipped, they'll have NV gear too."

Michael nodded, as though expecting the statement. "Yes, but we're hoping that having some of their vehicles destroyed will throw them into disarray. At the very least, it will slow their progress to a crawl as they check every yard of road. We didn't only mine the highway – we also mined the surrounding areas they'd have to take, and deliberately chose sections where there weren't any options other than the road. That lends itself perfectly to snipers lying in wait. If we can hit a few of their buses, we could eliminate hundreds of them before they get anywhere near us. By repeating this process again and again, we hope to be able to whittle them down by a significant number."

"What about the big guns?"

Michael fielded that question, too. "Shouldn't be an issue if they can't get across the river. Their max range is about fifteen miles. That's over twenty."

Richard, one of Arnold's security force, stepped forward. "That was for conventional units. If they've got special munitions, they could hit us from up to twenty-plus miles away."

Michael looked like a deer in the headlights for a moment and then recovered. "We have no information on what they're using for ammo."

"Right. My point is that they very well could have big guns that could reach us even from across the river. That's a very real possibility, especially if they aren't all that concerned with accuracy. All they need to do is get a spotter into one of the hills around us and they could call in the fire and adjust as necessary. Presuming they don't have a map, which they will."

Michael's tone hardened. "Which is why we need to eliminate the artillery before they get to the river."

Another voice called out, "What's this I heard about Arnold leaving?"

Elliot nodded. "Sadly, we had a parting of the ways over the best way to guarantee that our work here doesn't go to waste. Arnold felt that the best option would be to abandon the valley to the Crew. I'm unwilling to vacate a place that's the only bit of civilization I know of left in the world. If that isn't worth fighting for, then I'm not sure there's anything worth living for in the badlands. Everyone knows what it's like out there. Nothing in life is free or easy, and sometimes you have to be prepared to fight to defend what's yours. I made the call to stay; Arnold didn't."

"I heard he took a bunch of his men with him."

"Fourteen, to be exact," Elliot said. "Look, if anyone wants to turn tail, that's their prerogative. Nobody is being forced to stay, of course. There's every likelihood some of us won't make it through this ordeal, so I wouldn't blame anyone if they decide to leave. But I'd also remind you that you've lived in safety and comfort for years because of collective effort – you and your neighbors pulling together and overcoming obstacles as a team. I believe that we can defeat this threat, acting as one. Between all the mines and booby traps, our natural defenses, and our determination, we can preserve our way of life. I'm of the opinion it's worth going to the mat for."

Another voice from the back, female, spoke out. "No guarantee we'd live very long if we left, either. It's hell out there. We've all heard the reports. At least here we know the terrain and we can trust each other. I'm going to stay. This is our home, and I'm willing to defend it."

A chorus of voices rose with affirmations and it quickly became evident that the possibility of an exodus had been avoided.

Elliot allowed the crowd to digest the news and then called out, his voice strong, "We're going to need to assemble sniper crews to hit the trail. Figure eighteen men and women – three groups of six. We'll also need people to assign to blowing the bridge. The rest will be deployed in the canyons and strategic locations in the valley."

Richard spoke up again. "They can get across north of the bridge. There are three other crossings up by Espanola."

"That's why we'll equip the bridge crew with sufficient explosives to destroy those as well. First order of business will be to blow the Rio Grande bridge, then ride hard to the north and blow the others. They'll have to backtrack, and the highway runs far out of their way – with a few mines strategically located to buy us more time."

When the assembly broke up, Sierra stopped Lucas with a hand on his arm. "Lucas, I know you're still angry, but we need to talk."

Lucas shrugged off her touch. "Not a lot to talk about, is there?"

Sierra's voice quieted, and Ruby, sensing the tension, led Eve and her piglet a discreet distance away. "That's where you're wrong," Sierra said.

Lucas's jaw clenched. "So talk."

Sierra sighed. "Lucas, our night together was…it was everything I could want."

"But not enough to keep you from running off first chance you got. What's that old saying about actions speaking louder than words?"

"I know, but you have to put yourself in my position. Imagine you had a son. And you found out he was alive. You fulfilled your obligation to get Eve to safety, you met someone…special…but your son is still out there, and you're his parent. What do you do?"

"I'm smart enough to know he's not really out there."

"That's what you keep saying. But you don't *know*. That's just a guess. I'm telling you that if there's even a remote chance he's alive, you'll find him. That's what being a mother is all about. You don't give up on your child. You never –" Sierra choked up momentarily, and wiped away a tear. "You never give up," she said, staring defiantly into his eyes. "Otherwise, what kind of human being are you?"

"Word that comes to mind is 'alive.'"

"It's not worth living if you allowed your child to die when you could have saved him."

Lucas looked away. "Sierra, that was just something Garret said to get to you. And it worked. But you have to recognize it wasn't real. It's just technique, nothing more."

"Maybe. But if you're wrong, my son's alive, and he's out there, and I need to do everything I can to find him. I have no choice." She paused. "That's why I left. You would have done the same."

Lucas didn't say anything. Like arguing angels on the head of a pin, there was no way of responding to a hypothetical built on a probable lie. He took a calming breath, and when he spoke again, his voice was low. "You didn't just leave, Sierra. You snuck away without telling me."

"Because you would have stopped me."

"Damn right I would have," he agreed.

"So I did the only thing I could." She cleared her throat. "Lucas, I don't want you to hate me. I want to stay here with you. But I also need to do what's right."

"What's right is to stay alive."

Sierra nodded silently, but Lucas could see the wheels turning behind her eyes. He stiffened when she moved close to him and tiptoed to kiss him, and turned away as her lips rose to his.

She surprised him by grabbing his jaw, forcing his mouth back to hers, and kissing him hungrily. When she finally pulled away, she was panting slightly.

"That's real, Lucas. Out of everything, that's the most real. If I could undo leaving when I did, believe me, I would. Please...don't let one bad decision ruin it for us. That's all I ask."

Before he could answer, she was walking away. Ruby's eyebrows rose as he watched Sierra depart, hips swinging with a rhythmic stride that commanded his attention.

Chapter 44

The Crew army was able to roll out of Albuquerque before sunrise, the repair crews having again worked through the night on vehicles that were proving increasingly unreliable with every mile. Duke and Aaron had scoured the city for parts and had spent most of the past eighteen hours negotiating or outright seizing whatever was on the list the repairmen required. The local militia had given the Crew a wide berth after advising them to keep their convoy outside the town limits, and Magnus had made a strategic decision not to take the city just to prove that he could – they'd seen hundreds of armed militia waiting as they'd rolled toward the main entrance, and Albuquerque wasn't worth losing men over.

Tires were proving the hardest items, which Magnus had anticipated from the warnings of the repair crew chief. Duke had sourced any that appeared in reasonable shape, but even the best of the rubber was questionable from age, and nobody had much confidence in their new acquisitions.

Luis had materialized in Albuquerque and, after introducing himself as the head of the Locos, had reported on Cano's death – another blow to Magnus's plan, albeit a minor one.

"You don't know who did it?" Magnus had snapped when Luis finished.

"No. I assume it was a raiding party from one of the bandit gangs in the area. I asked around town, and apparently there are more than a few of them."

To Luis's relief, the Crew boss hadn't asked about the man who'd radioed in the location of Shangri-La, being obviously preoccupied with weightier matters. He'd ordered Luis to report to Jude with the same dismissive disdain that Cano had shown, eliminating any hope Luis had fostered of better treatment.

Magnus had debated running at night when the pavement was cooler, to save wear on the remaining tires, but circumstances prevented him from doing so, there being too many vehicles that required patching up to make the final distance to Los Alamos. As it was, even with a predawn departure, he had slim hope of making it by nightfall. The highway north was littered with abandoned cars and trucks, forcing the tow trucks into duty every few hundred yards.

When one of them stalled with a screech like a wounded animal, he stepped from the Humvee and marched to where it had been attempting to heave a panel van off the road.

The driver opened the hood and recoiled at the smoke rising from the engine and the strong odor of burning oil. He looked over the motor and shook his head before turning to Magnus with a scowl.

"Must have thrown a rod or something," he reported.

Magnus signaled for another tow truck to push the ruined one from the highway, wincing as the first rays of the rising sun blinded him. Only a few miles out of town, and they were already stalled. A part of him realized that his vision of racing across the wasteland to eradicate his enemy had been overly optimistic; but he was committed now, and he had never been closer to his objective. Just one final hundred-and-something-mile stretch and the battle would be joined. Then he would be vindicated, the upstart enclave that dared compete with him leveled and its inhabitants slaughtered as a cautionary tale to others.

Ten minutes later, the dead vehicle had been forced off the road and the procession lurched back into motion like a fatigued snake. As the column crawled along, the highway degraded, flanked by deserted small towns already partially reclaimed by the high desert sands. As the heat rose with the morning, more tires gave out, including a front of one of the remaining pair of tow trucks – for which there was no spare. Another stop in the increasingly blazing conditions ended with Magnus making the call to leave the vehicle behind and to lead with the buses, whose bumpers and bulk were sufficient to push most obstacles from the road with judicious application of power.

The number of abandoned vehicles thinned to only a few, replaced by sand drifts that made all but one lane impassible in many places. The day wore on with progress made in fits and starts, this semi-rig losing a tire, that one blowing a line, and by late afternoon they'd only made forty-five miles instead of the hundred Magnus had hoped for. He was reclining in his Humvee, grateful for the AC as it bumped and rocked along, when a massive explosion sounded from the front of the column, followed closely by a second.

"What the hell–" he exclaimed as the windshield filled with brake lights.

The Hummer rolled to a stop and Magnus jumped out. Up ahead a cloud of black smoke drifted west along the rise, and voices cried out in alarm. He ran toward the site of the explosion and stopped in his tracks at the vision that greeted him – two of the lead buses lay on their sides, distended – blown apart by mines, as a glance at the gaping craters left by the devices instantly told him. The second bus had been towing one of the howitzers, which had been thrown like a rag doll a dozen yards from the bus to land upside down on the pavement.

"Mines!" one of his Crew lieutenants called from near the wreckage, but Magnus was already in motion, face distorted with rage. He approached the first bus, where a group was searching for survivors and, after studying the destruction, moved to the second to confirm the casualties. Each bus had carried fifty men and their gear, so in a heartbeat he'd lost ten percent of his fighters, and he wasn't more than halfway to Los Alamos.

A string of elaborate curses streamed from him as he paced by the wounded men being dragged from the twisted carcasses of the buses. Only a few looked like they'd make it to nightfall; blood covered most of them, and several had limbs twisted at impossible angles.

Jude came at a run and stopped by his side. "Good Lord," he exclaimed.

"Check the big gun and see if it's salvageable," Magnus ordered.

"Of course. I'll set up a triage area for the injured." Jude hesitated. "This means we're going to have to slow down and put some men in front to sweep for mines. There's no other way."

Magnus nodded. He'd already come to the same conclusion. "Look for an alternate route. There's a small road to the west that runs parallel I keep catching glimpses of. If the main highway's mined, maybe that will be clear."

"I'll send a detail to look it over, but if it was me, I'd mine all the routes – I'd expect us to try to find another way and have taken precautions."

"Just do it," Magnus ordered, and scowled at the steep rises on both sides of the highway. "And get those ruined buses out of the road. There's no way we can go around them."

"I'm on it," Jude said, turning to issue commands.

Magnus grabbed his arm to stop him. "It's not a good sign that you failed to anticipate this. You're my main strategist." Jude had done two tours in the Army as a sergeant before going to jail for a triple homicide during a home break-in gone horribly wrong.

"We had no reason to expect it, Magnus. Nothing indicated they knew we were coming."

"Your job is to foresee every possibility. Failing to just cost us dearly. See to it there are no more oversights."

"You can depend on me."

"I already did, and I have a hundred fewer fighters to show for it. This happens again, I'll make it a hundred and one," Magnus snarled, his message clear.

Jude swallowed dryly and moved to the rear of the column to organize his men. Magnus continued to stare at the carnage, his face a stony mask. In the end, Shangri-La being forewarned wouldn't matter – sheer numbers and firepower would overwhelm them – but his victory would come at a much higher cost.

He glowered at the wounded moaning on the hot pavement as

though they'd personally insulted him and then stormed back to his vehicle, waving away the flies that had appeared out of nowhere, the shadows of vultures orbiting overhead a reminder of nature's uncaring efficiency.

Chapter 45

John, the leader of the first sniper team dispatched by Elliot to attack the Crew convoy, peered through night vision goggles at the stopped column of vehicles. He had a clear line of sight from the rise on the east side of the highway, and as darkness fell he'd watched the buses crawling forward as a score of Crew gunmen checked for mines in front of them on foot.

The sight of the two detonations that afternoon had sent a thrill through the snipers: the buses had lifted into the air, plumping like overcooked hot dogs before tearing apart and slamming back onto the asphalt. It had taken a good hour for the remaining tow truck to shift enough of the wreckage for the rest of the vehicles to get by, from which point their progress had been nearly nonexistent as the minesweepers located six more antitank devices hidden among the sand drifts that covered the highway.

Whoever was directing the Crew must have decided that there was too much risk involved in continuing after dark, the men's ability to spot devices at night virtually nil, and the force had parked in a long line as the fighters pitched tents outside the buses. Fuel was far too precious to squander running engines all night to fend off the heat.

The tanker truck was near the back of the lineup, and John and his lieutenant, Chris, had discussed in hushed tones the best way to proceed. Chris had favored putting the .50-caliber machine gun to work on the fighters once they'd retired for the night, whereas John wanted to take out the fuel truck first. There were positives to both approaches, and they'd finally agreed to launch a strike on the tanker with the two AT4 antitank weapons they'd been given while a shooter rained death on the tents with the machine gun.

"The problem's the sentries. Looks like they've got NV gear, and there are enough of them to waste us within seconds," Chris pointed out.

"I think we have to do this three-pronged. Chris, since you've got experience with AT4s, you'll be in charge of the tanker, with Eric laying down covering fire for you. Brett and I will take out as many of the nearest guards as possible with our night vision scopes, and Martin can work the Browning with Abe on ammo."

Martin, who'd been in the National Guard for a couple of years before the collapse, nodded from his position nearby.

"Better hope they don't have any infrared," he said, "or Chris won't get close enough to pull it off." While the AT4s were rated as accurate for an area target at up to five hundred yards, in order to have a certainty of destroying the tanker, Chris would have to get within a couple of hundred, at most.

"Doesn't look like they do, or we wouldn't have gotten this far."

The team consisted of six men, all combat veterans or ex-military with substantial training. This group had been entrusted with a Browning, a thousand rounds of ammunition, and the pair of AT4s, in addition to their usual assault rifles. The other teams were waiting at strategic points further along the highway – one where it cut through a canyon and beneath which they'd rigged explosives by digging from the shoulder, and the other by the Rio Grande bridge.

There had been heated arguments over whether to equip each of the sniper teams with Brownings, but after much debate, Lucas had spoken up and pointed out that the machine guns would be more valuable to them defending the canyons than deployed in the field. Lucas hadn't needed to say that the odds of John ever returning to Shangri-La with his were slim. Everyone understood that there would be sacrifices made to protect the many, and John had, as one of the more seasoned fighters left after Arnold's abrupt departure, agreed to head up what he privately believed was a suicide mission.

One of the horses snorted from where it was tied out of sight on the far side of the rise, and John cringed. The guards were too far off to hear, but if they got unlucky, the mission – and their lives – would be over before it had even started.

"How long do you want to wait?" Chris asked.

John glanced at the glowing dial of his watch, a mechanical model that had lasted him decades. "Another couple of hours, at least. We'll need to let the guards get nice and complacent. Figure they'll probably be pulling four-hour shifts, so I'd say we hit them toward the end of the first, at…eleven."

Time seemed to slow as they waited, but eventually the campfires dimmed and the fighters climbed into their tents. The air grew eerily silent, the only sound the occasional clank of a tool from the repair crew working on one of the rigs by solar-charged work lamps. The moon brightened in the night sky and the stars glimmered in a dazzling display, the high altitude and dry air making for a breathtaking celestial spectacle.

The sentries kept to the area near the highway, patrolling it with lackluster enthusiasm, and their movements slowed as the night wore on. At eleven John gave the signal, and Martin and Abe moved the heavy Browning M2 into position on its tripod. The gun weighed almost 130 pounds, and it took both of them to get it where they wanted it before Abe scrambled back to the horses for the last two ammo cans. They'd carried eight to their firing location in preparation for the coming onslaught, but there was no reason not to use the whole thousand rounds.

By the time Abe made it back, Martin had locked and loaded the machine gun and was ready. Each can held a hundred rounds linked together in a belt, and the M33 ball ammo would blow through brick or cinderblock like tissue paper, making it devastating even at considerable range. At the three hundred or so yards they were from the highway, it would destroy engine blocks and incapacitate vehicles, in addition to ending the lives of many of the Crew fighters.

John waited with Brett, their night-vision-equipped AR-15s switched to single-fire mode to deal with the sentries. Surgical precision would be better than indiscriminate spraying with the guards, and they wanted to conserve ammo to lay down fire for their egress – assuming any of them lived through the next few minutes.

Chris skirted the ridge and stuck to what little scrub there was as he edged toward the tanker, painfully aware that he was completely exposed if any of the guards chose to do a sweep of the area. His assault rifle was strapped to his back, and he toted an AT4 in each hand, their weight growing with every step. They'd agreed that Martin would open up with the Browning when the first AT4 projectile detonated, hopefully creating enough pandemonium for him to escape with his life.

His boot caught on a rock and he nearly went down, sending a spray of sandy gravel down the slope. He eyed the truck and guesstimated he was still a hundred and fifty yards away, at least.

The snap of a round narrowly missing his head was almost instantly followed by the bark of one of the guards' guns. A moment later another took half his jaw off, and Chris's world went black as the big Browning opened fire from up the hill.

The machine gun's roar was deafening, and spent brass arced through the air as Martin strafed the guards he could see by the moonlight. John, Brett, and Eric began shooting as well, and between them made short work of many of the sentries, who were exposed to incoming fire they'd clearly never expected to contend with.

When the first ammo can ran dry and Martin loaded another belt, John called to the others, "Cover me. I'm going to try for the truck."

He didn't wait for a response – his best chance of reaching Chris was now, before the rest of the Crew could mount a counterattack. He had the element of surprise, and if it bought him thirty seconds, that might be all he needed.

John threw himself over the ridge and raced for Chris's crumpled form. Bullets sprayed sandy soil around him but missed by a wide margin. His men's weapons answered those of the Crew, and no more rounds struck his proximity. He reached Chris and scooped up the AT4s, and then sprinted toward the truck, closing the distance as the guns on the ridge peppered the column of vehicles.

He had just made it to within decent range when the Browning went silent again. He held his breath, praying that Martin hadn't been hit and was merely changing out ammo cans. One second turned into twenty as the smaller AR-15s popped above him, and then an incoming round knocked the wind out of him like a punch to the sternum. He looked down at his plate carrier and rolled to the side as more rounds pocked the earth. Another slug struck his thigh, causing him to scream in pain. He winced at the burn and maneuvered one of the AT4s into position, peering down the sight in the moonlight at the stainless steel tank that seemed miles away now.

His finger squeezed the trigger and the projectile streaked away as more rounds struck the surrounding dirt. Flares ignited overhead, and the hillside was suddenly bathed in light. The shooting from the Crew increased markedly as John rolled toward the second AT4, but two rounds through his throat ended his life just as the tanker exploded in a massive orange-white fireball.

At the M2, the third can ran dry, and Martin struggled to load the fourth, ignoring the rounds slamming into the crest just below him. Abe grunted beside him and Martin glanced at him as Abe fell to the side, the dark dot at the side of his forehead seeming too small to end a life.

Brett's and Eric's weapons kept popping with the regularity of a target shooter, and Martin dismissed the fleeting idea of bolting for the horses.

He opened fire on the Humvees, loosing fifty rounds at them before shifting his aim and emptying the remainder of the belt at the men scrambling like ants toward the buses. He cut down as many as he could and was loading the fifth can when Brett's rifle fell silent.

"I'm out of ammo," Brett called to Martin. "Does Abe have any?"

"Yeah," Martin yelled, fumbling with the Browning.

Martin's expression was grim when he cocked the machine gun, ready to send another hundred rounds of destruction down the hill. He knew it was just a matter of time before he was killed, but he was going to take as many of the scum to hell with him as he could.

He screamed a battle yell and hammered at the Crew shooters, and when a stray round snuffed out his life, he didn't know what hit him. One second he was worrying about how he could get the sixth can into play, and the next he was falling back as though pushed to the ground by a giant hand, dead before he hit the ground.

Chapter 46

Lucas had tucked in for the night. The long day's preparations for the coming battle had drained him; Elliot and Michael had demonstrated an alarming lack of tactical know-how in mounting a counterattack. Some of the ideas the younger man had thrown out had been ludicrous, whereas others had been workable but at too great a cost in both man-hours and equipment. Lucas had wound up being dragged into the discussion as a mediator and had done his best to limit the hair-brained flyers and keep everyone focused on the achievable.

He'd suggested they focus on a workable plan to contend with shelling, possibly weeks of it, and enlisted a team to stock the underground winter quarters with supplies that would keep the population alive for a month. Lucas had also concentrated on booby-trapping the alternate routes into the valley, using explosives to create natural barriers that would force any attackers to approach on foot through narrow gullies where they could be cut down by only a few defenders. He'd set up strategic outposts on these secondary routes and deployed several AT4s and grenades for maximum defensive impact.

One of the most contentious issues had been where to locate the remaining pair of .50-caliber Browning machine guns. One would be at the final stretch of the main canyon, where it could hold off an attacking force virtually indefinitely. The terrain was their biggest asset, since the Crew would have no alternative to traversing a narrow section with steep walls, a funnel from which there would be no escape. But the second gun was undecided – Lucas thought it best to locate it at the Rio Grande bridge, out of range of assault rifles at a thousand yards from where the Crew would likely be stopped when the bridge blew, but Michael and Elliot had felt that it would serve better as a last defense to the main cave that led into the underground interlinked chambers.

Lucas had argued that if the Crew made it far enough for that to be a factor, they were done for, so the emphasis should be in preventing that at all costs. Michael had pushed for a last-ditch defensive effort to safeguard the lab, the women, and children. Lucas had finally prevailed, but they'd lost valuable time waffling when he could have been attending to other matters – like ensuring the ragtag army of defenders was prepared for the worst, which was coming their way with the inevitability of a runaway train.

A soft rapping interrupted his thoughts. He rose from his bed and pulled on his jeans and shirt before padding to the door to unlock it.

Sierra stood silhouetted by the soft ambient lighting from the hall, wearing the white dress from the celebration party – a time now so removed from their current crisis it seemed a lifetime ago. She looked up at him and raised her chin slightly, her skin bronzed from the sun, and offered a flash of white teeth at his surprised expression.

"Sierra," he whispered. She took a step forward and held her finger to his lips. The heady aroma of the vanilla-scented soap made in the valley rose from her as she pressed herself against him and lay her head against his chest, pushing the door closed with a bare foot.

"Lucas, don't say anything. Please. I'm scared, and I know that soon we could all be killed. I want to be with you before that happens, before the world turns upside down and we lose each other. I know you're angry with me and you feel betrayed, and you can still feel all those things tomorrow. Tonight, just hold me."

Lucas, against his better judgment, wrapped his arms around her. He could feel the flutter of her pulse, delicate as a butterfly's wings on his skin, through the sheer fabric of the dress. They stood together for a long moment, and then she rose on tiptoes and kissed him. He met her lips and remembered everything from their prior tryst, her passion and urgency and the lingering glow of their lovemaking, and the embrace became something more than comforting a frightened woman.

She pulled away from him, twisted the lock shut, and pulled her dress over her head. Lucas began to speak, but she shushed him and returned to his arms, and then they were lost in each other, his best intentions discarded at the feel of her supple skin and her curves and a hunger that demanded to be satisfied no matter what the cost.

Chapter 47

Magnus was so enraged he could barely see. Blood pounded in his temples as he listened to the reports from his subordinates in the command tent – mercifully, located on the opposite side of the vehicles from the attack. Jude was reciting the damage in an emotionless voice, and his lieutenants, including Luis, who had been ordered to attend, waited to answer any questions that arose that Jude couldn't field.

"Eight of the buses are out of commission. Bullets wrecked the engines. Another six are sitting on flats. But the worst on the equipment side is the fuel. We have nothing but what's in the tanks," Jude explained.

"Enough to get us there?" Magnus asked.

"Maybe. But we'll never make it back."

"I'm not concerned with that part. We'll figure something out." Magnus thought for a moment. "Can the flats be fixed? Patched? Or were the tires completely destroyed?"

"Most can be patched. We can use the generator to run the compressors to inflate them, and we have plenty of patch material. I just don't know how long they'll last in this heat, as the altitude increases."

"They just need to get us to Los Alamos."

"Right." Jude paused. "Now to the men. We lost two hundred and seven, with another forty-six wounded seriously enough to take them out of the fight. Another twenty with wounds that aren't critical."

"Damn. That leaves us with, what, six-something to mount the attack?"

"Correct."

"How do you plan to attend to them?"

"We're working on a system. I put Luis in charge of that."

"Who?" Magnus snapped.

Jude indicated Luis among the men, who cleared his throat. "We're thinking that we'll need to set up a medical unit here. Many of the men can't be moved."

Magnus frowned. "We can't divide our army to care for a few wounded. Move them."

"Most will die if we try."

Magnus shrugged. "Then they'll die. I'm not leaving medics and supplies we might need for the battle."

"But–"

"You heard me. Now what about the attackers?" Magnus demanded.

"We recovered four bodies. We believe at least one, possibly more, got away."

"Only four men did all this? Impossible."

"We know there were more – it's a question of how many. The machine gun was gone. Just empty ammo cans and hundreds of shell casings."

"Can't you track them?"

"Not at night. We could be riding into an ambush. We've lost enough men already without throwing fifty more into an unknown scenario." Jude regarded his men. "We'll just have to be alert to the possibility of another attack as we travel. We can put scouts on horseback ahead and on either flank. With radios."

"This is proving disastrous, and we haven't even gone into battle yet," Magnus fumed. "Over a third of my men dead…"

"We knew this would be costly," Jude reminded him.

"Not the trip, you fool. The trip was supposed to be the easy part."

There was a long, tense pause. Luis shifted and took a small step forward. "Maybe we should call for reinforcements?"

Magnus's eyes narrowed as he studied Luis with obvious disdain. "We're not waiting for anything. We've still got our long guns. We'll pound them to pieces before we attack. I'd be surprised if there's anything left once the howitzers are done with them." His voice strengthened. "Now all of you – get out of my sight. I need to think."

The men moved to the entry and Magnus snapped his fingers. "Not you, Jude. You stay."

Luis and the others left, and Luis circled back around to the far side of the tent to see if he could hear anything. He'd thought his suggestions had been good ones, but of course Magnus had rejected them – the same genius that had gotten so many of his men killed on this wild-goose chase thought himself above listening to anyone.

He heard Magnus's distinctive guttural voice and froze as he made out the words.

"I'd say kill him now, except that we need every available man who can fight."

"I put him in charge of something harmless to make him feel like he had authority. I'm sorry he popped out with that idiocy," Jude said.

"Cano was too patient. When this is over, we eliminate the Locos on the way back to Houston. If he's any example of them, good riddance. I don't need weakness in our ranks."

Jude's tone softened. "Maybe he'll take a bullet in the fight."

Magnus chuckled. "See to it. Now how long is it going to take to get rolling again? We can double-load the buses for one day. It won't kill the men."

Luis didn't wait to hear any more. He turned and was creeping away when he heard a sound from his left. He reached for his pistol as a voice whispered from the gloom.

"They talking about you?" Duke asked.

Luis had spent time with Duke and Aaron sourcing supplies in Albuquerque; they were the only two who didn't treat him like a leper.

Duke tried again. "Wouldn't buy any green bananas if it was. Not long for this world, I reckon."

"You were spying on me," Luis said, his words hushed.

"No, I was taking a leak. Couldn't help but hear. You, on the other hand – didn't see you peeing."

Luis didn't say anything. Duke motioned for Luis to follow him out of earshot of the command tent. When they were well away, Duke stopped and faced Luis. "So what are you gonna do? Sounds like your new boss is going to wipe the floor with you."

"I don't know," Luis admitted. "Why? What do you care?"

Duke looked around and leaned into Luis. "Not sure this is the winning hand anymore. I'm thinking it might be time to hit the trail."

"Where can you go that they won't find you?"

"Me, they won't care about. You, on the other hand…sounds like you really pissed off Magnus. I hear he holds a grudge."

"Then…what?"

"There's one place they can't get you."

Luis shook his head. "I don't follow."

"Where we're headed."

"What are you talking about? Have you lost your mind?"

"What if I told you I knew some people there?" Duke asked, the story of Eve and Sierra well circulated among the troops.

Luis absorbed the question. "They're dead. Or will be soon."

"That's not the way it's played out so far, though, is it?"

Luis frowned. "There's only three hundred of them. Remember? They don't stand a chance – we outnumber them and outgun them."

"Like they didn't stand a chance tonight? Seems like a handful of men took out a lot of Magnus's force in less time than it takes me to zip up." Duke paused. "So far your glorious leader has underestimated them at every step, and now he's down a third of his men, his vehicles are trashed, and he's facing a long road that's not only mined but could hide ambushes. I'd say the other team's been pretty smart to this point – they brought the battle to him, dealt some body blows, and have everyone second-guessing just how easy this is going to be. If they keep playing things like they have, my money's on them, not Magnus. I don't care how many hoodlums he trucks into the wilds."

"We'd be heading into certain death, assuming we even made it there. The howitzers will finish them. It won't matter how clever they are. He's got truckloads of shells – enough to destroy a small city."

Duke looked off into the darkness. When he turned back to Luis, his face was creased with a smirk.

"What if he didn't?"

Chapter 48

Brett and Eric had dragged the heavy machine gun to the horses, fueled by adrenaline and the knowledge that they were the last of the sniping detail left. They returned for the ammo cans and spotted a swarm of Crew working their way up the slope – too many to tackle now that their position had been exposed.

They trotted back to the animals, each toting two of the heavy cans, and were in the saddle and galloping away moments later, the glow of the burning tanker behind them.

They rode hard for twenty minutes, and then Brett eased up.

Eric turned to him. "What are we slowing for?"

"We can't just ride away."

"Why not? It's only the two of us."

"We've still got four hundred rounds and the gun. That could inflict some serious damage."

"We did inflict damage. Now it's time to live to fight another day."

Brett shook his head. "Not enough. They didn't send us out here to turn tail with half our ammo. John didn't give his life so we could bug out."

"Going back is suicide."

"I agree. So we have to hit them where they aren't expecting it."

"What are you talking about?"

"Think about it. They assume we've taken off. Battle's over. They're probably scraping their dead off the ground. So we circle around to the opposite ridge on the west side, hammer them hard and fast, and then bail once we're out of ammunition – not before. If we're lucky, we can neutralize at least another hundred, which is a hundred less we'll have to take on in the canyons." Brett paused. "Plus, it will seriously blow their minds."

Eric shook his head. "They're probably tracking us right now."

"Not at night, with mines. We know there aren't any here. But they don't."

"I don't know…"

"I do. We'll get into position and hit them a few hours before dawn. We'll be gone before they can react." Brett smiled. "Last hundred rounds will go into the vehicles that are towing the big guns."

"Why not try to hit the howitzers?"

"The ammo will probably just bounce off. But if they can't move them…"

"I can always try to take out the trailer tires while you're hammering them with the Browning," Eric mused, slowly coming around.

Brett nodded. "Not a bad idea."

Three hours later they were on the opposite hill, behind a rock formation, watching the Crew encampment through their night vision goggles. The M2 was set up and ready for action, cans of ammo next to it.

Brett nudged Eric and pointed to a large white tent. "Must be something special in there. Maybe we should hit that first?"

"Nah. If there was anyone in it at this hour, it would be lit. It's dark as your mama's…"

Motion near one of the trucks drew Brett's attention and he swiveled his head to see. There, in the heavy shadows, two men darted along one side of a tractor trailer to where a howitzer was connected to the tow bar. He watched as a third man led three horses away from the column of vehicles, moving toward the ravine that cut through the hill where they were positioned.

Eric whispered to Brett, "What the hell's that all about?"

"Don't know," Brett said, watching intently as the pair reached the long gun. One of them unslung a satchel from his shoulder and placed it on the top of the weapon while the other watched, holding an assault rifle. The first man gave the watcher a thumbs-up, and they ran together to the next gun and repeated the process.

"I'll be damned..." said Eric in wonder. "We have anyone working on the inside?"

"Not that I know of."

"Looks like we do now."

A flashlight beam swept the side of the truck, and three guards appeared around the cab, startling the two men, who froze. Another beam joined the first, and then the night erupted with automatic rifle fire as one of the saboteurs shot at the guards while the one who'd placed the satchels ran toward the man with the horses.

"What do we do?" Eric asked, and then Brett was firing the Browning, cutting down four more guards who were coming at a sprint to intercept the shooter by the howitzer.

Under Brett's covering fire, the two men made it to the horses, and the one with the rifle extracted something from his pocket and held it toward the trailers. Both satchels detonated with loud whumps, and then they were on horseback, riding for all they were worth as Brett emptied the M2 at anything that moved, buying the riders time.

More Crew gunmen emerged from the buses, and Brett loaded a new belt and gunned them down, ignoring the snap of bullets and the whine of ricochets off the rocks near him. When there were no more fighters to shoot, he turned his aim to the trucks and buses, inflicting as much damage as he could with his final rounds, pounding the remaining howitzer's tow vehicle before the machine gun was empty again.

He was changing the ammo cans and locking the third belt in place when an RPG exploded directly below him, sending a shower of rock skyward and deafening both Brett and Eric. They exchanged a dazed look and struggled to their feet to make for their waiting horses, narrowly avoiding another explosion that would have killed them both had they remained in place. Eric stumbled several times as he staggered to his animal, and when Brett helped him the final yards, his arm came away slick with blood.

Eric climbed into the saddle, his face white from shock, and Brett swung up into his, lips in a tight line.

"I'm hit pretty bad, Brett," Eric managed in a ragged whisper.

"Just hang on, Eric. Let's get out of here and we'll deal with it."

Brett gave the twisted remains of the Browning a final look over his shoulder as he spurred his horse into the gloom, ignoring the burning pain in his leg from gashes caused by flying rock chips, and offered a silent prayer of gratitude that he'd survived the second pitched battle of the night.

It was only after a few minutes that he realized Eric's horse was racing after him without a rider. He slowed and considered turning around, but shots from the crest convinced him there was little to be gained, and he ducked down and urged his horse to greater speed, confident he could easily outrun the Crew fighters following on foot and be long gone by the time dawn had broken.

He set off after the trio that had sabotaged the Howitzers, unsure of why they'd acted as they had or who they were, but aware that whoever they were, they had a common enemy, and in the post-collapse world that was as good a basis for cooperation as any.

Chapter 49

It was late morning by the time Brett had led Luis, Duke, and Aaron through the maze of canyons and into the verdant valley hidden from discovery by the ring of peaks at the top of the world. They'd ridden hard through the night and their horses were blown out by the time they arrived; on the final stretch to the compound the animals were on their last legs.

Duke had explained the situation when Brett had caught up to them. After a tense exchange, Brett had agreed to show them to safety. His distrust of Luis was based on his appearance and prison-yard demeanor, but he'd accepted that the former cartel thug was genuine in his hatred of the Crew and his commitment to seeing them defeated, and in this situation, any cooperation against their common enemy had to be considered.

Elliot, Michael, and Lucas were waiting outside the main building when they rode up, the sentries having radioed their arrival so they could be met and interrogated by the leadership. Duke's face split with a wide grin at the sight of Lucas's familiar dusting of beard under the straight brim of his ubiquitous beaver-felt hat. Lucas nodded in greeting as the older man lowered himself from the saddle, followed by Aaron, who offered a tight smile.

Lucas's gaze locked on Luis and his jaw clenched. "Friend of yours?" he asked.

"You could say that. Mutual objectives is more like it. Allies," Duke explained. "This is Luis. Former head of the Locos. Now on the run from Magnus, who wants his head on a pike."

Lucas didn't respond or drop his eyes. "Locos, huh? Lost a bunch, I hear."

"That's in the past. Now I'm…a free agent," Luis said.

Lucas had explained who Duke and Aaron were to Michael and Elliot, but Luis was an unknown. "Or a spy," Lucas said.

Luis shook his head. "News flash – Magnus knows your location. He knows your strength. The Apache sold you out. There's nothing to spy on."

"Why are you here?" Elliot demanded.

"To help," Luis said simply. "My survival odds are best if you win. So I'm placing my bets on you. I know all about Magnus's strategy, his force's size and weak points, his approach, his resources. I bring a lot to the table, so I'm not coming begging."

Duke nodded agreement. "He blew up two of the remaining three big guns. Took them out of the game. That alone should get him a medal."

"How?" Lucas asked, his suspicion obvious.

"I'd gotten my hands on a decent amount of explosives in Albuquerque for Magnus. We rigged up a couple of detonators to a wireless receiver, and kaboom," Duke explained.

"Why were *you* working for that scum?" Lucas asked Duke.

"I figured if I followed him, eventually he'd lead me to you."

"And why were you in such a rush to find me?"

Duke laughed dryly. "Believe it or not, it started off as a business proposition. Little late now, I suppose. But I'm here, so all's well that ends well, right?" He looked around. "Nice digs. Brett here told us some about it. Seems like a good situation – except for the Mongol horde that wants to burn the place to the ground." Duke paused. "How's the little girl and her mom?"

Lucas managed a small grin. "Her aunt. They're both good."

"I never doubted they would be, with you riding herd."

Lucas wasn't finished with Luis. "How did you figure an explosion would knock out the guns? They're designed to take a lot of abuse."

"Went for the loading and targeting systems. These are computer driven, so destroy those, and they're inoperable. We were going to detonate the third one as well as the trailer with the shells, but the guards interrupted before we could get to them."

"He's got hundreds of shells," Aaron said. "It'll be ugly if he gets to put them to use."

The questioning continued for a good hour as the stable hands took the horses to the barn. The inhabitants were milling about making preparations for the battle. Elliot's radio crackled and a voice rang from the speaker – the leader of the team that was to blow the bridge.

"They're on approach. I see…buses and trucks. Over."

Elliot pressed the transmit button. "Artillery? Over."

A pause. "One gun being towed at the back of the column." Another pause. "Estimate they'll be on the bridge in about two minutes."

"Any chance you can get them all when it collapses? Over."

"Negative. Maybe the first few vehicles. It's a long column. I'm signing off. Over and out."

The plan was to blow the bridge and attack the force with the Browning, further thinning the ranks and making getting across the river a major obstacle. Days of planning, of setting shaped charges, of checking and rechecking the work, were about to come to fruition – hopefully in a deadly plunge into the Rio Grande.

~ ~ ~

Jude stopped the column as it neared the bridge, the trek that had begun before dawn finally over. According to his reckoning based on an old map, once across, they could be at Los Alamos in an hour or two and be able to make their way through the canyons under cover of darkness – although any advantage they might have had due to surprise had clearly been lost. Still, they had plentiful night vision gear, and Magnus's plan was to rush the valley after softening it with nonstop shelling while his troops moved into position. Jude wasn't convinced that would work as well as Magnus believed, but he also knew better than to argue. As it was, Magnus was blaming Jude for failing to prevent the attacks that had wreaked such havoc on the force.

He studied the bridge and the far bank with his binoculars and stiffened when he heard the heavy crunch of boots on gravel behind him. He didn't need to turn around to know Magnus had come for a look himself – the man exuded a presence that was palpable.

"What are you waiting for?" Magnus asked.

"Checking the bridge." He swept the area and shook his head as he lowered the spyglasses. "I want to get some men on it to search for mines. I don't want to take anything for granted. This would be a natural point to block us, at least temporarily."

"Delaying the inevitable."

Jude held his tongue. He privately thought that Magnus had overlooked the possibility that the occupants of the valley had fled in advance of his attack, and that they'd wind up having expended all their energy and hundreds of men for nothing. That was what Jude would have done in the face of an overwhelming force headed at him – he'd have launched token attacks and mined the roads to buy everyone time to get to safety. He'd bet that was what Magnus would discover when he finally made it into the valley, but there was no way Jude was going to voice the possibility.

Ten minutes later, the four men he'd sent to examine the understructure of the bridge reported back that from their vantage point on the bank they didn't see anything suspicious. A sweep of the surface of the road found no mines, and Magnus was pacing by his vehicle when the men returned and pronounced it clear.

Jude scowled as he regarded the river and the smaller wood footbridge downstream. "I don't like it. Something's off. Why didn't they blow the bridge?"

"They probably don't have enough explosives. Used them up on the mines," Magnus said.

"Maybe," Jude said. "I want to have a look myself."

Magnus watched him descend the steep bank and work his way to the wood structure. Jude crossed, surveying the highway bridge from the lower, smaller one, and then Magnus's radio crackled as Jude's voice reported.

"I can't be sure, but it looks like there's some suspicious material on the far end. Over."

"What does that mean?" Magnus growled. "Suspicious material. Be clear. Over."

"It means there's a ridge of debris that could be nothing, or could be…something." Jude paused. "We should get a team across the bridge to take a hard look before we put any vehicles on it. Over."

Magnus weighed his impatience against the possibility of calling it wrong, and erred on the side of the conservative. "All right. Come back and do what you need to do. Over," he said, and strode back to his Humvee with a shake of his head.

~ ~ ~

Richard watched the drama at the river play out through his binoculars from his concealed position on one of the hills a half mile west of the bridge, the Browning beside him cocked and loaded, sights set for the longer range.

"Come on, come on. Cross it. Just cross it. It's safe. Really, it is," he muttered, and then sucked in a sharp intake of breath when he saw a group of men move onto the bridge and probe the surface for mines. They returned to where several others stood at the front of the long procession of vehicles, and then one of them broke off and made his way down the bank.

"Damn. They're not going to fall for it," he said under his breath. His impression was confirmed when the four men who had checked for mines crossed the bridge and began working their way below it. "They're onto us. We're going to blow it," he said, and flipped the cover up on the wireless transmitter that would detonate the numerous charges required to collapse the high-density reinforced span.

The gunner looked at him. "You sure?"

"Open up once it blows. Don't wait. They'll spot us sooner than later, so give them everything you've got." Richard eyed the red button and nodded once. "Here goes nothing."

He depressed the button and the end of the bridge lifted into the air, buckling where it met the shore, and then sagged as a cloud of dust and smoke rose into the air and blew out both sides of the span. The boom of the explosion reached them over two seconds later. Richard peered through the binoculars and cursed.

"Damn. It didn't completely collapse."

"Should I start shooting?" the gunner asked.

"Have at it. Make every round count."

The big gun opened fire and stuttered after ten seconds before falling silent. The gunner fumbled with the cocking lever to clear a jam as Richard watched the reaction at the bridge. His eyes widened behind the glasses as two of the Humvees rolled forward, their identical .50-caliber M2s pointed up the hill at his position, and then they were firing in tandem. The world around him disintegrated as hundreds of high-caliber armor-piercing rounds disintegrated the rocks providing their cover, shredding him and his men to pieces in seconds.

Chapter 50

Michael started at the distant sound of the detonation as the bridge blew, the sound faint in the valley, and exchanged a look with Elliot. "That should slow them down," he said.

"Wouldn't make any assumptions," Lucas said, checking the time. "They're what, about twenty miles away now?"

"That's right. But there's no way across the river unless they go pretty far north, and that will further delay them."

"What about the wood bridge Arnold talked about?" Lucas asked.

"We decided to leave that. They can't get vehicles across it, and we figured it would invite them to try crossing it with horses, which would bring them out in the open for the machine gun to cut down."

"Arnold approved that?"

"It was actually my idea," Michael said. "Another trap."

"Assuming everything works perfectly. What if it doesn't?"

"So far it has."

Lucas didn't want to argue, but he'd never been consulted on leaving the smaller bridge intact. He would never have done so, but his sway with Elliot only went so far, and he couldn't counter what he didn't know about.

"See if you can raise Richard on the radio," Elliot said.

Michael nodded and held his handset to his mouth. After several tries, he lowered it and shook his head. "If they're shooting, which I assume they are, they probably can't hear me."

"That's one possibility," Lucas agreed. "I'd get everyone into position just in case. All noncombatants to the caves and the hospital area. Snipers to the outposts. Same for the demo crew." They'd concealed a number of Bouncing Betties in the canyon in strategic locations, but also had charges set to induce rockslides, which would require men to trigger them at appropriate points in the Crew's approach.

"You really think that's necessary? I hate to get everyone into the field if we're still hours from needing to be on alert," Michael said. "We want to avoid the fatigue factor, if possible."

"No matter what happens, this is the beginning of a long process. Could be many days of battle. A few hours one way or another won't make much difference."

Michael looked to Elliot, who nodded. "Lucas is probably right. Call an operational meeting for ten minutes from now, and get all the team leaders ready to be there and deploy immediately afterward." Elliot turned back to Lucas. "I trust you'll join us?"

"Glad to."

A high-pitched whistle split the air, and the earth trembled from an explosion on one of the surrounding peaks. Over a minute later, a roar drifted across the valley from the boom of a distant howitzer. Lucas glared at Michael. "Get everyone into the bunkers. They'll eventually get the range right."

"But…it's too far away," Michael protested.

"To be accurate, sure. But it doesn't need to be. Not with hundreds of shells — and those have to be base bleed models, which have far greater range." Lucas frowned. "Call your meeting in the bunker and get everyone moving."

Several minutes went by, and then another shriek confirmed Lucas's warning — a mushroom of smoke and rock blew from the valley floor several miles east of the compound. He turned to Elliot. "Remember the guide gave them precise location information. Anyone with a map could pinpoint where to concentrate the fire."

People were running with weapons in hand, and the team leaders were yelling orders, trying to organize and calm everyone in the face of the shelling they'd never thought would happen. Lucas didn't have to point out that Arnold had been right. More shells landed, falling every fifteen to twenty seconds, and within minutes the blasts were closing on the compound, with only occasional detonations badly off the mark. Duke stood by Lucas's side as he advised a pair of men on the best way to keep their animals from panicking in the face of the shelling, and shook his head when he was done speaking with them.

"Doesn't look like they were ready for this, pardner."

"Yeah. But they'll figure it out. The shelling's to soften us up. They can't physically make it to the canyon quickly, even if they get the vehicles across the bridge. But the artillery…" Lucas's voice trailed off.

"Any way to stop the big gun?"

"If Richard isn't responding, not for hours. We don't have anyone down there other than his group. It'll take at least three or four to get men on horseback with some AT4s."

Ruby's voice called to Lucas from behind him. "Terry's plane could get you there quickly."

The men spun to the older woman, who was standing with Terry, eyeing the distant hangar.

"True," Lucas said. "But there's no airstrip nearby, is there?"

"Depends on what you mean by airstrip," Terry said. "There's a section of Route 30 that's straight as an arrow. I could probably set down there."

"Or you could drop napalm on them," Ruby reminded them. "We made all those bombs. Wouldn't they work?"

"Not against artillery," Duke said. "Although…they could make the area around the gun pretty ugly and might detonate some of the shells, which could put it out of commission."

"That's probably your best bet," Terry said. "I set you down in broad daylight, they're going to hear it and they'll be waiting for you. Be smartest to wait for nightfall, but if that's the case, might as well just ride out." Another shell exploded, this one only three hundred yards from the buildings. "Problem is Richard was the one who was going to drop the napalm. And he isn't here." Terry sighed. "Don't suppose any of you were ever in the military, were you?"

Aaron shrugged. "I was in the Marines for four years. Saw a decent amount of combat."

"Think you could keep your nerves steady enough to drop some napalm?"

An explosion rocked the valley from off to their right. Aaron squinted at the hangar. "Compared to this, it would be a vacation."

Terry led them across the compound as the shelling continued. He stopped near the cave entrance and leaned toward Ruby. "You should get below. Where are Eve and Sierra?"

"I'm sure they're already down in the bunkers."

"Might want to check to be sure," Lucas said.

Ruby took the hint. "Okay. Be careful, Terry."

"Always."

Ruby made for the entry to the subterranean complex as the men continued to the stables and mounted up. They rode across the field and arrived at the hangar less than ten minutes later. All pitched in to load the glass milk jugs with plastic fins glued to their tops, taking care to handle them gently lest they inadvertently detonate the Armstrong's mixture affixed to the sides. When they were done, they pushed the plane clear of the hangar, and Terry started the engine, which caught on the third try and settled into a steady hum. Aaron climbed into the back, Duke shook his hand, and then the old Cessna was accelerating down the dirt strip as its prop clawed at the sky.

Ruby found a frantic Sierra in the lower bunker, which was chaotic with frightened children crying at each new explosion. They had both been assigned to work in the field hospital set up to deal with the inevitable wounded, and Sierra was roaming through the oversized rooms with a panicked expression.

"Where's Eve? Have you seen Eve?" Sierra asked when she spied Ruby.

"No. I thought she'd be with you. She isn't down here anywhere?"

"I told her to come. She was right behind me, but now I can't find her."

Ruby stiffened as a thought struck her. "Where's Ellie?"

"The pig? How would I know?" Then Sierra gasped as she

realized what Ruby was getting at. "You think she went to get it?"

"She loves that animal."

They made for the stairs that led two stories up to the surface, fighting the crowd coming down. At the top, they could see that the explosions were getting nearer to the compound, although still randomly landing in a relatively large spread.

Sierra's hand flew to her mouth at the sight of one end of the sleeping quarters in rubble, and then they were sprinting toward it, Sierra screaming Eve's name over the incessant din from the detonating shells. At the entry, Sierra exhaled in relief at the sight of Eve's dress inside, her knees skinned and her torso streaked with dust, cradling Ellie. Sierra ran to the little girl and scooped her into her arms.

"I told you to come with me!" Sierra chided, her tone ragged.

"Ellie was here. But she's fine. Just scared."

Ruby tugged on Sierra's sleeve. "Come on. No telling where the next shell hits."

They were halfway back to the cave when the sound of an engine roared overhead, and Terry's plane soared by no more than three hundred feet above their heads, narrowly clearing the tree line at the edge of the valley before disappearing on a circuitous course to reach the convoy from a direction it would least expect.

Chapter 51

The Cessna vibrated alarmingly as it fought for altitude, skewing sideways when it hit a gust of rough air from the north before straightening and continuing on its course, the engine thrumming so loudly that Aaron could barely hear himself think. Terry banked over the trees and set a bearing over the lowest peaks, passing close over them.

Once the little plane was clear of the valley, the earth dropped away, the area surrounding the mountains around Shangri-La three thousand feet lower, and Terry tapped the altimeter and gave Aaron a thumbs-up.

"Eleven thousand feet. That's about max for this thing running ethanol," he called out in a loud voice.

"How long until we get there?" Aaron asked.

"Oh, probably no more than fifteen minutes. Want to sneak up on them from the southeast."

"Won't they hear us coming?"

"Nobody's going to be able to hear anything down there if they're firing that big gun without hearing protection. Plus, the prevailing winds are from the north, so we'll have that going for us, too."

"How far above them are we going to be?"

"Couple thousand feet, at least, to stay out of range of their weapons."

"Sounds like a lot."

"Nobody said this would be easy. But I'll slow to almost stall speed, and you can dump a bunch of bombs once you get the hang of it. Do one at a time until you sort of get it down, and then go for broke. Less time we're over the target, the better, far as I'm concerned."

"We should be able to get closer. I mean, an AK's only accurate for three hundred yards."

"Yeah, but they're still dangerous at double that. And if they have any .50 calibers, up to couple thousand or more, then we're screwed. Altitude there is about six thousand feet. No way could we get to thirteen or fourteen to stay above those."

"Not easy hitting a moving target, even with an M2."

"You feeling particularly lucky today?"

Aaron fell silent as the plane bounced gently along, moving at 110 knots. He inspected the napalm jugs and counted twenty in all – there were still another twenty back at the strip, but they wouldn't fit in the confined space. He tried to envision how he'd go about his approach, trying to remember the speed of fall of an object from his high school physics class. Thirty-two feet per second stuck in his mind, but there was something about acceleration…

He recalled terminal velocity as around 240 feet per second, but how long would it take to reach that? At two thousand feet, would it be…less than ten seconds? More?

Math hadn't been his strength in school, and he wondered if Terry was any better. He was going to ask when Terry called out to him and pointed ahead, where puffs of smoke were rising from the horizon along the river.

"Thar she blows. Be there in three minutes or so."

"Any idea how long it will take for the bombs to hit the ground? In other words, how far ahead of time do I drop them?"

"That's a tough one. I mean, there's your velocity moving down, but also your momentum forward from the speed of the plane. If we were standing still, you could just drop it straight over the target, but beats me how far in advance to let loose. I'd start at maybe twenty seconds and keep dropping them to see what works."

"That's as close as you can get?"

"Without a calculator, it is."

"Then fly straight along the vehicles so it doesn't go to waste."

"Thanks for the tip. You can open the hatch whenever you want."

Aaron took the hint and slid the rear door open and was instantly buffeted by wind. Terry yelled to him as they neared the column. "I'll say go when you should drop the first one. Then do it every couple of seconds and watch for the effect. Try to remember which one gets closest, and that will tell you how many seconds on the next pass."

"Not very scientific."

"Not much in life is."

Aaron waited for the go-ahead, a milk jug in his lap and another in his hand.

"All right. On my count. Five-four-three-two-one… Go!" Terry cried. Aaron released the first jug, counted to two, and released the next. He repeated the maneuver ten times, looking down to see the detonations once he'd released the fifth.

Liquid fire exploded along the side of one of the buses a good distance from the howitzer, scalding the men near it. The next struck one of the equipment trucks, immersing it in burning liquid. After all ten were released, none had landed near the howitzer, although they'd certainly caused substantial destruction among the fighters.

Terry banked and called over his shoulder, "Looks like the fifth one was the closest. I'll adjust my count accordingly."

"Let me know when to start dropping them."

"You got it. Only this time, drop them as fast as you can."

They did a tight loop and returned along the smoldering column for a second run. On Terry's count, Aaron pitched jug after jug from the plane, taking care to avoid detonating the Armstrong's mixture with an errant strike against the fuselage. He was dropping the last one when a row of holes appeared along the right wing, the tip of which sheared off moments later.

Terry fought for control and Aaron gripped the seat belt for dear life, almost missing the results of his bombing run. Two of the napalm jugs exploded near the howitzer, which fell silent as the crew was immolated. Then the plane was yawing at a precarious angle, and

Terry was screaming at the top of his lungs while he fought with the controls.

"Hang on. We're going down."

Chapter 52

Magnus surveyed the wreckage from the napalm and screamed orders at his men. He was now down to half his original force, and his patience was at an end. He didn't care about the buses, but the loss of the howitzer threw his entire plan into jeopardy, and he wanted his fighters on their way at a gallop within the hour.

Jude convinced him to stay with the column with a small security contingent as the repair crew attempted to fix the howitzer; the goal was to at least get the optics working well enough to do some primitive sighting. They'd lost their lead gun detail, but there were enough ex-soldiers in the Crew's ranks to replace them.

Magnus watched as his riders swarmed across the wood bridge. The cement road was too unstable to support them, the twenty-foot gap where the charges had gone off barely held together by the rebar that remained. Jude led the charge. The horses were eager to run after a week cooped up in the trailers, and the force rode up the highway at a good clip, the sound of their steeds' hooves thunderous.

They passed through Los Alamos without a fight, which surprised Jude after the attacks they'd endured. The air strike had been the most unexpected, and even Magnus was unable to hold Jude accountable for failing to predict it. Nobody had seen an operating plane for years, and the idea that Shangri-La had any took them by complete surprise – for which eighty men had paid with their lives before one of the M2 gunners had shot the thing out of the sky.

Once off the road, Jude followed the Apache's directions into the canyon to his right. He'd slowed to a trot once through town, wary of ambush now that the canyon walls rose sheer on either side. The late afternoon sun shone at such an angle that the crest above blocked its light. He put two riders well out in front of the main force to watch for mines, the men's reluctance well hidden by their bravado.

Forty-five minutes into the maze, the first disaster struck when one of the advance scouts triggered a Bouncing Betty, which liquefied the pair and shredded fifteen of the front riders to pieces. The men stopped in their tracks, and Jude ordered more fighters forward on foot, leaving their horses to be led by others. Jude had never seen the result of a bounding mine, and was shocked by how many of his men had been killed by only one of the devices, even at considerable distance. If the advance riders had been closer to the main group, he could have easily lost fifty men with one explosion instead of seventeen.

The advance men moved painfully slowly across the dry wash, and the following riders stayed in a narrow band to prevent straying from the area the walkers had confirmed safe. They discovered ten more of the mines over the next hour and marked their locations using broken branches driven into the ground beside them.

Once out of the larger canyon, the second tributary was narrower, forcing the riders to group together more tightly than Jude would have liked. He occasionally communicated with Magnus on his handheld, but reception worsened as he pushed deeper into the canyons, the cliffs effectively blocking the signal.

He'd just begun to relax when another Bouncing Betty detonated, this one in the midst of his men, killing scores instantly as the shrapnel ripped through flesh and bone at blinding velocity. The screams and moans of the dying and wounded were as horrific as the sight of body parts strewn around the blast zone, disembodied arms and heads of men and animals alike littering the canyon floor, which was awash in crimson.

Shooting from snipers above began almost immediately after the explosion, taking down more of the riders as they attempted to return fire. Jude sighted a series of caves just below the crest and ordered the men with AT4s to fire at will.

A series of explosions above silenced the shooters, leaving the canyon echoing from the roar. Jude ordered his men to dismount and continue on foot, using their animals as cover in case there were more snipers ahead.

"What about the wounded?" one of the nearest gunmen asked Jude as he surveyed the carnage.

"We have to leave them. Take ten of your best and care for them as well as you can, but there's not much we can do until this is over."

The sky was darkening when the boom of the howitzer resumed, and a muted cheer rose from the men as shells whistled overhead. Jude scanned the surviving force and estimated that he still had over four hundred able-bodied fighters against almost half as many defenders. He'd understood the assault would extract a high toll, but they were closing in on their objective, and he suspected he'd already seen the worst of what could be thrown at them.

~ ~ ~

Brett watched the approaching Crew and whispered to the young man next to him, "Hold on. Wait until there's no turning back."

The man nodded, the detonator switch in his hand trembling slightly. Brett noticed the tremor and inched closer. "You going to be okay?"

"Yeah. Just a little nervous, is all."

"I can do this part if you want."

The young man shook his head. "I set the charges. I'll push the button."

"Fair enough."

The attacking force advanced, and when Brett calculated they were beyond the point of no return, he gave his companion the nod. The man flipped the switch, and a rapid-fire sequence of explosions rocked the ridge to their right.

~ ~ ~

Jude looked up to see whole sections of the canyon detaching and snowballing toward him with relentless force. He leapt on his horse and ordered his men forward, urging them to a run as they raced to avoid the huge rockslide.

Most made it, but the stragglers were crushed under tons of stone and vanished beneath the rubble like drowning men pulled beneath a roiling sea. Jude's men were recovering, the dust in the air thick as fog, when more sniper fire chattered from above, accompanied by the clink of grenades landing on nearby rocks. Jude drove his horse onward, shouting instructions to his men, who returned fire at the sniper positions until more AT4s could be brought to bear. The grenades exploded, yielding more screams, and then the AT4 projectiles did their work and the snipers fell silent before they could inflict any more damage.

~ ~ ~

Brett stared at the young man's sightless eyes beside him and shook his head to clear it. The explosion had deafened him and all he could hear was a loud ringing, like he'd stuck his head in a church bell and someone had struck it with a sledgehammer.

The steady drumbeat of the shelling shook the ground as he crawled from his hiding place and made for the final defense point. Arnold had underscored the importance of stopping the attackers before they reached the valley, where it would be a bloodbath of one-on-one fighting, and Lucas had echoed that strategy – the Crew would either be stopped in the canyons, or Shangri-La could lose everyone to Magnus's men.

He staggered along, unaware of the blood trickling from his right ear, clutching his M4 reflexively in his hands, the only one of ten snipers left alive after the antitank weapons had done their job. That he'd lived twice after facing seemingly certain death surprised him, but he didn't pause to think about it. He had to reach the final attack group and do what he could as long as he was drawing breath.

~ ~ ~

Magnus's decision to send Jude into the canyon before dark had proved disastrous – one of their supposed edges being their night vision equipment. He would never have led a frontal assault given the conditions they'd met, and would have retreated and held the area under siege while waiting for reinforcements and more artillery, even if it took months. Only his fear of Magnus's retribution had made him continue forward, and it had cost too many of his men their lives.

According to the Apache's directions, they only had one dogleg to go before they would ascend into the valley, at the other end of which lay their final target. They'd run the deadly gauntlet, and those that remained were ready for blood, the memory of the damage inflicted on their peers vivid and fresh. They would show no mercy and kill every man, woman, child, and animal they found.

Some part of Jude's reptilian brain sensed imminent danger as their force entered the final dogleg. The darkness that would cloak them was also a hindrance to spotting mines, and he recognized the new challenge instantly – either they'd have to make a best effort in the fading light or wait until night and attempt navigating the ravine using NV gear. Neither was a good option, but every minute he was in the narrow branch he knew he was at risk from ahead as well as above.

He was ordering another ten men forward on foot when the percussive booming of an M2 echoed from the other end of the canyon. Men around him dropped from their horses, their flak jackets useless against the high-velocity slugs. He estimated the range at over six hundred yards and yelled for his fighters to take cover among the rocks as the stream of rounds from the big gun cut them down like a giant scythe. Jude's fighters answered the shooting with fire of their own, but at that range the M2 had them badly outgunned. He called to the nearest man with an AT4 strapped to his back and the gunman crawled toward him, staying low. When he reached Jude, he looked frightened but determined.

"See the muzzle flash up there? Probably six hundred yards, at least," Jude said.

"I make it about that."

"What's the best you've ever done with an AT?"

"They start to fade at four, but I might be able to do it with a few tries. Have to adjust for the drop, but they'll hit something."

"He's got us pinned down here. I'll get as many tubes as it takes, but you've got to take him out, understand?"

"I'll do my best..." the man said uncertainly.

"Make it happen, or we're all dead."

The man nodded and freed the antitank weapon while Jude transmitted a call for more AT4s on his handheld. Several minutes later, two more Crew fighters reached him during a pause in the shooting – no doubt while the sniper was changing belts – and handed him their AT4s.

The first projectile sailed in an arc that struck fifteen yards below the machine-gun position, exploding harmlessly against the canyon wall. Jude gritted his teeth and handed the fighter another tube, which he adjusted for the range and fired as the Browning began its deadly song again.

This time the projectile sailed over the position and exploded well past it, in the valley. The fighter shook his head and blinked away sweat as the last tube was thrust into his hands. Rounds chewed the ground around them, blowing chunks of rock into the air, ricochets whining as he leveled the tube and peered through the sight.

A splatter of warmth struck Jude's face and he gasped as the man fell forward, most of his skull gone and the AT4 unfired. Jude was reaching for the antitank weapon when shooting from behind him drew his attention – different caliber than the AK-47s his men used.

He realized too late that he'd been lured into a trap and was now boxed in by shooters on both sides; he could tell from the distinctive chatter of AR-15s and M4s picking his men off from above and behind while the big gun ahead obliterated everything in its path.

For the first time in the fight, it dawned on him that he might ultimately fail Magnus, and it was with that thought that he wiped the blood from his face and pointed the AT4 at the M2 position, determined to end the onslaught or die trying.

Chapter 53

Lucas glanced at the sky outside the cave when the howitzer resumed shelling. Elliot was with him, and his face went gray at the first incoming explosion.

"So much for the plane idea," the older man said.

"Worked for a while," Lucas said, his expression grim.

"Arnold was right about the shelling. It's going to destroy everything if it keeps up. I should have listened to him."

"Too late now." Lucas paused as another shell whistled several hundred yards away before exploding on one of the slopes. "Don't see any way around dealing with it up close and personal. Is there another way out of the valley on that side that doesn't take me past the Crew force?"

"Colt's watching the entrance of a trail that skirts the ridge to the south," Elliot said. "It's treacherous going and too narrow for more than one rider at a time. No way they'd know about it."

"Then that's the way I'll go." Lucas looked at the stables. "Poor horses. I hope Tango's okay." He paused. "Don't suppose you have an antitank weapon handy? Or some grenades?"

"All the AT4s have been deployed, but I'll radio to see if there are any spares. I think we've got some grenades in the complex." Elliot raised his radio and sent a message, and a response came back within a few moments. Elliot nodded and murmured an instruction, and then turned to Lucas. "An AT4 will be delivered to the stable along with a grenade. Sorry we don't have more ordnance available, but pretty much everything's in the field."

"As it should be."

Elliot eyed Lucas as he moved toward the stable. "Good luck."

Lucas didn't respond and instead picked up his pace.

Tango was obviously frightened and skittish, and it was all Lucas could do to get the saddle on him with the help of one of the stable hands. A youth entered the barn, carrying an olive green tube and a grenade, and handed them to Lucas, who slung the AT4 over his shoulder and dropped the grenade into his flak jacket pouch. He led Tango from the stable and was relieved to see that the shells were striking further from the compound than earlier – so maybe the plane had been able to damage the targeting optics sufficiently so it was firing blind.

He galloped across the valley to the spot Elliot had indicated and found Colt behind a sandbagged embankment, with two AR-15s by his side and a dozen spare magazines lined up like sentries. Colt looked better than he had earlier in the week, but was obviously still recovering from his ordeal.

"You're headed out?" Colt asked.

"Somebody's got to tackle the gun. It's wreaking havoc."

"I'm monitoring reports from the canyon. Crew's getting its ass handed to it so far. Can't believe they came straight at us instead of using one of the alternate routes."

"They might be doing both. Warn the teams on the other approaches not to let down their guard."

"We mined those gulches too, so they'd get plenty of advance warning. Apparently those Bouncing Betties are doing a number."

Lucas nodded. "Anything I need to know about this trail?"

"Pretty steep in places, and a sheer drop about halfway down. It lets out just north of White Rock. Then straight ride up the Rio Grande to the bridge from there, maybe three miles."

"Any other way across the river?"

Colt shook his head. "Not really. Some shallow spots, but with the rains..."

"Got it."

As Lucas guided Tango down the ravine, the sound of explosions and gunfire from the north informed him that the battle had been joined for real. He trusted the big stallion to set a pace he was comfortable with until they were clear of the trail and could gallop to the river. The descent was hair-raising, the track little more than a ledge along a canyon wall, but after an hour it widened and the worst was over. Lucas urged Tango faster, and the sounds of fighting diminished as the stallion cantered to the water, the regular roar of the howitzer growing louder as they neared the bank.

It was getting dark as they traced the river north, and Lucas scrutinized the surging current, searching for a place to cross. Tango was strong, and if he could find a spot where the water was only a few feet deep, he would manage.

The sun dropped behind the mountains, and Lucas spotted a promising spit of gravel where the river widened considerably, the rush slowing with greater width to accommodate the volume. Lucas directed Tango onto the moist gravel and the horse obediently plodded into the river with tentative steps as the water rose to his belly.

The stallion almost lost his footing on the slippery stones twice but recovered quickly, and then they were across, no more than a mile south of the gun. Lucas rode as close as he dared and then dismounted and tied Tango to a tree before disappearing into the dense brush along the riverbank.

Ten minutes later, he had the Crew base in view from the rise along the river. There were only a few gunmen in evidence, a pair guarding a large tent and the rest working the howitzer, four men hauling shells from a nearby truck while three loaded it. Lucas freed the AT4 and sighted on the gun, estimating his range at no more than two hundred yards, and debated inching closer. The risk of detection was minimal, given the cover from the plants, so he edged along the rise until he was as close as he dared.

Lucas drew a bead on the howitzer and squeezed the trigger. Instead of a projectile streaking to the gun, he was rewarded with a snapping sound and a fizzle. He tried again and nothing happened.

After a third attempt yielded no better result, he set the AT4 down and felt for the grenade. Nothing about this adventure had been easy so far, and he wasn't surprised that things were holding true to form. Now he'd have to do it the hard way, which would involve evading the guards, taking out the gun crew, sabotaging the howitzer, and making it to safety without getting killed.

He considered tossing the grenade at the artillery position, but that wasn't a sure thing, depending on where it landed. He needed to get close enough to guarantee the gun's destruction, and the best way to do that was to drop the grenade into the recoil mechanism so it couldn't fire. That meant much more risk; but he saw no other choice and so removed his hat so he'd be mistaken for another Crew member as he approached the artillery loaders and skirted the encampment, sticking to the shadows while evading the guards who ringed the command area.

Once clear of them, he strode toward the howitzer, M4 in hand, rubbing his face so he looked like another tired Crew gunman. The artillery team barely glanced at him as he approached, and he was no more than twenty yards from them when another shell blasted from the howitzer and he opened fire, cutting the shirtless men to pieces with three-round bursts he hoped would be masked by the echo of the howitzer detonation.

It was over in ten seconds, and Lucas bolted for the gun, not waiting to see whether he'd drawn the guards' attention. He covered the distance in moments and was at the howitzer in a flash. He removed the grenade from his plate carrier and pulled the pin, and then wedged it into the recoil mechanism just as shots rang out from the guards.

Bullets ricocheted as he sprinted with all the speed he could muster, his boots crunching on the gravel as dirt fountained into the air around him. Then the grenade exploded behind him, and he threw himself behind a cluster of rocks as more shots blew chips from the stones. He brought his M4 to bear, wincing at the intensity of the incoming fire.

He jettisoned his spent clip, slapped a fresh one into place, and leveled a few bursts at the guards he could see in the rifle's night vision scope, but it quickly became obvious that the Crew fighters had him pinned down – it would be only a matter of time before they tossed a grenade at him or, worse, fired an AT4 in his direction and ended the show. His magazine emptied in moments and he fished another from his vest, mind working furiously on an out.

Lucas continued to exchange volleys and paused when he pulled his last magazine from his flak jacket and slammed it home. He continued firing, but he knew in his gut that he would be dead within a matter of moments. More rounds pelted into the rocks around him as though to confirm his assessment, and he ducked down and cringed, secure that he'd at least saved Shangri-La from further shelling.

The shooting accelerated, and then his worst fear was realized when the heavy fire of an M2 blasted at the rocks from one of the Humvees, making it impossible for him to do anything but wait for the end.

Chapter 54

Brett was almost to where the .50-caliber Browning was chewing the Crew apart when an explosion silenced it in a spray of rock and dirt. He continued toward the weapon and stopped at the sight of the two-man gun team, both dead, blown clear of the sandbagged trench. The gun rested on its side, smoke rising from the soil around it. Brett lumbered over to it, his balance precarious as he reeled from his injuries. Other dead Shangri-La fighters lay sprawled along the trench, victims of the intense shooting from the attackers.

A glance over the bags revealed the shadowy forms of hundreds of Crew in the canyon below, who were taking fire from behind from at least twenty of the defense force. He could barely make them out in the growing darkness and knew that within moments it would be too dark to see without night vision gear. He felt for his NV goggles, but he'd lost them at some point during the battle, and he groaned as his fingers closed on a shattered set near the gun – of no use.

Brett heaved with all his might and righted the Browning, setting the tripod crookedly on the rock between the sandbags, and checked the ammo belt, which trailed from an ammunition can that had been blown askew by the blast. He glanced around, spotted another can, and moved to it. A pull at one of the handles confirmed it was full, and he dragged it back to the big gun and opened the top so he'd be ready to reload – assuming he lived long enough for that to be an issue.

He blinked away dizziness and peered down the sights. When he squeezed the trigger, a grimace of fury on his dirt-smeared face, the big gun bucked like a living thing in his hands as he sent a hail of rounds into the Crew's ranks. The belt was expended in mere seconds, and he rushed to reload as bullets snapped past him, and then he was firing again, controlling the bursts more accurately, showering death down upon the exposed Crew fighters.

When the second belt was finished, Brett searched around in the gloom for more ammo cans, and found one several yards behind him. He hauled it to the gun and fitted the lead round into place, cocked the weapon, and continued the onslaught, killing scores with each salvo.

The Crew fighters were caught in a pincer, defending a low position from a crossfire assault, a recipe for disaster no matter what the circumstances. The Browning blasted away and the Shangri-La assault rifle fire picked them off, there being little cover to shield them from both angles.

When grenades lobbed by the defenders began landing in their midst, the rout grew worse, and soon the surviving Crew fighters were in full retreat, concentrating on clearing a way back down the canyon. They were able to overwhelm the Shangri-La gunmen and make it past, Brett's fire cutting them down as they ran for the dogleg.

When another belt was exhausted and he could see no more in the darkness, Brett groped in his flak jacket for his radio. He held it to his lips and transmitted. His voice came out as little more than a croak, and his ears howled with a dull ache.

"This is Brett from the canyon end point. The Crew's in retreat back down the canyon. No more than fifty left, but they wiped out our guys. Send more fighters. Repeat, they're in retreat, but we need more fighters with NV gear. I can't hear anything – ears are damaged. Over."

Brett fell back, the stars overhead pinwheeling when he closed his eyes, deaf to the acknowledgement message that blared from the handheld and numb to the pain in his ears and the wounds from ricochets.

More fighters arrived ten minutes later, but by then Brett was dead, his life drained from him onto the rocks beneath, a serene expression on his youthful face. Their leader smoothed his eyes shut with a gloved hand and then adjusted the NV goggles strapped to his head before turning to his men.

"You heard him," he said. "They're trying to escape. Let's make this the most difficult trip of their miserable lives."

The gunmen nodded in unison. The sight of the hundreds of dead Crew glowing in their goggles gave proof that they'd prevailed, and now they would finish the battle for good. The leader made his way down a trail that ran along the crest, the satchel of grenades hanging from his shoulder and the M4 in his hands ready for what was to come. The men followed in silent determination, the only sound their boots on the dirt and the hiss of their breathing, NV goggles lighting the way.

Chapter 55

Lucas was preparing to unleash his final bursts when shooting erupted from his left. A scream from one of the guards carried from the road, and then a grenade exploded by the Browning and it fell silent. The gunmen shifted their focus to the new threat and a vicious firefight ensued, muzzle flashes lighting the night. Lucas held his fire, conserving his few precious rounds of ammo, and only after it became obvious that nobody was shooting at him any longer did he dare peer over the rocks.

The command tent opened and four gunmen emerged, Kalashnikovs at the ready, a mammoth of a man in their midst. One of them ran toward the river and called over his shoulder, "Magnus! This way. Hurry!"

Lucas raised his M4 and tried to sight on Magnus, but the Crew leader was moving too erratically, so Lucas settled for the nearest bodyguard. A three-round burst sent the man reeling backward, firing his rifle into the air, and Lucas shot him again to put him down hard.

More shooting drove Lucas back behind the rocks, and then a figure appeared out of the darkness behind him, firing as he ran to him. The gunman threw himself down as rounds snapped overhead, and Lucas rolled away and brought his M4 to bear on the new arrival.

"If I wanted you dead, you would be," Arnold said, and rattled another burst at the Crew shooters.

"Thought you left," Lucas said.

"I came back."

"Just in time."

"Better late than never, right?"

They both fired at a gunman who was using the corner of one of the buses for cover. Lucas aimed below it, trying for his legs. The man screamed, confirming that at least one of the slugs had done some damage. Lucas leaned toward Arnold. "Magnus is getting away."

"What? Where?"

"He took off down the river." Lucas exhaled loudly. "Lay down some cover fire for me, and I'll go after him."

"I don't know where all the shooters are."

"Do your best. He's got three bodyguards with him." Lucas paused. "You got any spare ammo?"

"I'm on my last mag."

"Damn. All right. Toss another grenade at that bus, and when it goes, I'll make for the river."

"Got a few more of those left," Arnold said, and extracted one from the pouch on the front of his flak jacket. He worked the pin loose and lobbed it high into the air. They waited for it to explode, and when it did, Lucas leapt up and ran for the river, the dirt around him geysering as shots narrowly missed him.

Once at the water, he slowed and swept the bank with his scope, searching for a sign of Magnus or his men. He spied motion downriver and stuck to the brush line as he followed the water, wincing at the sound of each footfall on the loose gravel. He stopped periodically and surveyed the way ahead in the green glow of the eyepiece, determined that the source of his misery not escape.

~ ~ ~

Magnus had been in the command tent with his security detail, listening in disbelief to the panicked radio report about his force's rout from one of his surviving lieutenants. He was shaking his head as though he wasn't hearing correctly and interrupted the man's transmission with a growled threat not to return without Eve's head.

Magnus had thrown the radio to the ground in disgust, his chest heaving beneath the bandoliers of grenades over his flak jacket, and glared at his men as though daring them to say anything.

An explosion rocked the tent, and everyone but Magnus hit the ground. He glowered at the entryway and stormed to it as his guards rose. "What was that?" he demanded, but was interrupted by gunfire from nearby. "Who's shooting?" he yelled, and one of the guards poked his head out of the tent to see.

"Our men. They're firing at the howitzer. The explosion was from there."

"Why are they shooting at their own people? That's insane."

"I didn't see anybody."

More shooting erupted, and soon the sound of at least six AK-47s filled the air, answered by a higher pitched rifle from the artillery position. The gun battle intensified, and then the M2 came into the mix, its bass boom as distinctive as a fingerprint.

The explosion of a grenade rocked the bus beside the tent. The .50-cal stopped firing, and assault rifles joined the fray from the east. Magnus's guards exchanged worried looks, and Magnus yelled at them, "Get me out of here!"

The head of the detail nodded and pushed from the entry, and the rest of the bodyguards surrounded Magnus, shielding him with their lives. The leader sprinted down the bank and called to him as he stepped from the tent. Magnus hesitated for a split second and then zigzagged toward the leader as one of the guards behind him went down shooting.

There was just enough starlight to make out the bank, the moon still low in the night sky, and Magnus trotted after his man as his other two gunmen guarded his rear. He had no idea how everything had gone so wrong so quickly, but he vowed he'd return with an even larger force and raze the earth. Visions of retribution filled his mind as he neared the river, and then shooting rattled from behind him, and one of his men screamed in agony.

~ ~ ~

Lucas spotted a Crew bodyguard and dropped into a crouch, steadying his aim as he fired a burst. The guard jerked as bullets shattered his front ceramic plate, and Lucas fired another three-round volley to ensure he was neutralized. Another bodyguard returned fire and Lucas dove to the side; the man obviously was equipped with a night scope, judging by how narrowly the shots missed. That changed everything – it was now three against one, and at least two hostiles with NV gear.

He debated whether to continue, and then the leaves beside him shredded from a full-auto burst, making the choice for him. He rolled into the brush with his rifle in front of him and glued the scope to his right eye, waiting for either a muzzle flash or movement. His patience was rewarded after fifteen seconds when another long burst rattled in his direction, and he stitched the area where the shooting had come from with three bursts of his own.

A body fell onto the bank, and Lucas nodded grimly. One down, two to go. Those odds he could deal with, after all he'd been through. Lucas scanned his surroundings and spotted a faint trail that paralleled the river. He moved cautiously onto it, staying low, finger on his trigger guard as he crept along the bank.

Lucas heard a rustle ahead and saw a pair of men disappear around a bend. He increased his speed and followed the curve…and barely escaped being shot when the surviving bodyguard opened up at him from behind a tree.

Lucas tucked and rolled, angry at himself for his overconfidence. That had been a mistake made in the heat of pursuit – one that had almost gotten him killed. He remained motionless, the bushes so thick he could barely make out anything, and thanked Providence that the bodyguard would have the same success seeing him.

More shooting missed him by several yards, and Lucas emptied the remainder of his magazine in methodically grouped bursts at the source, imagining a grid as he did so. He freed his Kimber and waited for more shooting and, when none occurred, pushed to his feet, shouldering the M4 sling and reaching for the monocle in his flak jacket pouch.

He didn't see anything but empty bank, but his nerves were sounding a shrill warning as he made his way along the track. Assuming the bodyguard had bought the farm, that still left Magnus, who'd been carrying a pistol, nothing more. But Lucas didn't want to assume he'd hit the bodyguard – the man might, even as Lucas moved forward, be lining up the reticule of a scope on his head.

Two minutes went by, and when Lucas was still alive and had advanced past the point from which the bodyguard had been firing, he stopped and regarded the bank. Magnus couldn't disappear into thin air, and he couldn't fly and didn't appear to have much stealth or physical grace, so if he was moving, Lucas was confident he would see him eventually.

The game of cat and mouse came to an end when the snap of a twig no more than fifty yards up the bank echoed off the water. Lucas was instantly in motion and spied Magnus's bulk running toward the nearby hill. Lucas slipped the monocle into his pouch and assumed a two-handed military stance to squeeze off five rounds from the Kimber. None hit Magnus, who twisted as he ran and fired back at Lucas. His aim went wild, the bullets missing by a wide margin.

Hitting a stationary object at fifty yards with a pistol was difficult at night, even if man-sized. A body in motion was nearly impossible, Lucas knew, but that wasn't going to stop him from trying. He fired again and again, trying to anticipate the Crew boss's movements, but in vain – the big man was more agile than he looked, and the gloom was working in his favor.

Lucas ejected a spent magazine and inserted a spare. He gave chase, but slowed as he neared a dense clump of the tall brush that dotted the hillside. Magnus could be behind any of the bushes, waiting to blow Lucas's head off.

Lucas dropped to the ground in order to present as slim a target as possible and slid the monocle from his plate carrier. All he saw was scrub and rock, the side of the hill scored with small gullies. He waited, breathing heavily from the run, and then the earth near him sprayed into the air as more shots blasted from up the hill – these no more than thirty yards away. Lucas returned fire but didn't hit anything.

Magnus was already on the move again, and Lucas pushed himself to his feet and gave chase, firing as he ran. Magnus emptied his pistol trying to hit him, and Lucas increased his speed as the warlord veered left and leapt across a six-foot gully before vanishing around an eroded rock formation.

Lucas slowed as he rounded the stones, but not in time to avoid a sledgehammer blow to his gun hand that knocked the Kimber from his grip. Magnus had jumped Lucas from a depression in the formation, leaving him with only his Bowie knife and a numb arm. The big man followed with a kick to Lucas's solar plexus that his ceramic body armor absorbed most of, but the force knocked the wind from him and doubled him over. Lucas was reaching for his knife when Magnus's knee caught him in the jaw, knocking him backward in a staggering fall, the pain blinding.

Magnus grinned in the dim moonlight, the occult symbols on his face lending him the appearance of a devil. He clenched and unclenched his hands as he neared, grunting like a wild beast. Lucas freed the knife with his left hand, but another kick whacked it from his grasp, and a spike of agony radiated from his wrist.

"I'm going to tear you apart, punkass," Magnus growled, and rushed Lucas before he'd recovered. Magnus's tree trunk arms wrapped around Lucas's chest, crushing his ribs with viselike force. Lucas struggled for breath, but his lungs couldn't expand, and he began to tremble as he fought for air, Magnus's foul breath against his face. The warlord bounced Lucas like a rag doll, and the only thing that prevented all his ribs from cracking instantly was his body armor.

Magnus's eyes gleamed at Lucas's agony. Lucas tried to head butt him, but it had no effect but to amuse the madman, who tightened his grip even more. Magnus whispered in his ear, his voice a hiss. "You like that? Still wanna play? Do you?"

A snapping sound stopped Magnus cold, and Lucas drove a steel pin through Magnus's eye. The warlord roared in agony and released

Lucas, clawing at his eye, and then pawed at his bandolier in a panic as he realized where the pin had come from. Lucas dropped to the ground and dragged himself to the edge of the gully, tumbling into the wash as Magnus howled like a wounded beast.

The grenade blasted fire and stone in every direction, washing over the ground and sucking the oxygen from Lucas's lungs at the bottom of the gulch, six feet below where Magnus had been atomized. The concussion of the explosion left Lucas dazed but alive, every muscle in his body aching from the mauling. Gagging at the stink of incinerated flesh from above, he probed his ribs beneath the flak jacket and was amazed that none appeared to be fractured.

A minute later, he emerged from the far end of the gully, lacking the energy to crawl back up the slope, and began trekking along the river to where silence had descended over the riparian expanse.

Chapter 56

Fewer than a third of the inhabitants remained alive and unwounded when the sun rose over Shangri-La, and another twenty-eight were suffering from injuries that varied from life-threatening to flesh wounds. The shelling had devastated the infrastructure, although the underground structures had mercifully remained intact, and most of the buildings above had sustained damage of one kind or another.

Elliot had been one of the lucky ones, but Michael had been injured during the shelling, suffering a broken arm and several deep lacerations along with a mild concussion. He stood beside Elliot with his arm in a sling and stitches crowning his head where he'd almost been brained when blown through the air by an exploding shell.

At five in the morning, Lucas had brought news of Magnus's demise, as well as Arnold's reappearance in the clinch. Elliot had listened with a wooden stare, in mild shock at how badly the valley had been brutalized. When Lucas finished his report, Michael had nodded slowly, clearly in pain. "Arnold wound up losing half his force after you left the river."

"He did? How? He was mopping up Magnus's remaining guards by the time I made it back to him."

"He joined our canyon defense force and cut off the retreating Crew. Some of them escaped, but not many. We took heavy casualties stopping them, his men among them."

"Arnold's okay?"

"Yes. He'll be here shortly. He wanted to hunt down as many of the remaining Crew as he could."

The uninjured stood in a semicircle around Elliot and Michael, with Arnold nearby and Lucas by his side. Dawn had brought with it an unforgettable image of the extensive damage the valley had suffered from the artillery barrage. Elliot stepped forward, his shoulders stooped and fatigue lines etched into his countenance, to address the survivors.

"The good news is that many of us are alive and that we defeated the miscreants who were determined to annihilate us. The bad is obvious: we've lost too many good people in defending our home, and it's no longer safe here. As such, we've discussed the matter at great length and decided that we should move somewhere safer."

A hum rose from the crowd, and Elliot held up a hand. "This is not a unilateral decision for me to make. We'll put it to a vote. My reasoning for wanting to leave is that some of the Crew members escaped, and even though their leader is dead, there's no guarantee that his successor won't continue with his plan for cornering the vaccine, which necessarily involves our destruction. If so, we'll never be secure here."

The vote was overwhelmingly in favor of moving the facilities to Colorado, which had been one of the alternate destinations Elliot and his advisors had looked at before deciding on the valley. There were several remote locations there with access to water and power, one with some mechanical engineering work required, but achievable. Elliot had assured the crowd that the vaccine development equipment, as well as the pharmaceutical lab, could be transported on carts, and after the vote, the decision was made to vacate the valley within the week, taking the wounded with them.

Elliot's radio crackled as the gathering broke up, and a voice announced that a pair of riders were on their way from one of the alternate valley entry points. The throng watched as two dots materialized at the eastern edge and rode toward them at a steady clip.

Ruby gasped when she saw who it was. Terry and Aaron, scraped and bruised, atop a pair of filched Crew horses. When Terry dismounted, she ran to him and hugged him.

"I...I thought you..."

Terry shook his head. "The plane's no more, but we walked away. Barely."

Aaron nodded as he climbed from the saddle, Duke beaming at him from Lucas's side. "Barely is right," Aaron said. "We got our wing shot off, but Terry was able to put her down on a long stretch of empty road. Lost the wheels halfway through, but all told, could have been worse." Aaron paused as he took in the damage around him. "Like we could have been here, looks like."

"I figured they couldn't kill you that easy," Duke said, slapping him on the back.

"Too mean to go quietly," Aaron agreed. His voice softened. "How many?"

"About two hundred," Duke answered.

"God."

"Like you said, could have been worse."

Lucas shook his head at Duke, and then his gaze moved to Sierra, who was watching Eve as she played with two little girls, chasing Ellie around in a circle, the prior day's horror already fading with the mercifully short memory of youth. A hint of a smile tugged at his mouth, and he turned to Duke. "So what was this business proposition?"

"I was thinking of setting up shop, maybe around Santa Fe. But Colorado might be a decent spot, too."

"And?"

"Could always use a partner. I'm not getting any younger."

Lucas nodded. "Aaron seems fit."

Duke frowned. "That mean you ain't interested?"

"We can talk later, but right now it means I've got unfinished business," Lucas said, his attention drawn back to Sierra. "Might want to gather up all the AKs and ammo you can find in the canyon, though. Be a nice start for the business, and some things never go out of style."

"I'm already ahead of you on that. You know what I'll be doing all week." Duke paused. "How about you? Be nice to have another pair of hands to help, even if you don't want to make it permanent."

They were interrupted by Luis, a bandage around his arm where he'd been wounded by a Crew bullet. "Magnus has a ton of gold in his vehicle," the ex-cartel boss said in a low voice. "I was going to go after it myself, but I figure it's way more than I can carry, so might as well share the wealth."

Duke absently drummed his fingers against his leg. "How much we talking?"

"Hundreds of kilos, at least."

"Where did he get that kind of weight?"

"Dallas Federal Reserve had almost five hundred in their vault. The rest I heard he confiscated from jewelry stores and coin dealers in Houston and Austin." Luis shrugged. "I haven't seen it for myself, but the word was he brought a third of his fortune to finance the attack. I figure it's worth a trip to investigate before the scavengers get to it."

Duke grinned. "I love me a treasure hunt." He paused. "But Lucas bagged that elephant. He should get a share."

Luis shrugged. "If it's there, I have no problem with that. A third, a third, and a third works for me."

Duke offered his hand. "Might not have to trade any more after this."

Luis looked him up and down. "Or you might want to take on more partners."

Lucas walked away, unconcerned by the discussion of rumored wealth. There wasn't much in the world that he wanted at the moment that gold could buy – it wouldn't bring his grandfather or Bear back, it wouldn't keep him safe, nor would it shield Sierra and Eve...

If anything, it could make him a target.

Still. Couldn't hurt to ride down to the convoy and nose around with Duke.

He approached Sierra, who, like Ruby, had come through the

shelling unscathed. She beamed at him. He cleared his throat, and she waited expectantly.

"We need to talk, don't we?" he began.

She took his hands in hers with a slow nod. "That we do, Lucas."

"Don't want to have to worry about you running off every morning."

Sierra got a faraway look in her eyes and stared at the peaks. "Me either."

"No need to ask whether we're going to Colorado, is there?"

She regarded Lucas with the beginnings of a wistful smile. "I'm glad you made it in one piece."

"Same here."

She sighed and squeezed his hand as the morning sun warmed her face, the flecks of gold in her eyes glowing as they caught the light. "We definitely need to talk."

Chapter 57

The communications room in the basement of the church Magnus had taken over to use as his headquarters suddenly felt too small, even with only two men in it. The Houston Crew radio operator relayed the message he'd received to Snake, stammering in disbelief as he read from his notes. The transmission had come in fifteen minutes ago, and Snake had been summoned for an emergency conference.

"Magnus is dead," the man repeated. "The whole army was wiped out except for a few dozen survivors. They made it back to Albuquerque and are awaiting instructions." The operator looked up at Snake with fearful eyes. "There's no mistake."

"You're absolutely sure this is genuine?"

"Yes. The sender knew the passwords and the code phrases."

Snake shook his head. "A thousand men. Gone. And Magnus... I figured him as immortal."

"What are we going to do?"

"Who else have you told?" Snake demanded.

"Nobody. I called for you when I decoded it. I don't want to cause a panic."

"That was smart. Very smart." Snake nodded.

The operator straightened in his seat. "What happens now?"

"You're to tell no one. I'll deal with breaking the news. This has to be handled delicately, or there's going to be complete chaos. Magnus was the glue that held Houston together. Without him and clear leadership… Well, I don't want to think about it."

The operator nodded his understanding. "I'll keep it secret."

"That may not be possible for long," Snake said, processing the news. "This was over an open channel?"

"Yes. But it was coded."

"Still."

Snake turned away, and the operator swiveled back to the console. A flash of steel in Snake's hand blurred as he whirled around and drove his dagger into the operator's spine. The operator stiffened and went limp as Snake withdrew the blade, leaving the man lying in a pool of blood.

Snake exited the radio chamber and pulled the door closed. A guard nodded to him, and Snake ordered the man to ensure nobody entered the room until he returned.

An hour later, Snake was sitting in Magnus's private dining room as a lunch of freshly dressed beef filets, field greens, and spiced wine was served for himself and three of the inner circle.

"Gentlemen, I have good news from Magnus!" Snake began. Servers placed heaping platters of mouthwatering fare before them, and a steward poured generous portions of wine in their cups.

"Yes?"

Snake signaled the servants. "Leave us. I'll call for cleanup later."

The wait staff trooped from the room. When the heavy mahogany door shut behind them, Snake leaned forward, his eyes glittering with manic excitement.

"The transmission was slim on details for security reasons, but apparently everything's going to plan, and they've reached Shangri-La…and taken it!" Snake announced, his voice jubilant. He snatched up his cup and held it aloft in a toast. "Magnus estimates that he'll be back before the week's up. So today is one of celebration!"

The men joined Snake in the toast and drained their cups. Only Snake didn't finish his wine and, soon after toasting, excused himself and made for the restroom to flush his mouth with soap and water. He'd swallowed none of the port, but wanted to take no chances, his future now assured if he played his cards right.

When he returned to the chamber, the three men were dead. Their faces were blue and bloated, foam frothed from their mouths and noses, and their eyes bugged from their skulls like some internal pressure had swelled to the bursting point. Snake sat back down, sliced into his filet, and chewed a bite with a look of approval.

"Unfortunately, my homies, the world's only big enough for one of us, and this go round I'm gonna be running the show." He nodded to the nearest corpse and winked. "Don't be throwing shade, big dog. I know you're happy for me. I'm sure Magnus would have wanted things this way." He paused, forked another heaping portion of steak into his mouth, and smacked his lips appreciatively. "You'll have to trust me on that."

Thanks for reading *The Day After Never – Covenant*,
(Book III in the Day After Never series.)
I hope you enjoyed it.

Book IV in the series continues with:
The Day After Never – Retribution

About the Author

Featured in *The Wall Street Journal*, *The Times*, and *The Chicago Tribune*, Russell Blake is *The NY Times* and *USA Today* bestselling author of over forty novels, including *Fatal Exchange*, *Fatal Deception*, *The Geronimo Breach*, *Zero Sum*, *King of Swords*, *Night of the Assassin*, *Revenge of the Assassin*, *Return of the Assassin*, *Blood of the Assassin*, *Requiem for the Assassin*, *Rage of the Assassin* The *Delphi Chronicle* trilogy, *The Voynich Cypher*, *Silver Justice*, *JET*, *JET – Ops Files*, *JET – Ops Files: Terror Alert*, *JET II – Betrayal*, *JET III – Vengeance*, *JET IV – Reckoning*, *JET V – Legacy*, *JET VI – Justice*, *JET VII – Sanctuary*, *JET VIII – Survival*, *JET IX – Escape*, *JET X – Incarceration*, *Upon a Pale Horse*, *BLACK*, *BLACK is Back*, *BLACK is The New Black*, *BLACK to Reality*, *BLACK in the Box*, *Deadly Calm*, *Ramsey's Gold*, *Emerald Buddha*, *The Goddess Legacy*, *The Day After Never – Blood Honor*, *The Day After Never – Purgatory Road*, and *The Day After Never – Covenant*.

Non-fiction includes the international bestseller *An Angel With Fur* (animal biography) and *How To Sell A Gazillion eBooks In No Time* (even if drunk, high or incarcerated), a parody of all things writing-related.

Blake is co-author of *The Eye of Heaven* and *The Solomon Curse*, with legendary author Clive Cussler. Blake's novel *King of Swords* has been translated into German by Amazon Crossing, *The Voynich Cypher* into Bulgarian, and his JET novels into Spanish, German, and Czech.

Blake writes under the moniker R.E. Blake in the NA/YA/Contemporary Romance genres. Novels include *Less Than Nothing*, *More Than Anything*, and *Best Of Everything*.

Having resided in Mexico for a dozen years, Blake enjoys his dogs, fishing, boating, tequila and writing, while battling world domination by clowns. His thoughts, such as they are, can be found at his blog: RussellBlake.com

Books by Russell Blake

Co-authored with Clive Cussler

THE EYE OF HEAVEN
THE SOLOMON CURSE

Thrillers

FATAL EXCHANGE
FATAL DECEPTION
THE GERONIMO BREACH
ZERO SUM
THE DELPHI CHRONICLE TRILOGY
THE VOYNICH CYPHER
SILVER JUSTICE
UPON A PALE HORSE
DEADLY CALM
RAMSEY'S GOLD
EMERALD BUDDHA
THE DAY AFTER NEVER – BLOOD HONOR
THE DAY AFTER NEVER – PURGATORY ROAD

The Assassin Series

KING OF SWORDS
NIGHT OF THE ASSASSIN
RETURN OF THE ASSASSIN
REVENGE OF THE ASSASSIN
BLOOD OF THE ASSASSIN
REQUIEM FOR THE ASSASSIN
RAGE OF THE ASSASSIN

The JET Series

JET
JET II – BETRAYAL
JET III – VENGEANCE
JET IV – RECKONING
JET V – LEGACY
JET VI – JUSTICE
JET VII – SANCTUARY
JET VIII – SURVIVAL
JET IX – ESCAPE
JET X – INCARCERATION
JET – OPS FILES (prequel)
JET – OPS FILES; TERROR ALERT

The BLACK Series

BLACK
BLACK IS BACK
BLACK IS THE NEW BLACK
BLACK TO REALITY
BLACK IN THE BOX

Non Fiction

AN ANGEL WITH FUR
HOW TO SELL A GAZILLION EBOOKS
(while drunk, high or incarcerated)

Made in the USA
Thornton, CO
03/05/23 20:48:23

a83c6c36-7152-4496-ac87-0c03c04ce5f4R01